WINTER WHIMSY

The Boardwalk by the Sea
Book Three

Georgina Troy

Published by Green Shutter Books Ltd 2020

Winter Whimsy is the third in the series set in a fictional seaside village on the island of Jersey known as, The Boardwalk by the Sea. Each book is set during a season and focuses on one of four friends. Book 1 was Sacha's story, Book 2 was Bella's and this is Lexi's story.

I hope you enjoy getting to know her.

Dedication

To my sisters, Kate and Rachael, with love.

Before you visit the Lexi's fishermen's cottages...

Did you know that Georgina has a newsletter? She loves to share updates about forthcoming releases and regularly holds competitions for bookish goodies.

You can sign up to her newsletter by clicking here.

Acknowledgements

Thanks, as ever, to my wonderfully supportive husband, Rob and to my children, Saskia and James. Each of them never seems to tire of listening to me worrying about the book I'm working on.

To Karen Clarke for her structural edits, I know this book is much better thanks to your invaluable input.

To my three rescue dogs, Jarvis, Claude and Rudi who regardless of whether I want to step away from my work in progress, always insist on their daily beach walk and ensure I get some fresh air and exercise.

And most of all to you, the reader. I hope you enjoy the latest instalment in the Boardwalk by the Sea series. If you did, please consider leaving a review on Amazon or anywhere else you fancy.

If you haven't signed up to my newsletter yet, please do. I don't send out newsletters too often, but I do like to keep my readers up to date with any exciting book news or if I have a giveaway.

To discover more about Georgina Troy and my next book in The Boardwalk by the Sea series, Spring Siren:

Sign up to my mailing list
Follow me: Twitter, Facebook

CHAPTER ONE

December

Lexi opened the front door to her end-of-terrace fisherman's cottage and gazed down the hill towards the boardwalk. She took a deep, bracing breath as she watched the rough sea crashing against the cliff-face near the small beach where she had spent almost every day of her life. She loved it here. These cottages had been the only constant in her life, especially since her mother had passed away suddenly in a car accident, two years ago.

She had focused a lot of time on her dad since then and with the help of her best friends, Sacha, Bella and Jools had slowly found a way to get by without her fun-loving mother in her life. Now, though, her father had found himself a girlfriend Lexi simply couldn't take to. She recalled her conversation with Bella the night before when they'd met for a couple of drinks in the Ploughman's Pub.

'I don't know what it is about Gloria,' she'd admitted guiltily, 'but there's something about her I'm not keen on. I've thought about it and it's not because she's the first woman Dad has gone out with since Mum.'

'I know that,' Bella had said, having taken a few hours away from her boyfriend and stocktaking for the tiny antique shop she ran from the living room of her blue cottage on the boardwalk. She took a sip of her white wine. 'I bumped into them at the newsagents the other day. She seemed very pleased with herself about something. 'Maybe she's more fun than we imagine.'

They'd stared at each other in silence briefly, both processing Bella's comment.

'I don't mean sexually,' Bella grimaced. 'Just that we might not have seen the best side to her, that's all.'

Lexi hadn't let herself think about her father actually being intimate with anyone, let alone Gloria. 'Gross,' she shuddered. 'Thanks for putting that thought into my head.'

Bella had giggled. 'You have to remember he's only fifty-something and I guess attractive in an eccentric, arty, odd sort of way.'

'Maybe that's because he is a little odd and an artist,' Lexi said fondly, still struggling to shake off the thought of her father doing anything remotely physical with his girlfriend. 'Anyway, I don' t think she likes me either.'

'She probably sees you as competition for his attention.' Bella leant in closer to Lexi. 'You're an only child and maybe she thinks he's got money seeing as his paintings sell quite well.'

They had done, but not recently, Lexi had realised. She'd confided her thoughts to her friend. 'Since Mum died, he's found it difficult to paint. He always said she was his muse from when they met at seventeen. Now she's gone, he's lost his inspiration to paint. It's so sad,' she added swallowing tears.

'Well,' Bella placed a hand on Lexi's and gave it a gentle pat. 'And I know you won't like me saying this, but as your friend I feel I should.'

'Go on,' Lexi said, suspecting she knew where the conversation was going.

'Maybe this girlfriend will spark off feelings in him that will help him get into his painting again. Surely it would be a good thing for your dad? What do you think?'

Lexi couldn't ignore that what Bella had said made sense. And, however distasteful it may be to her to think of him replacing her mother with another muse, she needed to be grateful that he had found some way of moving on and resuming his artistic passions. She was also aware he needed to begin making an income for himself again.

'Lexi?'

She smiled at Bella, not wishing her to think her suggestion had upset her in anyway. 'You're right, I know you are. And if it helps Dad, then I'll just have to accept it.'

'Good girl.' Bella had risen and walked around the small table to give Lexi a hug. 'After all, you have the fishermen's cottages to keep you busy. Changing the subject away from your dad,' she'd said, giving Lexi a wink. 'How are things going on that front?'

'They're fine.'

Now it was the following morning and Lexi cupped her hands and blew on them to warm them up, wishing she had thought to wear gloves to come outside. She looked around her at the cottages, grateful to Bella for her comments the night before. It wasn't easy bringing up things that people didn't like to face and Bella was right; she needed to be happy for her dad if he was finding a way to move on with his life and get his career back on track.

Her friend was right too, when she said that Lexi had the fishermen's cottages to focus on. They were her link to her mum and not only gave her somewhere to live, but also a way to make money, managing them for holiday-makers. She made herself feel better with the thought that, whatever her father chose to do, she at least had these cottages as a way of making money.

The sound of a car engine coming down the hill distracted her. She turned and saw a taxi, surprised when it slowed and stopped at the end of her pathway. She hadn't been expecting any visitors to come and stay today. She tried not to appear too obvious as she peered in the taxi's direction, shocked to see that the man getting out of the vehicle was none other than Oliver Whimsy.

What the hell was he doing here? She tried to recall whether he had booked the cottage at the end of the row, where she had allowed him to stay for a couple of nights a few weeks earlier. Or, had she simply forgotten him booking a return? No, she was sure she hadn't. Lexi watched him pay the taxi driver and then carry his large suitcase towards her. He looked as if he had prepared to come for some time. The thought worried her.

He gave her a brief smile. 'It's freezing out here,' he said, shivering despite his bespoke overcoat, which Lexi suspected was made of something exorbitantly expensive, like cashmere. 'Do you mind if we go inside straightaway? We can sign any paperwork then.'

'Sorry?'

He lowered his case and rubbed his gloved hands together. 'Can I take it that you weren't expecting me?'

'No, I wasn't.' She was confused. 'Have you booked?'

He took a deep breath and sighed. 'I'm guessing your father hasn't told you what's happened, has he?'

An unnerving thought occurred to Lexi. To most people, her father was outgoing and charismatic, though at times a little dippy. What they didn't realise was that he could also be cowardly when it came to confrontation and avoided it at all costs. And she knew, of old, that if Oliver Whimsy was here and she knew nothing about it, then her father had made arrangements that he knew she wouldn't like. Dread pulled at her stomach like a vice slowly tightening.

'I have a horrible suspicion I'm not going to like this.' She turned around and opened her front door, stepping back to wave Oliver in. 'You may as well come inside. It's too cold out here. We probably have quite a bit to discuss.'

His face clouded over and he picked up his bag and went inside. She stepped in behind him and closed the door, using the few seconds it took her to take off her coat to try and gather her thoughts and prepare for what was to come.

'Please,' she said, joining him in the small open-plan living room and kitchen area. 'Take a seat.'

She watched him, unable to ignore how attractive he was; over six-foot tall and dark-haired with piercing blue eyes.

'Can I make you a coffee? You look frozen.' She may as well be neighbourly, she thought. At least initially.

'Yes, please. I could do with one.'

Lexi busied herself at the kettle. 'It's instant, I'm afraid.'

'No problem.'

She wasn't so sure. She stirred the drinks and handed one mug to him before sitting down opposite and waiting for what he had to tell her.

He stared silently at his drink. She could see he was mulling something over. Eventually he looked across the small space at her.

Lexi crossed her legs, wishing he would hurry up.

'I think it's time to tell me exactly what my father has arranged with you. Not,' she added, aware she wasn't being as hospitable as she usually was to her tenants, 'that I mind you being here. In fact, all three cottages are empty, so I'm more than happy for you to rent one of them. But I would like to know why you're here.'

He straightened up slightly in his chair. She was beginning to think he might feel even more uncomfortable than she did. She hoped it wasn't her chairs. No one else had complained about them. In fact, everyone remarked how comfortable they were in the short surveys she left for tenants to complete. She realised she was being ridiculous and waited impatiently for him to speak.

He took a deep breath. 'Your father hasn't mentioned that he's coming down here this morning to speak to you?' She shook her head. 'Right.' She saw a muscle working in his jaw. He was angry, but why? 'I don't know how else to say this,' he said, leaning slightly forward in his chair. 'I assume you're unaware that I now own these cottages.' He watched her silently.

Lexi had heard the words coming out of his mouth. She even understood what they meant. Somehow, though, she could not make her brain take in the reality of them.

Lexi could imagine her father renting one of the cottages to Oliver, probably for less than he should, despite knowing she wouldn't like it. It never occurred to her that her father could betray her in this way though. Oliver Whimsy, she decided, had to be wrong.

'I think there must be some misunderstanding between you and my dad.' She willed him to agree with her.

Instead he shook his head slowly. Looking down briefly at his mug of coffee he seemed to be struggling to find the right words. Eventually, he looked up at her.

'I'm dreadfully sorry. I can see that you're not happy with this news. I am, however, the new owner. The sale was completed last week.'

For a few seconds it was as if her head was in a bubble.

'He can't have,' she said, her voice a high-pitched squeak.

She swallowed a mouthful of coffee, trying her best to hide how much it stung as the steaming liquid scalded her throat. The pain distracted her from the tears that threatened to come.

'He has." Oliver looked, she thought, as if he could kill someone. 'He led me to believe that you were fully aware of the transaction. I'm sorry,' he said, looking angry. 'I think you need to discuss this with your father before we speak further. Can you let me know which cottage I can take my things to while you call him?'

'I'm staying in this one right now,' she explained, her attention turning to a silver-framed photograph of her grandmother and mother beaming at Lexi from the mantlepiece when she was around four-years old as she danced on the lawn in front of the cottages. She liked to keep them as free from her personal effects as possible in case she didn't have much time to make the place up for a new holidaymaker. This photo, however, went everywhere with her. It represented her happiest times with the two women who loved her above all else.

She realised he was waiting for her to speak so looked at him and continued, 'I live here when it's empty, so that I can keep an eye on the rest.' Her throat constricted with unshed tears. She coughed lightly, determined to know why he had bought the cottages. 'I don't understand why you want them. They're tiny, for a start, and you've only ever stayed here for a couple of nights.'

She could hear the bitterness in her own voice

and was embarrassed. It wasn't Oliver Whimsy's fault that her father had sold them to him. Lexi gave him a tight smile to soften her words.

'It's personal,' he said after a moment's hesitation.

'Personal?' What reason on earth could he have to feel connected to these cottages? As far as she was aware, he had no family on the island, and it wasn't as if he had shown any attraction to her. In any case, Lexi thought angrily, if he did like her, which she was certain he didn't, not in that way, then that still wasn't reason enough to pay what must have been a lot of money for this tiny terrace.

He shifted in his chair. 'I'm sorry, but I'd rather not say why.'

She stared at him, willing him to change his mind. She wasn't satisfied with his answer but could tell that he wasn't going to add anything further.

'Fine.' It wasn't at all, but what could she do about it now?

It occurred to her that if Oliver Whimsy was the new owner then he wouldn't need her hanging about. She put her cup down on the table next to her. The last thing she wanted was to get upset in front of a relative stranger. Especially Oliver Whimsy. She thought back to the first time she'd met him, at the recent Halloween party that Jack Collins' ex-girlfriend Nicky had held. No one on the boardwalk liked Nicky, simply because there was nothing much to like. Also, because she'd tried to cause trouble for Jack, Sacha's twin and the man who Bella had been seeing for the past few weeks.

Despite all that, when Nicky had called Oliver Whimsy over to join her on the dance floor that night and proposed marriage, he'd stunned everyone by glaring at her before walking away, leaving Nicky standing alone in front of all the guests. It was not the act of a gentleman, they had all agreed. Regardless of his good looks, his actions had made him unattractive to everyone. This was despite them agreeing that Nicky had put him in a very difficult position.

Lexi thought back to that night when, unable to stay at the hotel any longer and needing somewhere to stay, Oliver had turned up at the cottages. He had explained to her that there was nothing going on between him and Nicky and that the proposal had been, in his opinion, simply to antagonise Jack. He ended up asking if he could spend a couple of nights in the end property. Despite thinking he could have handled things better with Nicky, Lexi had let him stay.

However badly she thought he had behaved, she could not knowingly let him or anyone else find themselves without a roof over their head. But now, it seemed, he had liked the fishermen's cottages so much, he had bought them. She felt as if someone had punched her in the stomach.

'Look, why don't I take you to the cottage you

stayed in before?' she said, desperate to remove him from her home... *well, home for now,* she thought. She was determined not to show him how stunned she was.

'I'll come and set the place up for you before I go and speak to my dad.'

'That's very kind, especially under the circumstances. Thank you.'

Leading the way through to the hall, Lexi took the cottage keys from the window ledge.

'I'll make up the bed and then pop out and fetch a few essentials for you, so you have something in the cupboard and the fridge.'

She needed a little time to think through what she was going to say to her father. Also, time to let the shock sink in about what he'd done and the repercussions his decision would have on her life. What had he been thinking, selling her mother's cottages, and without consulting her first? He knew it was her livelihood and, more often than not, her home. She stood in the hall, trying to regulate her breathing. She didn't want Oliver to know how the sale would devastate her although he'd probably already guessed. She heard him pick up his case and without another word, opened the front door and led him to the end cottage unlocking it and letting him in.

'We always keep the heating on although it's rather low now. I'll turn it up a bit,' she said, going to the thermostat. 'We never turn it off completely, in case there's a sudden dip in the temperature outside.' She wondered why he was being so helpful under the circumstances. 'We don't want the pipes freezing. The frost we sometimes get here can lead to burst pipes and living so close to the sea on this hill, we sometimes get the full force of the winds coming in from the channel.' She knew she was waffling.

'If you want to make yourself comfortable, I'll quickly go upstairs and make up your bedroom. I keep the sheets and the towels for each cottage in their own airing cupboards, so everything's already here.'

She didn't know why she was explaining this to him, it wasn't as if he needed to know. But it kept her mind from focusing on the nagging thought that she was now having to face being homeless herself.

Lexi hated the thought of moving back into her father's house, especially now Gloria had essentially moved in. It wasn't the childhood home she remembered anymore. She hadn't lived there much for five years now, not since she had taken over the running of the cottages. And the last place she wanted to live was in her father and Gloria's love nest. She shivered at the prospect.

Lexi was sure she had been pleasant enough to Gloria when her father had introduced them, so could not understand the woman's dislike of her. Maybe Bella was right and that being his only child had stirred up a feeling of competition in his girlfriend that wasn't necessary. Or, Lexi wondered, as she took out the sheets and towels from the airing cupboard, it could be that she looked so like her mother. Everyone said so. Could it be the similarity between the two of them that Gloria had an issue with?

She focused on making up the double bed in the small but cosy bedroom upstairs before returning to join Oliver Whimsy downstairs. 'Right. I'm off to speak to Dad. Then I'll hurry back, so I don't keep you waiting too long.'

'Really, there's no need,' he said opening his case and taking out a shiny laptop. He placed it on the small table next to the armchair by the window and waited for her to make the next move. 'I'll be fine here. I've got plenty of work to be catching up on for the next few hours.'

She forced a smile and left him to get on with his work.

Standing outside, Lexi zipped up her coat battling conflicting emotions of anger.

Overcome by the urge to confront her father, she ran back to her cottage, grabbed her car keys and drove up the hill to her dad's house.

CHAPTER TWO

Lexi parked the car badly but didn't care. She ran inside the bungalow without bothering to knock. She marched into the kitchen looking for her father and was welcomed by the sight of him snogging Gloria. Lexi stared open-mouthed at the discomfiting scene of them locked in their passionate kiss.

Her father froze as Gloria gave her a triumphant smile over his shoulder. Seconds later, he sprang back. Any nerves Lexi had about confronting him disappeared. Pure rage coursed through her. She knew without doubt that Gloria had played a part and no doubt persuaded him that the sale was a good idea.

Lexi glared at her. She might be barely above five feet in height, but was determined to show Gloria she was a lot tougher than she looked. 'I'd like a private word with my father, if you don't mind.'

'Look who's come to visit us, Jeff.'

Her father shuffled from one foot to the other. He had always left awkward situations for her mother to deal with. After a slight hesitation, he gave Gloria a tilt of his head, indicating she should leave the room. As soon as she'd gone, he folded his arms and leant back against the work surface behind him.

'Ahh, Lexi. You've heard then.'

It was a statement rather than a question and his attitude infuriated her. What had happened to change him so much? Surely this couldn't all be Gloria's doing? She hoped not, because if that was the case then the woman had far more influence on her father than Lexi had ever imagined possible.

'I don't know what hurts more,' she said glaring at him, shocked to see his arrogant, unrepentant stance. 'The fact that you sold Mum's cottages so readily, or that it never occurred to you to mention it to me first.'

Her father struggled to reply. In the past, he'd spent a lot of time on his art, but was basically lazy when it came to anything else. Maybe his dislike of confronting people was why he'd decided to act behind her back.

'I can't believe you did this,' she went on. 'You know Mum always intended for me to run the cottages.' Her temper rose when he didn't reply. 'What do you think Gran would have said if she knew what you've done?'

Her maternal grandmother, Dorothea, known

to everyone as Thea had been a formidable woman. She had never married and brought up Lexi's mum alone, never thinking anything of it. Her own mother had done the same and Thea had always insisted that men were not to be relied upon. Lexi thought back to her earliest memories, of different people with colourful lives, coming and going, over the weeks and months, in the two cottages that her gran had rented out as holiday lets from the early sixties, when she had inherited them from her own mother. Her home had been the one at the end where Lexi now lived.

She realised her father was staring, shamefaced, at several blank canvasses leant against the wall. 'You do realise that I'm now essentially homeless,' she snapped. When he didn't reply, she added, irritated to think that she would now have to share her childhood home with her father and Gloria, 'I'll just have to move in here now, won't I?'

His mouth fell open in shock. Pleased to finally have some reaction, Lexi didn't wait for him to reply but marched out of the kitchen, down the short hallway, and burst into her bedroom. At least, into what had been her bedroom the last time she visited. However, instead of being greeted by her old single bed and the faded but familiar flowery wallpaper of her youth, she almost tripped over a stack of canvasses waiting to be painted. She turned, coming nose to nose with her father as he raced down the passageway to join her. 'Where's my bedroom?'

'You moved out,' he said, looking a little anxious. 'And I needed a bigger studio. Gloria said it made sense to knock through from your room into the studio. I happen to think she was right. It looks rather good.'

'It does, and generally I'd be very impressed,' she said trying not to lose her temper. 'But now that you've got rid of my bedroom and sold my home, where exactly do you think I'll be sleeping from now on?'

He chewed the skin at the side of his left thumb. 'Ahh, I hadn't thought that far,' he answered honestly.

'And,' she added, as something else occurred to her. 'Thanks to you and Gloria, I've also now lost my job.'

Lexi opened her mouth to say something else when Gloria strode back into the room. The smug expression on her heavily made-up face disappeared the second Lexi's father turned around to look at her.

'You poor thing Lexi,' she said, her face the picture of someone who truly was devastated. 'You're young, though, and shouldn't have a problem getting a job.' She walked up to Lexi's father and linking her arm through his gave him a gentle, collaborative smile. 'After all you're a grown woman now, of what, thirty-five?'

'Lexi refused to give her the satisfaction of

letting her see how much she was winding her up. After all that was Gloria's intention. 'I'm 29, Gloria.'

'Yes,' Gloria smiled, her perfect white teeth shining brightly in the overcast day. 'Then you're more than an age to stand on your own two feet.' She gave a silly laugh. 'I was eighteen when I was living in my own home, which I paid for by working. You can't really expect your poor father to still be supporting you at home, not at your age? Can you?'

Lexi clenched her fists, pushing them deep into her coat pockets. 'No, of course I don't expect him to give me a roof over my head. However, as I'm sure you are aware Gloria, those cottages were my mother's.'

'But your mother is dead.' Gloria raised her thick eyebrows as if to make her point, before she turned on her heels and flounced out of the room.

Lexi stared her father, his mouth open in stunned horror

'Seriously Dad? I know you're besotted, but are you going to let her get away with saying things like that about Mum?'

He cleared his throat and shook his head, looking bewildered. His paint spattered grey hair stood up at different angles as he pushed his hand through it.

'Look, Lex, Glory didn't mean what she just said. That is, she wouldn't have meant it to come out like it did. She is a good person. She's kind and looks after me very well. And she's right, your mum is dead and we should both learn to move on with our lives.'

Lexi could see she was not going to get anywhere. 'There's moving on and erasing someone from your life, Dad,' she said miserably.

She admitted to herself that Gloria had been right when she said that she was now a grown-up. Her father was also entitled to have a girlfriend and a bit of fun in his life. Lexi had just not expected things to turn out how they had done. After her mum had died, she and her father had become close, relying on each other for company and advice. Somewhere, this had all changed, and for some reason Lexi couldn't fathom, it had happened without her being aware of the change.

She stared at her father as she gathered herself. 'I'll leave you and Gloria be then, Dad,' she said quietly. 'I'll ask Oliver Whimsy to fill me in on the details of the sale and the fine print, so that I know where, if anywhere, I stand.'

It was time she left and sorted out her life. She was obviously not the most important person in her father's life anymore. As much as she didn't like Gloria, the woman was her father's choice for his girlfriend, and Lexi knew she had to respect that decision. But she couldn't go, or even begin to move on, until she got to the bottom of how this had happened.

'Don't worry Dad, it's fine. I still don't understand what the hell you were thinking, selling Mum's cottages like that, and despite what Gloria said, I'm only too painfully aware that Mum's dead.' She saw the hurt expression on his face, so added, 'And despite your bravado in front of her, I know how it still hurts you.'

'It does, love.'

She took a shuddering breath, trying her best to remain calm in the face of his betrayal.

'What happened to us, Dad? We used to be so close.'

He stared at her. For a moment, she thought she had touched something she recognised. He opened his mouth to speak, then looked down at his feet. 'Life moves on, love.'

It certainly has done for us, she thought miserably.

'Yes, but I just don't understand why you wouldn't speak to me about selling the cottages first? It was cruel and embarrassing to find out in the way I did.' He glanced up at her but didn't reply. 'Why did you go behind my back and sell them to Oliver Whimsy, of all people? He isn't even from Jersey. How could you do that? And how is he entitled to buy property without qualifications?'

She thought of the many people she had met over the years who would have given everything to be able to live on the island, but were stopped from doing so because they hadn't met the work and residential qualifications required to live in Jersey. It all seemed rather odd, as well as sudden.

'My lawyers dealt with it all,' her father said shaking his head. 'I don't quite understand everything that was said.'

Lexi studied him silently. She wasn't surprised. He had always been hopeless with any form of administration or paperwork, preferring only to use paper for sketching on. His artistic talents were purely for canvasses and art of any kind, which was why she had been the one, after her mother had died, to deal with any administration to do with the cottages. It was another reason why she was still bemused by the fact that he had managed to go behind her back and sell the properties.

Lexi thought back to Gloria's self-satisfied expression and it dawned on her that it was as a result of a job well done.

'Can I see the contracts please Dad?'

'Why? You would only upset yourself seeing it in black and white.' He shuffled from one foot to the other.

'Because maybe, if I see it on paper, it might help it sink in that it's actually happened,' she explained.

'One minute,' he said, before walking out of the room. She waited silently for him to return. Studying the room that had, until now, been as familiar to her as her hands. She could hear rustling and whispered conversation but waited patiently for him to return. She had to obtain the contract now, before Gloria persuaded him not to let her see it. Lexi needed to know what had happened and it looked like this was the only way.

He marched back into join her, brandishing a brown envelope. 'It's in here.' He opened it and withdrew what looked like a contract and handed it to Lexi. 'I can't let you keep it, I'm afraid. I'll need to lock it away again in your mother's—' He blinked a few times at his slip of the tongue. 'My desk. I have to keep it safe.'

Lexi quickly skimmed through the pages, taking in the amount the cottages were sold for, the fact that they were sold to a company on a date that was one week before. Then she turned the pages and saw her father's and Oliver Whimsy's names printed on the contract. Next to the names were both signatures. What stunned her was the name and signature of the witness for her father's signature: Gloria Sweeting.

Lexi sighed heavily. 'Well, that's done then.' She handed her father the contract and turned to leave.

'Wait.' Her dad followed her into the hall when she didn't do as he asked.

She reached the front door, wanting to get away from him and his vile girlfriend before the tears that were building up inside her began to escape and she made an exhibition of herself. *So much for trying to be understanding and move on with my life. How could they do this to me?* She put a hand on the handle to open it and without looking back at her dad swallowed to ease the tightening in her throat.

‘I'd better go and speak to Oliver Whimsy. In fact, he’s waiting for me to buy him a few essentials from the shops, so I’d better do that first.’

Lexi stepped outside slamming the door behind her. Not wishing to have to go back to her father’s house for anything, she pulled the car keys from her coat pocket, got inside her car and drove the fifty yards to the nearest shop. Unable to hold back the tears any longer, she parked in a space as far away as possible from the shop so that no one could see her crying.

Those cottages were such a huge connection to her mother. She hadn't ever considered that they would ever not be a part of her daily life. Lexi didn’t know what was breaking her heart the most, the fact that the cottages and her home had gone, or that her father was instrumental in tearing apart her life. She gave in to her sobbing, unable to stop. A few minutes later, spent from the release of her emotions, she pulled a tissue out of her coat pocket and wiped the tears from her cheeks before blowing her nose.

She took a deep breath and pulled down the sun visor to check her appearance in the mirror and grimaced. She looked like she was suffering from an allergic reaction to something nasty. Her eyes were puffy and swollen and her face pale. She couldn't possibly let anyone see her looking so revolting. Lexi wished she could simply go home, and that she hadn't offered to buy essentials for Oliver bloody Whimsy. She opened the compartment under the dashboard on the passenger's side and took out her sunglasses. It was overcast, but she had no choice if she didn't want gossip to start about why she was in such a state, as soon as she had left the shop.

There was a rapid knocking against her car window. The sudden unexpected sound gave Lexi a fright. She glanced up, horrified to have been caught in such a dishevelled state, to see Betty, a concerned expression on her gentle face.

Lexi grabbed her purse and shopping bag and stepped out of the car. She quickly locked the door and turned to the oldest resident on the boardwalk. 'It's freezing out here, Betty. What are you doing outside?'

'Never mind me lovely, what's the matter with you? I was watching you cry for couple of minutes and knew you needed to let go of whatever it was that had upset you so terribly. I didn't like to interrupt. You're usually such a cheerful little thing. Whatever it is must be bad.' When Lexi found it difficult to get her words out, Betty added, 'What's upset you so?

She took the old lady's hands in hers. They

were freezing, despite the leather gloves she was wearing. Recovering from her distress, her thoughts now turned to Betty and getting her out of the cold.

'Come on Betty, you can't stay out here, it's freezing. Were you going to the shop?' Betty nodded. 'Right, let's get you inside. I'll explain as we go in.'

She linked arms with Betty. The last thing Lexi needed was her lovely friend to slip over in the icy weather. She held the shop door open for her and followed her in, standing a few feet inside near an overhead heater while she quietly relayed her.

Betty listened in silence, her face a mask of concern. 'I can't believe Jeff did such a dreadful thing.' She took Lexi's hands in her tiny ones and gave them a gentle squeeze. 'Your father always was the less sensible one in his relationship with your mother, but I never thought he'd be this silly.' She lowered her voice further and added, 'I suspect he's been infected by that woman friend of his, what's her name, Gloria?'

Lexi nodded. 'I think you mean influenced. And yes, I have to agree with you. I think he has been, too. But what's done is done now. I've seen the contract. Oliver Whimsy, the man who came to the Halloween party, Jack's ex-girlfriend Nicky threw,' she explained. 'The one with all the drama and the proposal. Do remember us telling you about it?'

Betty thought for a moment before nodding. 'I think I do, yes. He wasn't very nice man, either, was he?'

'Whatever we all thought of Nicky, he shouldn't have left her standing in the middle of the dancefloor like that.' Lexi said, picking up a plastic basket and following Betty around the shop. 'But I think he might have had his reasons.'

'She's not a nice girl either,' Betty said, studying a carton of eggs. 'Maybe they would have been well suited after all.' She laughed quietly at her own joke.

Lexi smiled. 'I'm supposed to be getting him a few bits for the cottage,' she said, grabbing a crusty loaf, a carton of milk and box of teabags. 'What can I do now?' she asked, overwhelmed by her situation, once again.

Betty gave a reassuring smile. 'Don't you fret lovely,' she said. 'I know my place is small, but I'll always find a place for you there somewhere.'

Lexi put an arm around the older lady's narrow shoulders and gave her a hug. This was why she and everyone else on the boardwalk loved and respected Betty. Despite her being in her nineties, they could always rely on her to be there to offer words of kindness, good advice, or even a roof over their heads.

'I'm sure it won't come to that,' Lexi said sounding more certain than she really felt. 'After all you've got Bella's mum, Claire staying at your house and she seems rather settled now that she's seeing Tony.'

'Well, yes. I'm not sure how long that will be lasting.'

'Why, what's happened?' Lexi asked, intrigued to know what she might be missing.

'Never you mind that.' Betty picked up a pint of milk and packet of digestive biscuits. 'Let's concentrate on you for the moment.'

'I'll be fine, honestly.' She glanced at her watch and realised she been longer than she had intended. She needed to get the shopping back to Oliver Whimsy. Lexi knew she was feeling more in control after her shocking meeting with her father and was ready to discuss with Oliver how soon he was expecting her to remove her things from her cottage. As much as the thought devastated Lexi, she had no choice and couldn't put it off. It would only worry her if she didn't get organised as soon as possible.

Betty took her free hand. 'Look, Lexi. Why not come back to my cottage? Let me make you a hot drink and we can talk about things.'

She smiled at her kindly friend. 'Thank you, but I really must face this head on. I'll give you a lift home first though.'

'If you're sure?'

'I am, thank you. Just let me pay for these things and I'll drop you off at the boardwalk.'

'That would be lovely.'

Ten minutes later, having dropped Betty off outside her home and carried her few bits of shopping in, Lexi drove back up the hill and parked the car in her allocated space. She braced herself and took the bag of shopping to Oliver's cottage. She knocked on the wooden door and hearing his voice, walked in.

'Sorry I took so long,' she said. 'My visit to my father took slightly longer than I imagined.'

He was leaning against the work top in the kitchen area. 'Don't worry. I've been thinking about what's happened and feel rather bad for my part in undermining you.'

'It was nothing to do with you,' Lexi acknowledged, realising it wasn't fair to take it out on him. She placed her carrier bag onto the work surface. 'Right, let's put these things away and then I'll leave you to it.'

He went back to whatever he'd been doing on his laptop. Lexi sensed him looking over at her every so often as she tidied up and wiped around the sink area. She hurriedly put everything away and took out a fresh tea towel, hanging it on the outside bar of the oven.

'That's me finished then,' she said. I'll leave you to your admin. I'm going out for a bit, but feel free to come over to my, er, the cottage a bit later. We can talk through what you intend doing next and when you want me to move out.'

Without looking back, or waiting for him to answer Lexi left, closing the door behind her. Not bothering with the car, she zipped up her coat and walked down the hill.

What was she going to do? She'd never considered leaving. It wasn't as if there were many places close to the boardwalk that would be available to rent or that she could afford, as properties close to the sea were expensive. She wiped away a stray tear and pushed her hands deep into her pockets against the biting wind.

It broke Lexi's heart to think how much her life had changed in the last two years since her mother had died.

It was so cold that ordinarily she would pace her way down the hill. Today though, she was too lost in her thoughts to really notice the cold. She didn't wish to discuss what had happened to anyone else and was grateful that the freezing weather kept most people inside. Betty was the only person she was ready to speak to about her situation.

Like Lexi's fishermen's cottages, the properties around the boardwalk, where her friends lived, were all tiny. Try as she might, she couldn't imagine anyone of them would have enough room to take her in, especially since Bella's mum had moved in with Betty to help out when needed.

Lexi would have to find somewhere to live, then fetch the boxes she'd been storing at her dad's.

She was fairly sure she hadn't accumulated as much stuff as some of her friends had, like Bella with her antiques, or Jools with her second-hand books and her paintings. Lexi suspected she still had more than enough though. She would need to find storage, not just for her own possessions, but those of her mother's she had been unable to part with.

As Lexi descended the hill towards the boardwalk, the sound of the waves crashing against the sea wall below distracted her. She raised her gaze from the road to the beautiful grey and white tones of the waves as they broke over the rocks on the right-hand side of the boardwalk, and to the golden damp sand on the beach in front of her. Lexi had always lived close enough to smell the sea and hear the waves and didn't want to leave this place. But what else was she to do?

CHAPTER THREE

'Hey, Lexi.'

She heard a muffled voice she recognised and looked over to see her friend Jools waving at her. Jools' short magenta hair was temporarily hidden under a bright orange bobble hat and her mouth covered by a matching woolly scarf.

Lexi tried to force a smile and failed. Jools caught up with her and when she didn't receive Lexi's usual cheerful welcome took her by the shoulders and stared into her eyes, scowling. Jools knew her well enough to know that if she couldn't speak, something major had happened in her life. Lexi forced a smile and Jools' hands dropped to allow Lexi to resume walking.

She was grateful to her friend for walking in silence next to her, allowing her time to think. They were almost at the boardwalk when Lexi wiped her eyes and cleared her throat, doing her best to summon up the strength to speak. Her friend deserved an explanation.

'My dad sold the cottages.' It was a simple sentence but one that held so much meaning.

Jools walked for a couple of steps before stopping. She spun round on her boot heels and grabbed hold of Lexi's arm as she stepped in front of her.

'Sorry? What did you say?'

The sympathetic tears shining in her friend's wide dark eyes made Lexi's throat constrict from trying not to cry. She cleared her throat.

'Dad sold the cottages,' she said, her voice barely above a whisper. She could almost see the cogs turning in her friend's brain as Jools' expression changed several times in the next few seconds.

'But they've been in your family for donkey's years. Why would he do such a terrible thing? Especially knowing how much they meant to Thea and your mum.' She gave Lexi a heartfelt look. 'And to you.'

Lexi raised her shoulders in a shrug. 'I've no idea.'

Jools stared at her in silence before pulling Lexi into a tight hug. 'I'm so, so sorry, Lexi,' she said, before letting her go. 'I know how much those cottages mean to you.'

'They're my last connection with Gran and Mum.' Lexi took a deep breath to stop herself crying, the deep intake of freezing air catching in her throat and causing her to cough several times.

'I bet he hasn't even thought about the implications of what he's done. I always thought Jeff was such a cool dad.'

Lexi had thought so, too. 'I guess he was lonelier than I imagined.' She wondered guiltily whether she should have insisted on spending more time with him. Maybe then, he wouldn't have become so totally absorbed by Gloria. 'I think all this is about trying to please his girlfriend.'

'It's a bit bloody extreme though, don't you think?' Jools shook her head and pulled her beanie lower over her ears. She jumped back, pulling Lexi with her when an extra-large wave crashed over the metal railings along the edge of the boardwalk. 'That was a bit close.'

'It was.' Lexi brushed off droplets of sea spray from the sleeves of her coat. Irritation built up inside of her as they walked on. 'Why would Gloria persuade Dad to sell though, I just don't get it.'

Jools grumbled something to herself under her breath.

'Pardon? I missed what you said just now.'

'I said, it's probably because she's a nasty cow. She must know how vulnerable he still is after your mum passed.'

Lexi thought so, too. 'Which is probably how she persuaded him.' She began to shiver. She hadn't felt the cold since starting her walk, her mind too wrapped up in her problems.

'Do you think it's because she's jealous of him still caring for your mum?'

It made sense. 'I suppose so.' Lexi linked arms with her friend. 'Come on, it's too cold to be hanging about out here. Let's go to Betty's cottage. I was on my way there when I met you. I bumped into her earlier at the shops and she invited me to pop down and speak to her. Can you come, or do you need to get back to your gran at the book shop?'

'I'm coming with you now. It's been so quiet lately that we've closed for the afternoon. I told Gran to have a nap and that I'd see her later.'

They hurried along, passing the second-hand bookshop where Jools had lived with her Gran most of her life. Her friend knew what it was to have lost a parent, but had always seemed perfectly happy with her home life.

As they walked to Betty's tiny cottage at the far end of the boardwalk, Lexi thought back to when her father first told her he was seeing Gloria. His eyes had been shiny with happiness. Although it had been a little odd to imagine him with someone other than her mother, Lexi had hoped that seeing someone might give him something else to focus on and lift him from his depression. She had never seen anyone as devastated as her father had been over her mother's death. Lexi had never wanted him to remain alone but hadn't expected him to change so utterly either.

'It's hard to imagine your dad with someone,' Jools said, shouting over the sound of the waves. 'He's mostly liked his own company what with his painting and all that.'

There had been little painting though over the past two years, Lexi knew. Maybe it was the lack of money being brought in, because he hadn't created anything new to sell, that had prompted him to sell the properties. But why not confide in her? That's the bit that stung the most. Him going behind her back and letting her find out what had happened from someone she barely knew, when it was already a done deal.

'Gran knows Gloria,' Jools said as they reached Betty's front door.

'She does?' Lexi was intrigued. 'What does she think of her, do you know?'

Jools gave the door a couple of raps with her knuckles. 'She said she's a sly bugger. Those were her words. She doesn't like her at all.'

'Neither do I,' admitted Lexi. 'Not now.'

The door opened and Claire, Bella's mum, held an index finger up to her lips. 'Betty's having a doze,' she whispered. 'If you want to see her, can you make it later on?'

'Of course we can,' Lexi said quietly, smiling. 'I hope we haven't disturbed her.'

Claire had only been back living on the boardwalk for a few months and they were all still getting used to her being there. Claire had spent most of Bella's life away from the island travelling, despite having a daughter who she had happily left for her mother to bring up.

'No, it's fine, but she needs her rest. She went out this morning without me knowing and it's too cold out there.'

'Please give her our love and tell her we'll pop round some other time.' Lexi smiled again, relieved that she had insisted on giving Betty a lift home earlier and not letting her walk home.

As they walked away from the cottage, Lexi asked Jools, 'Don't you think it strange that both you and Bella were essentially brought up by your grandmothers?'

'I suppose so, but it's always been that way so I haven't ever really thought about it.'

'It's nice though that Bella and her mum are becoming closer,' Lexi said as they passed the bluebell blue painted walls of Bella's cottage.

'Look,' Jools shouted, pointing in the direction of the small lane that meandered its way down the hill. 'There's Jack. He must have been to visit his parents.' She waved him over. 'Hi, Jack?'

Jack joined them and gave them a kiss on both cheeks before falling into step with them. 'I've just eaten lunch with my folks,' he grumbled.

'You don't sound very happy about it,' Lexi said, wishing she was able to have one more meal with both of her parents.

'They drive me nuts,' he said, linking arms

with both women and holding them close. ‘They argue over the silliest of things. I’m sure if you put them in different rooms, they’d find a way to disagree with each other.’

Lexi couldn't help smiling. Jack always amused her. She could see why Bella and he made such a perfect couple; they had a similar sense of humour.

He glanced in her direction. ‘You all right Lex? You don't seem yourself.’

‘It’s her dad, Jeff,’ Jools said.

Jack shrugged. ‘Er, yes, I know who her dad is, Jools.’ He winked at her to show he was only teasing. ‘What’s he gone and done?’

Jools leant past him to peer at Lexi. ‘Sorry, I don't mean to be rude about your dad, but what he’s done really is a step too far.’

‘Will one of you put me out of my misery and tell me what it is?’

Lexi wasn't in the mood to discuss her problems in detail, so gave Jack a brief outline of what had happened. ‘Hey, guys, if you want to talk about this, please let’s do it somewhere warm. I’m freezing. Why don’t we go to Sacha’s cafe and treat ourselves to some mugs of her hot chocolate?’ She knew the hot chocolate would help her feel a bit better. Sacha's was the best she had ever tasted. If that couldn't cheer her up nothing would.

Lexi and Jack agreed.

‘I think it’s going to rain any minute now.’ Jack

turned the palm of his hand up to see if he was right.

Without another word they all ran along the boardwalk.

'You to go ahead,' Jack said. 'I'll go and fetch Bella, she'll want to be there for you, Lexi.' He gave her a quick hug, then headed off.

'It's going to be high tide soon,' Jools said. 'Never mind the rain, I think these drops are coming from sea spray. Come on, let's get inside that café.'

They hurried as quickly as they could up to Sacha's Summer Sundaes café, panting slightly by the time Lexi pushed open the café door. The large sea front window was steamed up, but the warmth of the cosy place immediately soothed her. They took off their jackets and, spotting Sacha behind the counter, smiled when she indicated a free table at the back.

Once seated, Jools said, 'I love it here, it's such a hive of activity, don't you think? Although that said, it does mean that Sacha seems to be constantly working.'

Lexi looked over at Sacha. If she didn't know better, she would think that her friend had stepped right out of a Californian surfing magazine with her sun-kissed, blonde wavy hair. She and her brother Jack looked so similar. As usual, Sacha had a big smile on her face as she took another order. She had worked so hard to make a success of the café and Lexi was proud of her.

A few minutes later Sacha walked over to their table. 'Hi, girls. How's it going?' Before either Lexi or Jools had a chance to answer her, she frowned. 'Are you alright Lexi? You don't seem your usual bubbly self.'

'I'm waiting for Bella to join us,' she explained. 'Jack's gone to fetch her now and then I'll tell you all about my morning with Dad.'

'There's nothing wrong with him is there?' Sacha asked, pushing her notepad and pen into her rear jean's pocket.

'Not yet,' Jools said, scowling.

A couple entered the café and Sacha waved at them. 'I'd better see to these customers, but I'll come back when Bella and Jack get here. Can I get you anything in the meantime?' She straightened the beach hut cruet set in the middle of the table. 'Would you like your usual hot chocolate to be going on with?'

Lexi and Jools nodded. 'Please,' they replied in unison.

'Two hot chocolates with extra chocolate sprinkles coming up,' she said giving Lexi's right shoulder a gentle squeeze before making her way over to the counter.

They took off their coats and hung them on the back of their seats. Jools pulled off her beanie hat and stuffed it partially into the pocket of hers before running her fingers through her short spiky pink hair. She then pushed up her sleeves as far as her elbows and turned to face Lexi.

'I've been thinking. You mustn't worry about it too much. I promise we'll find a way to help you. I know there's nothing you can do about cottages being sold. But you can bunk up with Sacha, Bella and me at different times and we'll find you a job. You must not ever think you're alone in all this. We're here for you, just like we know you are for us.'

Lexi appreciated her friend's reassurances. She knew that her three best friends would put her up temporarily, but she hated the thought of having to rely on them. Each of their homes was small. Jools lived with her gran, Bella rented out her two spare rooms to Jack and Alessandro – Sacha's boyfriend – and Sacha only had the one room in her flat above the café.

They had always been there for each other and the reminder that she wouldn't be alone for this made her feel slightly better. Yes, her life was going to change, but she did have friends. Good ones. It wasn't all bad she tried to tell herself, noticing for the first time that she had pulled a paper napkin into tiny pieces that were lying partially in her lap. She scooped them up and put them in her pocket to dispose of later.

She opened her mouth to thank Jools for her kind words when the door burst open and in raced Bella, her face pink from the cold, followed by Jack. Bella scoured the busy room looking for them and seeing Jools waving at her, rushed over. 'I'm glad I've found you both.' She pulled out a seat and sat down immediately.

'Hi ladies,' Jack said, stopping to give Lexi and Jools a kiss on their cheeks. 'Sorry, can't stop. I promised I'd help Sacha out with this lot.'

When Jack had gone to the kitchen to help his sister, Bella looked from Jools to Lexi. 'Jack told me what Jeff has done. I can't believe he'd be that stupid.' She mumbled something under her breath as she struggled out of her jacket. 'Sorry Lexi I don't mean to insult your father, but really. What the hell was he thinking?'

Sacha arrived at the table with three hot chocolates and a plain coffee for Jack. 'Right, now we're all here, please tell me what's happened. I'm dying to know what's been going on.'

Jack joined them and picked up his coffee. 'I'll take those,' he said, indicating her notepad and pen. 'You sit down and chat to these three while I take the orders for a while. I've heard what's gone on already.'

Lexi watched him go, wishing she didn't have to repeat her story again. Her heart was pounding at the thought of what her father had done and the last thing she wanted was to become emotional while telling Sacha and Bella her upsetting news.

'You're not going to believe it, Sacha,' Bella said.

Lexi took a deep breath and gave them a brief version. She could see the anger in her friends' faces as they listened intently. She dared not look at Jools, who was sitting on her right. She could almost feel her fury and knew that hearing it all again was winding her friend up.

Sacha shook her head slowly. 'I'm stunned. I hope he was apologetic.'

Lexi swallowed the lump in her throat. 'I think he feels a little bit guilty, but that's irrelevant now. He can't change what he's done.'

Bella picked up her mug and blew on the foamy hot chocolate. 'And Oliver Whimsy has bought them. Wow. How did he seem when he told you?'

'He was embarrassed more than anything, I think.' Lexi pictured Oliver's shocked face when it dawned on him that she had no idea about the sale. 'Now he's going to be living in one of the cottages. It's very odd.'

'I can't believe it.' Sacha shook her head again.

'Neither can Lexi.' Jools gave Lexi's hand a squeeze. 'We're obviously all shocked about this, but she needs our help. She's going to be out of her home and out of a job soon, so we need to put our heads together and come up with a plan.'

Mortified to find herself in such a vulnerable position, Lexi had to fight back the tears that were threatening to appear. She took a tissue from her sleeve and blew her nose. Then, picking up her mug, took a sip of the delicious chocolate concoction. 'This is heavenly, Sacha. Thanks.'

'Don't forget that you can always come and stay with me for a bit. My sofa isn't very big, so you'll have to share my bed. And,' she added, before Lexi had a chance to reply. 'I've always got food and drink here, so you'll never go without sustenance.'

Lexi sighed touched by her friend's thoughtfulness. 'Thank you.'

'You'd do the same for me.'

Sacha was right, she would. In fact, Lexi had put each one of them up at various times over the years when they had argued with family, returned from travelling with nowhere to stay, or simply been the worse for wear after a night out. This was different though. She was the one having to take their help and being in this position made her anxious.

'I love you all for caring about me so much.'

Bella slammed her hand on the table. A couple of customers glanced over to see what was going on, but soon turned away when all four glared back at them.

'Why are they being so nosy,' Jools grumbled.

'Shush,' Sacha glared at her. 'You'd be interested if you heard someone making that noise.' She frowned at Bella. 'What did you do that for anyway?'

'Sorry. I think I was imagining the table was Jeff, or Oliver Whimsy's face.'

'Oliver hasn't done anything wrong, though,' Lexi argued, not wishing her friend to take it upon herself to march up and give him a mouthful, which would not be too hard to imagine.

'He's only made a business transaction.'

'I suppose you're right,' Bella shrugged. 'You can come and stay with me.'

'No, I can't. You have more people in your house than anyone else and your bed is smaller than Sacha's. I'll sort something out, don't worry.' Lexi smiled at each one of her friends in turn.

She loved them all, and knowing they cared this much for her gave her a bit of confidence and made her feel much better. 'Thank you, but I bumped into Betty at the shop earlier and she made the same offer. I can't accept, although, if I am desperate, I promise I'll come and sleep on one of your sofas.'

'You could always try and make things up with your dad maybe?' Jools raised her thin eyebrows. 'It's the least he can do to let you move back into your old bedroom for the time being, or until you're sorted,' Jools said, looking very satisfied with the suggestion.

The three friends stared at her expectantly. 'Ahh,' Lexi braced herself for the anticipated angry reaction and filled them in on the reason why that wouldn't be a possibility. She waited for the stunned silence and three wide-eyed stares to vanish.

'OK, now this is too much,' Bella said. 'Your dad needs to have a word with himself.'

Sacha looked around before saying, 'I think we should probably lower our voices a little, if we don't want everybody in here to know Lexi's business.'

'To be fair,' Lexi explained not wanting them to be completely furious with her father. 'His studio was pretty small to begin with, so I can see why he wanted to extend it into my bedroom.'

Sacha leant in closer to her across the table. 'I would agree if he then hadn't sold the cottages, but to sell your home right under your nose, not tell you and then, on top of that, remove any chance of you returning to his home, seems...' She hesitated for a moment. 'Well, it seems incredibly harsh and not very like Jeff, if you don't mind me saying.'

She didn't mind at all. She hated being at odds with her father but had reached the same conclusion as her friend.

Sacha groaned. 'He's obviously going through some sort of midlife crisis. It's that bloody Gloria, I know it is. Mum can't stand her. She was only saying yesterday how that woman was boasting to one of the women in the bakery that she was your father's new muse.'

The notion made Lexi gasp. Her mother had always been her father's muse. He really had moved on. In every possible way. The thought devastated her. She put her hand in her pocket, fished around for an old tissue took it out and blew her nose. She didn't want to make a scene and cause her friends any more worry than she already had by crying. Lexi rarely gave in to tears but seemed to be doing it rather a lot already today.

'It's fine. I'll get used to all this soon.' She focused on taking a sip of her hot chocolate, the creamy, sugary liquid soothing her slightly.

'No,' Sacha said, a determined look on her face. 'We are your friends and we'll find a place for you to stay. If necessary, you can take it in turns to stay with each of us.'

Jools nodded. 'Try not to worry, about any of this. We can sort it.'

Lexi needed to be alone, to think things through. 'No, I'm fine thanks. I'll let you know how I am, but don't want you to fret about me. I can't imagine Oliver Whimsy will expect me to move out immediately. Well not tonight, at least.'

'He better bloody not,' Jools grumbled. 'I'll come with you.'

Lexi shook her head and motioned for her friend to stay seated. 'No, thanks. I need some alone time to think.'

Lexi gave each of her friends a grateful hug and waved at Jack, who was now dealing with two giggling teenagers at the counter. She pulled on her coat and zipped it up, needing to get outside.

It was harder than usual to walk up the hill as the wind had picked up and she was walking into it. As she neared the cottages, memories of her playing on the front lawn came back to her. She could almost see her mother planting the orange and yellow marigolds in an arc around the front.

She thought back to when her mum's heart condition had deteriorated to the point that she was unable to clean and manage the cottages. It had been an automatic progression for Lexi to take over the running of the three properties. They had all assumed her mother's illness would eventually be the cause of her death, so when her mother had died in a car crash it had been even more shocking to Lexi and her dad. The connection to her mother by keeping busy running the holiday lets was what had kept Lexi going. She had also, she realised, made the mistake of believing and acting as though the cottagers were hers and always would be.

She should have planned out her future a little bit better. Maybe if she had sat down and discussed how she felt with her father, instead of assuming that she would continue to do her mother's job, he might have understood the significance of the cottages to her.

The sky darkened. Lexi turned to stare down the hill and noticed the heavy, steel grey clouds working their way across the Channel from Guernsey. The horrible day suited her mood to perfection and, not wanting to get soaked, she picked up her speed and continued walking home.

The lights went on in the first building and she saw Oliver Whimsy's tall figure as he walked past the window carrying a mug of coffee. She might have told friends that none of this was his fault, but couldn't help wondering whether he'd have wanted to buy the cottages if she hadn't taken pity on him after the party and given him one to rent at the last minute. Was it her fault, or simply serendipity playing a cruel joke on her?

She hurried along the path to her temporary home. Her freezing breath came out in tiny clouds as she quietly unlocked her front door. She closed the door behind her, trying to picture living somewhere else on the island, but knew it wouldn't be the same. The pressure in her throat increased at the thought of having to move away.

Lexi took off her coat and hung it up by the front door. She desperately did not want to give in to the tears that were threatening to overwhelm her, but only managed to walk into the living area before the tears began to flow down her cold cheeks.

She sat on the nearest chair and cried for what seemed like hours. As the tears eventually petered out, she took a deep breath, exhausted by the release of her pent-up emotions. Walking over to the worktop, Lexi tore of a couple of squares of paper towelling, wiped her eyes properly and blew her nose. It was going to take her a little time to reconcile what had happened and be able to move forward.

She flicked the switch on the kettle and stood

leaning against the side of the cupboards. Didn't her mother always say that opportunities come when you least expect them? This did not feel like any opportunity though, it simply felt like the end of a very special part of her life. Taking hold of her favourite mug, she spooned in some hot chocolate powder. Lexi knew she was about to lose something she had always cherished and had naively expected to always be a part of her life.

What was she going to do next?

CHAPTER FOUR

Lexi swallowed the last mouthful of creamy hot chocolate and was washing the cup in the sink when someone knocked on the door. She wanted to pretend to be out, but the living room door was open and whoever was outside would know she was at home.

Lexi wiped a stray tear from her eyes and could tell by the puffiness of her face that it would be obvious to whoever was out there that she had spent some time crying. Her friends knew her well though, she decided, going to open the door. She pulled it back, expecting to see one of them outside.

'Oh.'

By the startled expression on Oliver Whimsy's face, he had not expected to be welcomed by someone who had obviously been distraught only a short while before. He seemed a little taken aback by the sight of her face, but only for an instant before covering up his shock.

'I'm sorry. I didn't mean to disturb you.' He looked past her towards the warm hallway. 'I was wondering if I could have a chat with you about a few things? If this is a difficult time though maybe we could meet up sometime tomorrow?'

'No, now is as good a time as any,' she said, resigned as much as she could be to her fate.

Lexi moved back to let him enter and waved him through to the living area. She closed the door against the brisk wind and watched him as he walked down the short hallway.

His shoulders seemed tense. What had really happened to bring him to the island?

'...here?'

She blushed aware that she had not been listening to what he was saying. 'Sorry, my mind's a bit all over the place right now,' she admitted. 'Would you mind repeating what you just said?'

Oliver studied her thoughtfully as he stood by her two-seater sofa, and somehow the room reduced in size around him. She wasn't sure if it was because he was so tall and broad-shouldered, or simply that his presence signified everything in her life was about to change.

'I was apologising for my unexpected arrival.'

Lexi thought of her father and Gloria's smug expressions when she had gone to confront them. She had to take a moment to calm herself to be able to speak without becoming emotional. 'It's not your fault you've found yourself in this awkward family situation. You simply made an offer to buy these properties and it was accepted. I can't hold that against you.'

He stared at her, frowning. 'That's as may be, but it's because of me that this is no longer your home. I gave your father a call earlier and have discovered that you're also now out of a job.'

She could see he was troubled by the situation and, judging by his fleeting sneer, that he wasn't impressed to have been a party to something underhand. Lexi didn't want his pity though. She would be fine. Hadn't her friends reassured her that she would be?

'I have a prospect to put to you,' he said, interrupting her wandering thoughts.

Lexi realised she still hadn't put away her shopping from earlier. She walked over to the cupboards and waited for him to step aside, then bent to put the milk in the fridge before straightening and folding her hessian shopping bag.

'Go on,' she said, intrigued to know what he had in mind.

'It's occurred to me that I'm going to be holed up here for several months.' He lowered his gaze finding the rug on the floor fascinating. 'You might have read about me recently in the papers.' He waited for her to reply.

'I don't often bother reading them that often, so no, I haven't.'

He seemed relieved by this information. 'I

could tell by the secretive glances when I stayed at the hotel the last time I was here that people have been making up their minds about me without knowing all the facts.' He studied her once again. 'It's usually the way these things work.'

Lexi had not wanted to admit it to him, but she had read something about him. She thought of the newspaper stories she had seen and discussed with her friends. He was right, she thought guiltily, they had all made up their minds about him without knowing him at all.

'I've never been in the media,' she said. 'I don't know how it works, but I gather they can put a twist on a story and make something out of nothing.'

He leant against the work surface and pushed his hands into his jean pockets. 'They've made me out to be something I'm not. I know that the incident at the hotel on Halloween with Nicky didn't help people's opinion of me, in fact it probably helped cement what they already suspected I might be like.'

He didn't sound as if he felt sorry for himself, Lexi noted, listening to his matter-of-fact statement.

'I have to admit that I did read something about it,' she said, deciding to be open. 'And you're right, it didn't show you in the best light.'

'No, it didn't.' He sighed heavily. 'I'm not here to make excuses for myself, or to make friends.'

Charming, thought Lexi, liking him a little less.

Oliver frowned. 'I would hope that when you get to know me, you'll form your own opinion. While I am here though, I have some business to attend to, and I'm also working on a book I've been signed to write.'

'Really?' Now that did sound interesting.

He must have noticed her interest. 'It's nothing too thrilling, I'm afraid. It's about setting up and running new businesses in the current economic climate.'

'Oh, right.' If that was the case, then Lexi wasn't sure why he was mentioning it to her. Maybe he thought it might impress her.

'I need someone to type the manuscript from my notes.' Lexi was beginning to see where she might come in. 'I gather from your father that you can type. He mentioned you'd trained as a personal assistant and worked in a couple of offices after leaving school.'

'He told you that?' Lexi wasn't sure if she was more surprised that her father had spoken to Oliver in detail about her, or that her father actually recalled her typing abilities. 'Yes, that's right. Why?'

'I was wondering whether you'd consider typing the papers up for me. I'll probably be a bit of a pain with editing, but I thought I could pass my notes on to you as I go. Maybe a chapter at a time. We could see how it goes. Is that something you'd be interested in?'

She considered his offer. 'What hours would you want me to work?' she asked trying not to sound too interested. 'I assume it'll be a paid role?'

He mentioned a sum, which seemed generous to Lexi. Then again, she had no idea how much a typist earned per hour nowadays, so he might be offering her something below the standard rate. She did not think so though. Lexi was glad he wasn't offering her charity, that would be too embarrassing. She wasn't up for accepting that. Nor, she realised, was she ready to admit how desperate she felt.

'Would you want me to come to your place to work?' Lexi hadn't typed up anything lengthy for several years and wasn't sure how fast her touch typing was now. She didn't like the thought of him witnessing her lack of prowess.

'Yes, please. Unless you'd rather work from here. I presume you have a laptop, or if not, I can get one for you.'

She didn't. 'Sorry, no. I try to keep my personal effects to a minimum and do most things, like dealing with bookings, invoices and banking from my phone. So, if you could, that would be helpful.'

'No problem. I'll get one ordered for you today.'

She wondered if he would do it himself, or whether he had an office of minions waiting for him to make requests for various things.

'When would you want me to start?' she asked without taking the time to think any further about his offer. After all, what other choice did she have?

'As soon as the laptop arrives, and I've got some edits worked through. Shall we say next Monday?'

Lexi nodded. 'OK.'

He went to leave. 'I forgot. One other thing. The cottages.' Her mood dipped again. 'As it's the middle of winter, I didn't think you'd have any bookings. Is that correct?'

'Yes, that's right. They're pretty much empty for the next few months.'

'Fine. I admit that I don't really know yet my final plans for them, but I'd rather they were lived in. I don't want to deal with squatters or burst pipes.'

Lexi didn't bother to mention that there wasn't really an issue with squatters on the island, but the thought of frozen pipes made her shudder. There had been an issue with one of the cottages when her mother had been alive. The pipes had frozen when they had gone away as a family for a week one winter, when she was twelve, returning to a nightmare of ruined cupboards, carpets and furniture. The temperature had risen and water had poured into the end property for two days. It had taken a couple of months to put things right and an insurance claim for the replacement kitchen, bathroom and new furniture and fittings.

'I'm happy for you to stay here until the other two have been rented out,' Oliver said. 'I don't suppose that will be until what, say, March?'

Lexi thought back to the previous year. 'It probably depends on when Easter is,' she said. 'Or how good the weather is in the February half term. Occasionally, families make last-minute bookings to come here for that week, and corporate types who fancy a bit of surfing in the wilder months.'

'Good.' He seemed satisfied with this news and nodded. 'Then shall we say we'll take it from there? Go by the diaries for now?'

Lexi didn't like to show how relieved she felt that she didn't have to immediately find somewhere else to live. Not yet, at least. She stared at him, not wishing to accept anything further from him, but aware that she didn't have much choice. 'Yes, that's kind, thank you.'

'No, Lexi,' he said quietly. 'Thank you. You'll be helping me out. I will have to go away occasionally, and it will be good to have you here to keep an eye on things.'

She liked the idea of being helpful, rather than accepting charity from him.

'Also, with regard to you typing for me,' he continued, pushing his hand through his slightly too-long hair. 'I can lose track of time when I'm working. If I have plans to leave the island for a bit, then I tend to work late, or have early starts during the days leading up to my departure. I was hoping that as you're close at hand, I could pass work on to you.' He looked at her, eyes narrowed. 'I might not stick to the nine to five routine. Is that something you would mind very much? I would pay you the going rate of course.'

If it meant that she could remain in her beloved home for one last Christmas, then Lexi was willing to agree to an awful lot. Anyway, would it really be so bad, working for Oliver Whimsy? It wasn't as if she was committing herself to years of spending time with him, just a few months. There wasn't any harm in giving it a try. It least it was a job. And it would mean that she wouldn't have to look for another one until the spring. What did she have to lose?

'OK,' she said, relieved. 'We'll give it a go and see how it works out.'

CHAPTER FIVE

Beginning of December

The following morning, Lexi drove her ancient estate car down to the boardwalk. She never minded lending her car, or her time to Bella. She enjoyed helping her friend deliver antiques and transport stock to the occasional market, where Bella topped up her income selling pieces to the locals. There was no parking on the boardwalk, but Lexi knew that if she was only stopping long enough to pack or unpack her car, then the Centenier – the parking control officer – wouldn't give her a ticket.

She was a few minutes early to meet Bella. Lexi covered her mouth with her scarf and pulled her beanie down further over her ears to keep them warm. She leant against the icy metal railings overlooking the beach and gazed at the waves crashing against the nearby rocks.

It would soon be high tide, and she realised that Jack's suggestion to collect Bella's stock for the market now was to ensure they weren't packing the car when the sea reached the boardwalk. A large wave broke over the end of the pier and smashed against the red and white lighthouse. The jade green sea was getting pretty lively.

Not wishing to tempt fate, Lexi ran to Bella's cottage and banged on the front door. Within seconds Jack pulled it open, his sun-kissed hair sticking up at all angles.

'Hi. Quick, come in,' he said. 'The sea is rough this morning. I was hoping to get in a bit of surfing, but Bella made me promise not to. She said it was too dangerous when it's like this.'

'And she'd be right,' Lexi said, shaking her head. 'Only an idiot would surf in this.'

He laughed. 'Are you trying to say I'm an idiot?'

'I'm not trying to say anything,' she teased.

He led the way through to the kitchen, passing several boxes that Lexi knew from experience would contain the smaller items Bella hoped to sell at the Christmas Market.

'You're ready, I see.' She stepped into Bella's galley kitchen, where her friend was taking the last few gulps of her tea.

'Want one?' Bella asked holding up her empty cup.

'We don't have time. Not if we want to get out of here before the tide reaches the sea wall.' Jack took Bella's cup from her and put it in the sink.

'He's right,' Lexi said, picturing the incoming stormy tide. 'We'd better load those boxes and get a move on. I'll get a hot chocolate from the café in the yurt at the market.' She knew that if they did stay too long her car was at risk of getting a stray pebble through the windscreen and didn't relish that happening. The last thing she needed now was unexpected bills to pay.

Fifteen minutes later, the car was packed and the three of them drove up the hill, away from the boardwalk, to the nearby granite barracks where the market was usually held towards the end of November, but this year had been delayed until closer to Christmas. Lexi parked as close as she could to her designated stall. Jack got out of the car and immediately roped in several other stall holders to help with the unpacking.

She liked the way each small room at the barracks held only two or three stalls. Because of Bella's slightly larger pieces, she was in a room with only one other seller. He had his back to them, unpacking loaves of bread as they went back and forth with the boxes.

Finally, relieved to be inside, away from the biting wind, Lexi began helping Bella unpack each box. Bella turned to smile at the other occupant, and Lexi noticed her friend's eyes widen. She looked at the object of her attention.

''Ello,' he said, in a French accent. 'I am Remi. I am pleased to meet you both.'

Lexi forced a smile and waited for Bella to introduce herself and shake his hand, before she did the same.'

'You're a baker?' Lexi asked, mortified that she was stating the obvious.

'I am an artisan baker.' He waved a hand across the row of baskets containing different types of loaves of bread.

'Ooh, tell us more.' Bella said, while it was as much as Lexi could do to stop staring at his beautiful dark brown eyes.

'I usually sell eight of my most popular loaves, mainly the rustic focaccia, soda bread and sourdough. Everyone expects me to bake baguettes, so I do. I also sell a ciabatta, publiese and a couronne, and because I'm living in the Channel Islands, I recently began selling the Jersey Cabbage loaf and the Guernsey Gâche, naturally.'

Lexi and Bella exchanged glances, impressed with Remi's different breads.

'That's a lot of choice,' Jack said as he came through the door. He looked over at Lexi. 'I couldn't help overhearing one of the *Centeniers* saying that you're going to have to move your car. It's in the way. If you give me the keys, I'll move it for you.'

Grateful not to have to leave the conversation with the handsome French baker, Lexi took the car keys from her pocket and lobbed them over to Jack. 'Thanks, Jack.'

As he walked away, Lexi turned her focus

again to Remi. 'Jack's right. That's a lot of different loaves to prepare.'

Remi smiled, his thin face lighting up. 'I use different 'erbs in some of the loaves also. Rosemary is one of the favourite choices of my clientele. I try different mixtures in my bakery at home. I usually take orders and deliver them to clients' 'omes, but one of them suggested coming to the Christmas Market. So 'ere I am.' He gave a lazy, one-shouldered shrug. 'I thought it was probably a good idea. You?'

Lexi motioned to Bella. 'I'm just here to help my friend with her antiques and collectibles.'

'You do not 'ave a stall?'

She shook her head. 'No, I'm in the hospitality business,' she said, aware that she was going to have to find something new to take its place. 'Or, at least I am right now.'

'That is 'otels, or restaurants, no?'

She wished now she hadn't made her job sound more important than it was. 'I manage some fisherman's cottages.' She pointed out the door. 'They're the three tiny ones in a row on the hill, just up there.'

He leant forward so he could see out of the door and peered up the hill. 'Ah, I see them. They are pretty. People on vacation hire them?'

'That's right.'

A couple, well wrapped up against the cold, tentatively stepped into the room. Lexi focused on picking up and pretending to look at a silver toaster Bella had on display. She couldn't bear being stared at if she was mooching in a shop, and was more inclined to look at items for sale if she wasn't being watched while she did it. Assuming others felt the same way, she left it to Bella to take notice of them while Remi finished setting up his stall.

She knew from experience, helping Bella, that people were more likely to buy cheaper items first, like Remi's bread, and maybe come back to the collectable stall once they had spent time considering an item that might have taken their fancy. The man began asking Remi questions about his loaves, but the woman, after a few second's hesitation, made her way over to Bella's stall.

'That's pretty,' she said, spotting the toaster in Lexi's hand.

'It is, isn't it? I have a similar one at home, but this one is particularly lovely.'

Bella pushed a small box into a larger one and shoved it under the stall. 'Is there anything in particular that you're looking for?'

The woman nodded. 'I thought this would be the perfect opportunity to buy something for my mother for Christmas.'

Lexi placed the toaster down. It was time for her to leave Bella to what she did best. Remi raised his hand in a slight wave as she passed his stall. She waved back and walked outside, only just avoiding bumping into Jack, who was on his way back in. They stepped back to let two women go inside.

'Do you mind if I borrow your car for a bit?' He held up Lexi's keys. 'Sacha asked if I could go and collect her Christmas puddings from the café. She came up earlier but forgot to pack them. And a couple of Christmas cakes she's made for the market.'

'It's not like her to forget something,' Lexi said, concerned. 'I can go and fetch them, if you prefer?'

'No, you stay here and warm up with some of the hot chocolate I know you're dying to try. I just need to pop down to the boardwalk, if that's OK?'

'Sure.' She was happy for him to go. He was right, she had been looking forward to trying out the hot chocolate, since discovering how delicious it was at last year's market.

She hurried across the busy yard to the yurt, knowing it would be warm inside and not caring about the inevitable queue. Opening the door, the heat warmed her face as she stepped inside. She scanned the dark space surprised, like she had been last year, by how many small groups of tables and stools they'd managed to fit inside. There were also at least twelve people waiting to place their order at the narrow counter. Lexi hadn't expected to find a spare seat and was simply relieved to be in the warmth for a bit. She rubbed her hands together, looking forward to holding a warm cup in them.

The two baristas worked expertly, pouring elaborate coffees, herbal teas and whatever other drink people chose from their extensive menu, written on chalk boards. Finally, Lexi held her cup in her hands and, paying for it, turned to see if she might have any luck finding somewhere to sit for a while. There wasn't really enough room to stand in the yurt once you had received your order, so it was an unspoken assumption that if you couldn't sit, you left and consumed your drink out in the cold.

'Hi, Lexi?'

She couldn't place the voice for a second, but the hint of a Scottish accent soon alerted her to Oliver's presence. She stiffened slightly, unable to immediately spot him in the dim light. She scanned the seating area for a second time and noticed him waving her towards a stool next to him, behind a man who was concentrating on zipping up his anorak.

'I think he's saving it for yer love,' the man said giving her a knowing smile as she waited for him to inch his way around the table to get out.

Lexi didn't thank him, grateful to Oliver for calling her over.

She squeezed between the table and a woman whose chair was pushed up next to it. 'That was kind of you. Thanks.'

Finally seated, she placed her drink container on the table and unzipped her coat, winding her scarf from her neck to make the most of the warmth in the room. 'It's perishing outside.'

'You should try living in the Highlands during the deep winter.' He glared at a man who knocked into his shoulder. 'I'm only stopping for a bit.'

Was this Oliver's way of telling her not to take his kindness the wrong way?

'I noticed people gravitating towards this place, and the strange bunting hanging above the entrance with pictures of Jersey cows' faces painted on it, and couldn't resist coming in.'

'It's good, isn't it? Do they have these markets where you're from?' she asked, hoping he would open up a little about his hometown.

'They do. This one is smaller than the ones I've visited, and somehow feels more traditional. Where I'm from, stallholders and artisans come from miles away to sell their wares, so there's much more going on. I think I prefer it here though. It's like going back fifty years.'

'I didn't think you'd be old enough to do that.' He didn't smile. Misery, she thought, trying to think what to say next. She didn't want to upset her new boss and landlord so soon after making a deal with him. 'That is to say—'

His eyes began to twinkle and he smiled. 'I'm teasing you. Although I have to admit that sometimes I do feel a lot older than I am.'

Intrigued, she asked. 'Why's that then?'

He shook his head. 'It's nothing.' He picked up

his cup and shook it slightly. 'One more mouthful and then I'd better go and let someone else have my seat.' He finished his drink and then, standing to take his empty cup to the recycling box, smiled at her. 'See you around. Have a good day.'

'Yes.' She couldn't help wondering why she felt a pang to see him leave. 'See you soon.'

His place was taken by a matronly woman Lexi knew vaguely. She occasionally stopped to stroke the woman's two spaniels while they were playing on the beach below the boardwalk. They chatted briefly about the latest dog food the woman had discovered for her dogs, and how she didn't like having to keep her dogs on leads on the beach between the months of May and October, during the day.

'I suppose I can understand why,' she said, the bobble on her bright pink hat bouncing as she nodded. 'But my dogs are well behaved and would never upset sunbathers or children playing.'

Lexi listened to her voice and noticed that the drink queue had now reached the door and did a U-turn back into the room.

'I think I'd better make space for someone else,' she said, relieved to find an excuse to leave. 'It was good catching up with you.'

She finished her drink, disposed of the cup, and pulled her beanie back over her short pixie haircut. After winding her scarf around her neck and zipping up her coat, she weaved through the throng of people to the outside.

'Bloody hell,' she coughed, her breath catching in her throat as soon as it was exposed to the cold air. 'It's freezing out here.'

'You talking to yourself again?' Jack jabbed her playfully in the ribs.

'Bugger off, Jack,' she said, spinning around to face him. 'It's alright for you to tease, you surf in this weather. I bet you even went in the sea today, didn't you?'

He linked arms with her as they strolled. 'Of course I did. Right, where shall we go now? How about the craft stall in that room there?'

Happy to agree to any suggestion that would take them away from the spiteful wind, Lexi nodded. She favoured the designs on one of the stalls. Everything was made from driftwood, shells and opaque glass the artist had picked up from one of the local beaches. She spotted something that would be perfect for her dad's Christmas gift. He might have done something to devastate her but he was the only family she had left, and she would still want to wrap up a present for him. It was a small flat piece of green frosted glass with a hole on one side. The stallholder had dabbed tiny specks of different coloured oil paint around the outside, which gave it the appearance of a tiny artist's palette. Her father loved anything creative or local and she could picture this piece on his studio windowsill. She felt a pang in her heart that they were no longer as close as they had been.

After studying other items on the stall, Lexi decided she had chosen the best gift for her father and that he could accept it in the spirit it was given or give it away. At least she'd made an effort to find something she hoped he would like. She paid for the tiny glass present and waited for it to be wrapped and placed into a small paper bag.

The weight of Jack's hand rested briefly on her shoulder. 'Good choice. For your dad?'

Lexi nodded. 'Do you think he'll like it?'

'I do.' He hesitated for a second. 'You know, I might have a proposition for you soon.' He winked at her.

Lexi froze, horrified to hear one of her best friend's boyfriends saying such a thing to her. She spun round to face him, shocked that Jack would act so out of character. 'Jack, I...'

'What?' His sandy eyebrows lowered in confusion. 'You thought...? Hell, no! I didn't mean—'

'Thank heavens for that.' Relief coursed through her. 'I didn't want to have to belt you one.'

Jack rubbed his chin. 'Charming. No, I was trying to tell you that I might have an answer to your housing problem. Or, at least Bella might. We have to work through the details, but I just didn't want you to worry unnecessarily about that Whimsy bloke buying your home from under you.'

His thoughtfulness cheered her. 'That's very kind of you both. Thank you.'

'Whimsy,' he said as they entered the craft room. 'What sort of stupid name is that?'

'It's my stupid name,' said an indignant deep voice from the other side of the room.

Lexi bit her lower lip. Jack had a habit of putting his foot in his mouth and saying the wrong thing. She decided to introduce them quickly before tempers got out of hand. Stepping between them, she pulled a face at Jack, who looked, she was pleased to note, embarrassed by his gaff.

'Oliver Whimsy, this is Jack Collins. He's Sacha from the café's brother and Bella's boyfriend. Bella runs her antiques business, The Bee Hive, from the little blue cottage on the boardwalk. You probably met at the Halloween party?'

Instead of shaking Jack's outstretched hand, Oliver looked confused. 'How many best friends do you have?'

'Three,' she said. 'The other one is Jools. You might not have met her yet either. She lives on the boardwalk with her grandmother. They run the second-hand book shop. She's an artist and has pink spiky hair, you can't miss her.'

'Right. There seem to be quite a few people living on the boardwalk. Apart from you.'

'Yes, I'm up the hill, but I can still see the boardwalk so I almost live there. There's also

Betty. She is the oldest resident.'

'She was a heroine during The Occupation when the Nazi's took over the island in the Second World War,' Jack explained proudly. 'I'm the surfer who helps out at the Summer Sundaes Café. Come in some time and I'll treat you to one of Sacha's specialities by way of an apology for being rude about your name.' The men shook hands. 'Even though you're the one who's bought Lexi's home and put her out of a job.'

'That's enough of that,' Lexi whispered, elbowing him.

'It wasn't done on purpose,' Oliver said. 'At least, I didn't know the circumstances until after the sale was complete.'

Not wishing to listen to the two of them act like stags, battling out supremacy, Lexi interrupted. 'I'm going to find Sacha and Jools and see how they're getting on at their stalls.' Without waiting for either man to answer she left the craft room and went to look for her friends.

She was delighted to find Sacha selling her cakes and buns in a room two doors along. Jools, the only other occupant, was displaying her brightly coloured abstracts of the cliffs and the red and white lighthouse either side of the boardwalk.

'How's it going so far, you two?'

'I've done quite well.' Sacha lifted an empty plastic container from behind her stall. 'I had two of these filled with Christmas puddings and

I've just sold the last one.'

'And I've managed to sell two of my larger paintings already,' Jools said, giving Lexi a wink. 'It's quite good for me and it's still early yet.' She lowered her voice as three people entered the room. 'How are things going with that Whimsy bloke?'

Lexi shrugged. 'Nothing much happening right now. He's ordered me a laptop so I can start typing up his work for him as soon as that arrives.'

Sacha and Jools exchanged surprised glances. 'You're going to work for him?'

Lexi had expected this sort of reaction from her protective friends. 'He's paying me and letting me stay at the cottage for the time being, so why not?'

There was a brief silence while they both digested this information.

'I suppose so,' Sacha shrugged. 'You could always come and help out at the café though, don't forget.'

Lexi knew there was barely enough work to keep Sacha, Jack and Milo busy. She couldn't in all conscience take wages from them. 'You don't need me.' She rubbed her hands together to warm them up. They might be inside away from the wind, but the door was permanently open and there was no heating in the bare granite rooms. 'Aren't you two freezing in here?'

Jools pulled a beanie out of her pocket and

pulled it on over her short hair. 'Not now I'm not,' she smiled. 'I have at least four layers on under this jacket, too.'

Sacha shivered. 'I'd rather be in my warm kitchen at the café, if I'm honest. Jack said he'd come and take over from me for a bit so I can go and warm up over a coffee in the yurt.' Sacha looked at Jools. 'I'm sure he'd keep an eye on your stall too if you wanted to join me.'

'Or, I could wait here for you?' Lexi offered. They looked at each other and she could see they were tempted by the offer. 'Go on, before the temperature in here changes my mind.'

They were making their way out when Oliver Whimsy arrived at the doorway. He stepped back to let them pass. Jools looked back at Lexi over her shoulder, and winked. 'We won't be long,' she said, thanking him with an icy tone in her voice as she left.

'Your friends, I presume?' he said, walking up to stand in front of Sacha's stall. 'I recognise the girl from the café.

'That's Sacha. Jools is the fiercer one with the pink spiky hair. She's a sweetie really.' She pointed at the paintings. 'Those are hers.'

He stepped closer and studied a couple of them. 'They're not bad at all.'

'You should tell her that, maybe she'll be a bit friendlier next time.'

'Maybe.' He turned his attention to Sacha's wares displayed neatly on the table between them. 'These look tasty. What are they? Donuts?'

'Jersey Wonders. You should try some.'

He nodded. 'I'll take half a dozen then,' he said. 'If I'm going to be here for a while it'll be easier if the locals don't all hate me.'

Lexi suspected it would take more than him buying a few donuts to soften her friends' opinion about him but didn't say so as she used the plastic tongs to drop six Jersey Wonders into a brown paper bag. She asked him for the money and once he'd paid, handed the bag over to him.

'They don't hate you exactly, they're just wary and concerned for me,' she said, putting his money in the tin and giving him his change. 'They know how much the cottages mean to me.'

'I recognise some of your friends from Nicky's disastrous Halloween party. No doubt they'll have a few preconceived ideas about me from that debacle.'

She couldn't deny that was the case. 'You've not really got off on the best of starts here really, have you?'

'It seems not. It's a good thing then that I'm not here to make friends.' She was about to add a snappy retort when Oliver opened the bag and held it out to her. 'Want one? Go on, it's pure bribery.'

She wasn't sure if he was teasing about not making friends. Could he be oblivious to how he was coming across to her, or did he simply not care what people thought of him? She realised he was waiting for her to take a Jersey Wonder and, hungry, couldn't resist.

'As you're trying to bribe me, why not? They are delicious. I've had lots of experience, tasting them at the café.'

They ate the small cakes in silence for a few moments. Finally, when Oliver had finished, Lexi asked, 'What's your verdict then? Good?'

'Exceptionally. I'll definitely have to keep on the right side of Sacha, if I want to be allowed into her café.'

'I thought you weren't here to make friends?'

'I'm not, but there's no point in antagonising people any more than I already have done, is there?'

There wasn't, she decided. She wasn't sure how well she was going to get on with him as her landlord and temporary employer. She knew that although she was easy going, she had her limits. Lexi hoped that Oliver Whimsy wouldn't give her cause to lose her temper with him, not when she needed a roof over her head.

If only there was somewhere else she could stay. If it was summer she could try to find a live-in job, but December was the worst possible time to find anything on the island now that the seasonal work had finished, and most of the hotels had closed down for the winter. There wouldn't be much chance of finding anything in hospitality until the run up to Easter.

A moment later Sacha and Jools returned. 'You two weren't very long,' Lexi said, instantly realising that Oliver could take her comment the wrong way. 'That is—'

'Thanks for looking after things for us,' Jools said. 'I don't suppose you had any sales.'

Lexi wished she could tell her otherwise but pointed at the bag in Oliver's hand. 'Only that one, I'm afraid. It'll probably get busier a little later.'

'I hope so,' Sacha grumbled. 'Otherwise I'm going to have to cart this lot home again.' She opened a container and replenished the Jersey Wonders displayed under a glass dome on the table. 'Jools and I were chatting about Christmas day,' she said, focusing her attention on Lexi.

Lexi felt her mood dip. She still hadn't heard from her father, despite leaving a message with Gloria two days earlier, asking him to call her when he had a moment. She had been suspicious when Gloria insisted he'd instructed her to tell Lexi he was indisposed. However, her father was a grown man and if he decided not to speak to her, she would have to just accept it. For now.

'With everything that's happened between you and your dad, I thought you might like to come to the café and spend Christmas day with us.' Sacha held her hand out to Jools in what Lexi realised was an almost choreographed chat they had come up with. 'My parents are going to family in Italy for the holidays, so we're spending the day at the café.'

'Yes,' Jools added. 'Gran, Jack and Bella are going to join Sacha, Alessandro and me at the café for Christmas lunch. Betty's coming too, and Claire, Bella's mum. Oh, and Tony, the fisherman and his kids, so it's going to be a fun day. You really should come, too.'

Lexi walked to the other side of the table to give her time to think of an answer that didn't offend them.

'Thanks, but I won't arrange anything just yet, if you don't mind. I'm sure I'll end up spending the day with Dad. We've never spent Christmas day apart yet, so I can't see him keeping up this coldness with me until then.'

She noticed Sacha was about to say something but stopped herself.

Sacha groaned and gazed at her thoughtfully.

Lexi could see a range of emotions crossing her friend's pretty face as she tried to work out how to break some news to her.

'You're worrying me now,' Lexi said, impatiently. 'What's happened? Go on, I can take it.' She wasn't sure she was up to hearing more bad news, but before her imagination began coming up with all sorts of terrifying options, she wanted to hear the facts.

Sacha took a deep breath. 'Your dad dropped off a box for you at the café.'

A box? 'Why did he take it there and not to the cottage?' Probably so he didn't have to face her, she thought, angry at him for being such a coward, again.

'He said you weren't in, and that you'd be bound to pop in here at some point.' Sacha shrugged. 'Which is true. You're here now, aren't you?'

Sacha had a point. 'Do you mind if I go and fetch it now?'

Sacha shook her head and took a step back. 'I left it in the storeroom. You know where that is, and where I keep the key. You'll find it on the middle shelf on the left, just as you go in. You can take it up to my flat, if you'd like some privacy.'

'No, it's fine.' She lowered her voice. 'I'll take it home.'

He stood. 'I'll carry it up for you, if you like?'

'It isn't too heavy,' Sacha said. 'Lexi shouldn't have any problem carrying it by herself.'

Oliver gave a slight nod.

'Lexi, you can come home with me to the shop if you like,' Jools said, giving her a proprietorial look. 'We're only a few doors down and it will save you lugging the box up the hill. I can leave you alone in my room if you want privacy.'

Lexi shook her head. 'I'm grateful for the offer, Oliver. And to both of you,' she said smiling at her caring friends. 'I don't want anyone to witness my reaction if whatever the box holds is upsetting in any way. Thanks for holding on to it for me, Sacha.'

'No problem at all.' Sacha held her arms wide

for Lexi to step into and gave her one of her bear hugs. 'Now, are you sure about Christmas?'

'I am, thanks.' Lexi hugged her back briefly before letting go.

Sacha narrowed her eyes and stared at Lexi thoughtfully. 'Fine. But if you change your mind, you know where I am.'

'Yes,' Jools added, standing up to hug Lexi. 'We don't want you spending the day alone. We know how much of a celebration your mum and gran used to make of it, and how you still miss them.'

Lexi took a deep breath to keep control of her emotions. She much preferred it when her friends were light-hearted and teasing each other amicably. She had been missing her mum and gran more than usual lately, and knew it wasn't just down to the fact that she would have to get through another Christmas without them.

'Thanks, I'll have a think and let you know, if that's OK?'

Sacha smiled at her. 'Of course. Whenever you're ready.'

'I forgot,' Jools said, her voice filled with excitement. 'We met Remi in the café, he was getting a coffee for him and Bella. He's a nice bloke, isn't he?'

Lexi nodded recalling the baker she'd spoken to earlier. 'He seems very pleasant. I only met him for the first time this morning though.'

Jools gave Oliver a brief glance before adding, 'He said to tell you that after the market finishes a few of them are going to the Fête dé Noué and meeting up later for couple of drinks in one of the pubs at the Royal Square. We said we'd go. Will you come along?'

'Yes, that would be lovely.' Lexi was a little embarrassed that Jools' invitation pointedly excluded Oliver. She hated to leave anyone else out, so looked up at him. 'You're welcome to join us too, if you like?'

'But don't feel you have to,' Jools said, frowning at Lexi. 'It was Remi's invitation after all, not ours.'

He looked from Jools to Lexi and shook his head. 'Thanks, Lexi, but I think I'll leave it. Right, I'd better get going. Have a good day, ladies.' He walked out and as soon as he'd left the room, Sacha glared at Jools.

'That was bloody rude of you.'

Jools looked stunned at the accusation. 'Why? He's not a very nice person.'

'You don't know that.' Lexi said, not wishing her friends to make assumptions about him based on her circumstances. 'We don't know him very well yet.'

'I know his type and I don't like him.' Jools scowled as she rearranged some of her paintings. 'Sorry if that bothers the two of you.'

Lexi didn't want to fall out with her friend, especially over someone she had only recently met. For all she knew, he could be the nasty person they initially thought him to be. And, she thought, going by Jools' reaction to him, she had a long way to go if she was ever to change her opinion.

'Look, let's forget it shall we? You two have a long day ahead of you. I'd better go and collect Betty. I said I'd give her a lift up here so she could spend an hour or so looking for Christmas gifts.'

'Thanks for reminding me about Betty,' Sacha said, immediately filling one of the paper bags with a dozen Jersey Wonders and another with a Christmas pudding. 'I know she'll want these and I'd hate to have sold out by the time she gets here. You can drop them down to her cottage.'

Relieved that the conversation had changed direction, Lexi agreed. 'You'd never be forgiven if you didn't save some for her. I'll get going and see you both in a bit.'

She left them chatting about what food to prepare for Christmas Day and went through to the back to collect the box her father had left for her. She didn't know what she had been expecting but was surprised to see it was a mid-sized delivery box, and probably one he'd received paint supplies in recently. The lid had been stuck down rather more securely than was probably necessary. Lexi lifted the box tentatively to gauge the weight and was relieved that Sacha had been right. It wasn't too heavy at all.

She carried the box into the café, waited for

Jack to pop the bag of Jersey Wonders on top, said her final goodbyes and left.

Lexi decided that as soon as she had dropped Betty off at the market. she would pop into the local shop and buy a few things to store in the fridge for a solitary Christmas meal, should she not be invited to join her father. She may as well be prepared if he didn't let her spend Christmas Day at his house, then the last thing she wanted to do was spend the day with friends, having to put on a brave face and pretending to have a good time. No, she much preferred the idea of spending the day quietly in the cottage reading a good book, transporting herself into a fictional world. Right now, it was preferable to being in this one.

First though, she wanted to see Betty, then hurry home and lock the door and sit quietly to open the box. She was a little nervous to see exactly what her father had thought so important for her to have.

CHAPTER SIX

Lexi arrived home half an hour later. She almost dropped her coat in her rush to remove it, while not letting go of the box, then hurried down the short hallway into her living room. It was warm enough in the cottage for her not to have to turn up the heating. She placed the box on the coffee table and went to the kitchenette. Picking up the kettle she gave it a light shake to see if there was enough water in it for a tea before switching it on. Then, after grabbing the kitchen scissors from the drawer, Lexi went and sat down, facing the box.

This is it, she thought, taking a deep breath. Opening the scissors, she slid one blade down the length of the brown parcel tape. Then, nipping at each side of the two folded pieces of cardboard making up the lid, she folded them back and stared inside the mysterious package.

The first thing she noticed was a note her father had enclosed, written in messy script.

I found this box in the attic recently. These photos belonged to your grandmother and your mum and I thought you would want them. I'm hoping they make up a little for what I've done, Dad x

He must be feeling guilty to go to the bother of bringing this to me, Lexi supposed. *Good.* Maybe the reality of what he had done might be sinking in, she thought angrily, still unable to believe that her father had sold the cottages behind her back.

Lexi reached in and took out a handful of old photos and began looking through them slowly. It was comforting to see pictures of her beloved grandmother. In one, she was sitting on the low wall by the pathway in front of the cottages, smiling at the camera, pointing at something behind the photographer. There were some photos of her mum, others of her dad, and quite a few of random people who had probably either stayed at the cottages, or worked there. There were so many photos, Lexi decided to separate them into two piles; one of her grandmother and mum that she could take time looking through, and one of the smiling people she didn't know.

She settled down on the two-seater sofa and made herself comfortable. This was going to take a good, few hours. Lexi's heart ached as she gazed at a photo of her grandmother and mother laughing together. Her mum was resting her head on her gran's shoulder. In another, they were holding their stomachs, bent forward in hysterical laughter, and Lexi couldn't help smiling at the simple joy in the picture she was holding. The bright colours of her mother's nineteen-eighties clothes and big shoulder pads, and her grandmother's orange and yellow striped dress, which wouldn't have looked out of place in the sixties. Such innocent times, or at least, Lexi thought, they had always seemed that way whenever her mother reminisced.

Lexi kissed the tip of her forefinger and pressed it lightly on the image of her grandmother's face, and then on her mother's. She knew she'd been very lucky to have had two such strong, kind women in her life growing up – she just wished one of them could be here now, to give her a hug and tell her everything would be alright. She placed the picture on the pile she wanted to keep for herself, and then picked up another few photos to look through.

So many faces and all seemed to be smiling. Then again, she thought, people had used reels of film in their cameras, with thirty-six shots at the most, back then. They'd have taken more care when snapping photos, usually keeping them for special occasions, or sentimental events they wanted to record. It's what made them so very special, Lexi decided, to know that these photos were taken for keeping and not to look through and delete when the moment has passed.

Even the photos of the people she didn't know

were all of smiling people, having a fun time at the holiday cottages. She wasn't surprised. Her grandmother had been a tough lady, but she was welcoming to everyone. Lexi sat back on the sofa and closed her eyes, visualising one of the days when she had brought her friends Jools and Sacha up to the cottages on their way for a walk in the nearby woods. They had been thirsty, and her gran had told them to take a seat at one of the three small metal tables she always set out on the front lawn, each with a bright yellow umbrella to shade them from the summer sunshine. She had gone inside and brought out three glasses of lemonade and three cornets, which she had made by twisting a sheet of paper and filling each one with sweeties.

'These are to keep you going on your walk,' she had said, giving them a wink. Lexi sighed. If only she could transport herself back to a day like that, even if just for an hour or so.

Several hours later there was a knock at the door. She stretched and stood up. Who could that be? she wondered walking through the hall.

'Jools, hi.' Lexi frowned. It was already dark and she realised it must be much later than she had expected. 'Come inside out of the cold.' She stepped back to give her friend space to enter the small hallway. 'Is everything alright?'

Jools put her hands on her hips and tilted her head, a grin on her cheeky face.

'What?' Lexi wasn't sure what message her

friend was trying to get across to her.

'You've obviously forgotten,' Jools said, her eyes travelling down to the photos in Lexi's hand. 'Photographs?'

'Take your coat off and come through. I've got something to show you.' Lexi led the way into the living room and indicated the large box on her coffee table. 'This is what Dad left for me. It's filled with photos of Mum and Gran. Other people's pictures are in there too. People who stayed at the cottages or worked for Gran, helping out during the holiday season.'

Jools pulled off her woolly hat and unbuttoned her coat, shaking her shoulders until it had dropped onto the sofa. She sat down on it and leant forward. 'Two piles?'

Lexi explained her reasoning for separating the photos. 'It's going to take me hours to do this properly, but I've been enjoying myself so far.'

Jools picked up the top photo on the pile with Lexi's mum and gran in them. 'Aww, they were lovely people, weren't they? I remember coming here for snacks and sweet treats.'

'Me, too.' Lexi cleared her throat to stop herself from becoming too emotional. 'I don't know if I'm being even more sensitive because it's almost Christmas and I'm going to have to spend another one without either of them here, or if I'm just being a sentimental fool.'

Jools reached forward and took Lexi's hand in hers. 'You're only human, Lex. You're bound to miss them both, especially at a special time of year and when...' she hesitated. 'Well, when your dad has done what he's done.'

Lexi sighed heavily. 'I suppose so.' Jools let go of her hand and put the photo she had been studying back on top of its pile. 'You didn't say why you're here,' Lexi added.

Jools grinned. 'You've obviously forgotten we were going join Bella, Remi and a few of the others from the market at the Fête dé Noué.'

Lexi stared at her blankly, trying to recall when she had made the arrangement. 'Oh, yes. Sorry about that. I've been so caught up with everything, I completely forgot. What time are we meeting them?'

Jools glanced at Lexi's wall clock and grimaced. 'We need to leave now really, especially if we want to catch the next bus into town.'

'I could drive,' Lexi said, preferring not to have to rely on the winter bus timetable. She could think of many occasions when she had missed one bus, only to have to wait for an hour to catch the next one.

Jools stood and pulled her hat back onto her head and lifted her coat. 'No. You're going to have a couple of glasses of warm cider, or,' she added when Lexi frowned at her, 'some of the mulled wine there's bound to be on offer at one of the Christmas stalls.'

Lexi knew Jools well enough to be aware that her friend wasn't going to give in. She may as well do as she had agreed and accompany her into St Helier to join the others. After all, she reasoned, it's probably the most Christmassy thing she would end up doing this year. 'Fine, then. Give me a second to quickly change and grab my coat and bag.'

Forty-five minutes later, Lexi linked arms with Jools in the cold December air as they walked through town. She looked up at the blue and white Christmas lights that must have taken weeks to hang up throughout the town, and smiled. She was glad she had made the effort to come now. The atmosphere in the town was certainly festive and the shops were open late, so that anyone needing to do last minute Christmas shopping was given the chance to do so.

'What does La Fête dé Noué mean, do you know?' Lexi asked, not expecting her friend to be able to answer. 'I suppose it's The Festival of Christmas, or some such thing.'

'I think it's simply Christmas Festival,' Jools said, waving to someone she knew, walking along the pavement on the opposite side of the road. 'Now, we can go in the shops, or just see what there is on the stalls? I think we'll find the others somewhere around the market.'

'Yes, near the warm drinks if they've got any sense,' Lexi laughed.

'Then we can all go and find somewhere to watch the parade.'

'Good idea.' Lexi gave her friend's arm a gentle squeeze. 'Thanks for making me come along to-night. I'm enjoying myself and we haven't even got to the market yet.'

Jools smiled at her. 'I'm pleased you're having fun and that you agreed to come. I wasn't sure if you'd want to, not after all that's happened. If you do nothing else over Christmas, at least you'll have this evening to remember. I think that everyone should have one special time to look back on each Christmas, don't you?'

Lexi agreed. Jools was right. It was important to make the effort to have something worth re-membering each year. She nodded. 'I do.'

They entered the Royal Square and immedi-ately spotted Remi. He was laughing at some-thing Bella was saying, and Lexi and Jools quick-ened their pace to reach them.

'Hi there,' Jools shouted, waving to get their attention.

Bella turned and beamed at them. 'I was beginning to think you two weren't coming, but Remi assured me you'd be here.'

Lexi didn't know how he could know such a thing, having only just met them. Her thoughts must have shown on her face because when she looked at him, she could see him grinning at her.

'I just had a sixth sense that you would be here,' he said raising an eyebrow at her.

She couldn't help smiling at him.

'And did you also sense that we would need a

hot drink to warm us up on this cold evening?' Jools teased.

Lexi laughed. She loved her friend's cheekiness. 'Well,' she asked. 'Did you?'

Remi threw his head back and laughed loudly. 'You Jersey girls have a way about you. So, ladies, what would you like to drink then?'

'Cider,' Jools said.

'Mulled wine for me, please.'

They greeted Bella while Remi bought their drinks, and Lexi was delighted to hear that her friend had eventually done well at the market earlier in the day.

'Remi sold all his bread,' Bella said. 'Which was rather annoying as I had hoped to buy a loaf for myself. It serves me right for not buying one and putting it aside.'

Lexi felt much better after a couple of drinks of the spicy warm red wine. 'Shall we go and have a look at some of the other stalls now?'

Later, as they watched the bright lights and listened to the music from the parade, Lexi thought how much her mother had enjoyed coming to this festival each year. She would have to find ways to make new traditions for herself, and new memories, she decided. For now, though, it was enough to be with two of her closest friends and a new one. After a fun evening, the three women caught the bus back to the boardwalk, while Remi went his own way to the part of the island where he lived.

'That was really good fun,' Lexi said standing in readiness to get off the bus at an earlier stop to her friends. She hugged Jools and Bella and promised to catch up with them the following day.

As Lexi walked the short distance from the bus stop to her cottage, she couldn't help smiling as she reminisced about the fun evening she had enjoyed. The twinkling Christmas lights, the street theatre, and all the festive gifts and trinkets on the stalls she had seen. She felt the gingerbread man in her coat pocket, that Jools had treated her to, as she passed Oliver's cottage. Glancing in the window, she spotted him sitting at the table, still working. Did that man ever take a break? she wondered.

Remi had seemed friendly. She smiled as she thought of the jokes he had entertained them with, and how some of their meaning had been lost in translation. She had enjoyed hearing about his bread making, and how much he loved his small business, and the stories about some of his more eccentric clients.

Lexi reached her front door and took out her key. She yawned. She wasn't sure if it was the emotion of the past week, or her concern about her uncertain future, but she was exhausted now and couldn't wait to lose herself in sleep.

CHAPTER SEVEN

Christmas Day

It had been a busy few weeks since the Christmas Festival. Lexi was thankful to have been kept busy with all the typing Oliver handed to her each day. She hadn't had much free time to think and couldn't believe that tomorrow was Christmas Day. She had met up with her friends the day before, at Sacha's café, and when Sacha had asked her about joining them, she told her that she would be spending Christmas with her dad. It was a lie, but Lexi knew it was the best way to stop her friends from insisting she join them. She always had fun at the café, but she wasn't in the mood for noisy fun. Not this year. She needed some time alone, to reflect on the enforced changes in her life and had no intention of putting a dampener on anyone else's festivities.

She had gone to bed the night before leaving

the curtains open, liking the idea of waking with the dawn. But when she had pulled the covers over her, instead of falling asleep all Lexi could think about was the disintegration of her small family. Her mother would be devastated, she knew that without any doubt. Unable to help herself, she ended up crying herself to sleep.

A distant cockerel woke her the following morning. Rubbing her eyes, she sat up and re-arranged her pillows. Relaxing back into them, Lexi stared out of the window to the distant rolling waves. It was going to be a beautiful day. That, if nothing else, would help cheer her up.

Lexi still found it difficult to believe that her father hadn't given her anything for Christmas. She didn't want or expect much, just a token gift to show that he cared and had thought about her at some point. Lexi wondered if he would like the glass palette, she'd bought at the Christmas market. She had popped around to the house a couple of days before hoping to see him but found that there was no one at home. Wanting him to know she had remembered him despite them currently being at odds, she pushed the box through his letter box and heard it land gently in the metal basket attached to the other side of the front door. Lexi knew the gift would be safe there. She had safely cradled it in cotton wool and then into a small box she had found in one of her cupboards and wrapped it with care.

Lexi wished she would be there to see his

face and gauge whether he liked it. Usually, her father was unable to wait until Christmas morning to open any gift and would have thanked her by now, or at least commented on it. She found it strange not to have heard from him at all. If only he had a mobile phone, she could send him a text, but he didn't believe in them. She would have to hope that he would call her from his landline when Gloria wasn't around.

She closed her eyes and tried her best to sleep for a little longer, but soon gave up.

'May as well get up,' she said, not caring that she was talking to herself. She made a promise to herself that when she did finally settle down in her own home again, she would adopt a rescue dog. She needed company and there always seemed to be dogs desperate for loving homes. The thought cheered her.

Showered and dressed, Lexi lit the log burner. Covering her legs with a pink blanket her mother had crocheted for her when she was a teenager, she settled down with a hot chocolate and the latest thriller she'd borrowed from the library. It took a little time but eventually she became absorbed by the heat of the summer depicted in the terrifying plot.

The night before, she had hung some fairy lights in the windows. It was her cunning plan to show anyone passing that she wasn't miserable and had managed to get into the Christmas spirit. She didn't feel at all Christmassy but had no intention of anyone else knowing that to be the case. Lexi settled down in her comfy armchair, her legs drawn under her as she read the book in front of the glowing log burner. She was cosy, and almost convinced herself that today was like any other wintery Sunday.

Lexi picked up her mug and was about to take a sip of her drink when someone banged on the front door, making her jump.

Hot liquid spilled down her favourite sweatshirt. 'Bugger,' she shouted, quickly putting the mug back onto the table and holding her top away from her chest so that it didn't burn her too badly. The rapping was repeated on the door.

Sighing heavily, she grumbled to herself as she went to answer. Why couldn't people just leave her alone? Surely that was a simple enough request?

She walked into the hall and glanced through the small window. Oliver waved to her and pointed at her front door. *Oh no, what did he want?* Forcing a smile, she opened the door. 'Is everything OK?'

He waved his arm to encompass the beautiful view in front of them. 'I thought you were going out today.' When she didn't reply, he added, 'I don't have anything much to do either, so I wondered if you'd like to join me for a walk. It really is a glorious day and would be a shame not to make the most of it.'

She thought back to her book, but now he

mentioned it, some fresh air would do her good. 'Why not. Come in for a second while I grab a coat.'

He did as she said. Peering into her living room, he smiled. 'I see you haven't bothered with Christmas decorations either.'

'Didn't see the point,' she said, surprised at her honesty.

'You do look pretty organised in here though.' He peered over her shoulder. 'Sorting out old photos, I see?

She went to secure the front of her log burner. 'Yes, something like that.' She didn't want to appear short with him, so added. 'My father gave me a box that he'd been storing since my grandmother died. They're photos of her when she was young, my mum and dad, and many of me.' She tidied them, aware how messy they must look, not wanting him to think he had an untidy tenant and ask her to move out sooner than they had agreed. She remembered the hot chocolate she'd spilled on her top. 'I'm just going to change this,' she said, pointing at the damp mark on her chest. 'I won't be a second.'

Oliver nodded and she saw him peer down at the photos as she went to run up the stairs. 'Why are they in two piles?' he shouted.

'Because one pile is of my family and the other is of people I don't know.'

'Other people?'

She pulled her top off and pushed it into her

laundry basket then grabbed the nearest pullover from her cupboard and pulled it over her head, pushing her arms into the soft cotton sleeves. 'Yes,' she called to Oliver. 'People who stayed at the cottages, or maybe worked here. I'm not sure.' She quickly brushed her hair and ran back downstairs to join him.

'Would you mind if I looked through them?'

Lexi shrugged. 'If you want to, of course you can.'

He beamed at her. 'Thank you. Hey, this room looks very cosy. It's nice.'

Lexi wasn't sure what to say. She wondered whether he suspected her of hiding from everyone. 'I didn't feel like spending the day laughing and joking with my friends,' she admitted. 'I've actually quite enjoyed being here by myself this morning.'

He followed her out to the hallway, and waited as Lexi pulled on her coat and wrapped her scarf around her neck before pulling up the zip. Grabbing her hat, she pulled it onto her head, picked up her keys and waited for him to leave before following him out and locking the door behind her.

'We can't go down to the boardwalk or my friends will ask us to join them.'

'And that would be a bad thing, because?' He grinned at her.

Lexi frowned. 'You want to go and join them?' Was she being selfish? she wondered.

He shook his head. 'No, I thought you might want to.'

'No,' she said. 'Do you mind if we take a walk up that way?' She indicated the lane wending its way up to the right, just before the turn-off to the boardwalk. 'We can walk along the headland. I don't know if you've been up there, but the views are pretty dramatic.'

'Sounds good to me.'

They began walking, the first few minutes in companionable silence. He wasn't such a bad man, was he? She wished her friends would give him more of a chance.

Lexi gave him a sideways glance. He seemed pensive, and she couldn't help wondering why he didn't have a significant other, or relatives with whom he might spend the holidays.

'Don't you have somewhere you'd rather be, or a special someone to enjoy the festivities with?' She hoped he didn't think she was being too personal, but decided he didn't have to answer if he'd rather not.

He was silent for a moment. 'It's complicated.'

That was it? Complicated? It didn't tell her much. Intrigued, she found that she did want to know more about him, after all. Who was this mysterious man, who had come to live on the island, who owned her home and now, temporarily at least, was her employer? He was young, handsome and supposedly wealthy. Surely there were places he would rather be than here, spending a quiet Christmas day with a relative stranger?

'Isn't it always complicated?' she said, eventually.

He laughed quietly. 'It does tend to be, as far as I'm concerned, yes. How about you?'

'How about me, what?'

'Significant other? Is there one?'

'No.' She didn't want him to feel sorry for her, so added, 'I'm happy being single.' She had been, since discovering that her fiancé of three years had been seeing someone else behind her back the entire time her mum had been ill, and before the car accident that finally took her life. Jools had been the one to discover his disloyalty and broke the news to Lexi, as kindly as she possibly could, but it had still devastated her. She had ended their relationship immediately. 'Being single suits me.'

'I know what you mean. No one to answer to and no one else's feelings to have to constantly consider.'

He sounded as if he had experienced the darker side of a relationship. Maybe his ex was high maintenance. She could picture him with a model, actress, or maybe some high society female, used to looking well-groomed at every hour of the day.

They might not have had the best start to their neighbourly existence, but he had been nice enough to her. She had witnessed his colder side at Nicky's Halloween party, where his exit had been so public and abrupt and, like everyone else, had been shocked.

His paced slowed and she stopped to see what was wrong.

'I can almost hear your brain cells whirring,' he said, amused. 'What are you thinking?'

'Nothing,' she lied, embarrassed to have been caught out thinking about him.

'You looked as if you were coming to some conclusions about me. Go on, what were they?'

She could see he was teasing her, but also interested to know what she'd been thinking. 'I was wondering why you didn't have anywhere else to go today.'

'I didn't say that I had nowhere else to go. I just don't choose to be there, that's all.' He gave her a sideways look, the skin at the sides of his eyes crinkling in his amusement.

He seemed to be enjoying her company and it pleased her, though she wasn't sure why his opinion of her should matter. 'You'd rather be alone here?'

'You chose to do that very thing,' Oliver replied. 'So why is it difficult to imagine me doing the same?'

He had a point. 'True.' She couldn't resist asking him, 'Can't you tell me something about yourself? We are neighbours, after all. And you're my boss, for now at least. I should really know who I'm living next-door-to-but-one.'

Oliver thew his head back, laughing loudly. The deep rumbling sound made her smile. If she saw a picture of him online, she'd think him very attractive. The thought made her blush.

'Go on then.' Lexi wasn't going to let him off the hook.

'I will. But first tell me more about the photos your father gave to you.'

Lexi was confused. 'Like what?'

'Well, why did he give them to you now? Are they a Christmas present?'

She hadn't considered that. 'No. I don't think so.'

'You said they were of family, your gran, parents and you. Don't you have any siblings then?'

'No.' It had been something she craved when she was small, but after meeting Sacha, Jools and Bella at primary school, Lexi had begun to think of them all as the sisters she'd never have. 'Do you?'

He didn't speak for a few seconds. Lexi looked at him to see if he was alright. He looked so sad that, if she had known him better, she would have given him a hug. Instead, she waited for him to speak.

'I have a younger sister. She lives in Scotland, near my parents.' They walked on a few steps further before he added, 'I had an older brother. He died a couple of years ago.'

'I'm so sorry. That must have been devastating.'

He nodded. 'It was, especially for my parents. My mother has found his loss especially difficult as my father was diagnosed with dementia soon after Alistair's accident.'

Finally, he was opening up to her. 'Your parents live in Scotland then, and you lived in London before coming here? Is that right?'

'It is. I've got a little mews house that I bought years ago, and love it there. There's not much room but it's quiet. It's one of the few properties of its kind that hasn't been messed around with. I know most people see it as modernising them, but I much prefer to not have that glass and chrome look people seem to like.'

It still didn't answer why he had come to the island and bought the cottages. Lexi tried not to ask him, but after a few minutes the opportunity was too tempting, especially as he seemed to be in the mood to share information about himself.

'So,' she asked, trying not to sound too interested. 'Why come to Jersey and buy property here? I suppose I'm trying to ascertain why exactly you would want my cottages?'

He stopped. Lexi turned to him unsure whether she had offended him. 'Is something the matter?'

He shook his head and continued walking. 'No, it's fine. I guess I'm not used to people being as direct as you are.' He laughed. 'To be honest, it's refreshing.'

Lexi had been accused of not holding back many times growing up, it was one of the things her mother used to worry about. Lexi remembered her mother telling her to try and keep a check on her curiosity, at least until she knew people better.

'Well? Are you going to tell me?' she asked, smiling at him so that he knew she was teasing.

'Maybe.'

Lexi gasped. 'Meanie!'

'My mother conceived my brother Alistair when she was staying here. That's why these properties mean so much to her.'

Lexi still didn't understand. 'OK, so does your mum want to come and stay here?'

'Now my dad is declining, he and my mother are unable to take long vacations to more distant places. But I thought they can come over from Scotland. Maybe spend several weeks here throughout the year. He remembers things from back then, just not more recent events.'

Lexi could feel her emotions getting away from her. As much as she loved her home, she couldn't deny that what Oliver had done was an incredibly generous, but also thoughtful, thing to do for his parents.

'They both miss my brother very much and I thought the cottages would be a way of helping bring him back to them in some small way.' He glanced at her. 'It sounds odd, now that I say it out loud.'

Lexi put her hand on his forearm and shook her head. 'Not at all. I think it's one of the sweetest things I've ever heard.' She stared into his eyes, surprised to find that she liked Oliver Whimsy rather more than she had ever expected to. 'You really do have a caring side, don't you?'

He laughed loudly. 'Well, I'm glad you think so,' he said. 'Although, by the sound of things, you didn't hold me in very high regard before.'

Lexi could feel her cheeks reddening. 'No, not really.'

'Well, thanks for your honesty. I think.'

She hadn't meant to insult him and wanted to change the subject. 'Right, you've told me about your parents and siblings, why did you decide to write your book now?'

They began walking up the hill while Oliver gave her request some thought. 'I'm not sure really. The publishers had asked me a few times, and I thought that now was as good a time as any to finally get it done. I knew that coming here would be emotional for me, you know, looking into my parent's past. I thought that focusing on a book about business would be a way to give me something to take my mind off it each day.'

It made sense to her. 'I see.' Lexi gauged that Oliver must be in his late thirties 'Aren't you very young to have achieved so much, business-wise, I mean?'

He stared at her briefly, perhaps wondering whether she was joking. 'Not really. I suppose I have done well for myself, but I've worked hard and have had some lucky breaks.'

'And are you enjoying writing the book?'

He smiled at her and tapped the side of his nose with his forefinger. 'Can't you tell from typing up my notes?'

Lexi frowned and gave his question some thought. 'Not really. I notice you're including more personal information in the book the further along it goes. Can you let me in on some of the things you'll be including in later chapters?'

'No,' he grinned. 'What would be the fun of you reading the notes when you receive them if I do that?'

Lexi could not hide her disappointment. 'You won't tell me anything now?'

'No. There won't be any surprises if I do.' He laughed to himself and she could tell he was teasing her.

'Will there be any surprises in a book about business?' she asked, doubting it very much.

'You'll just have to wait and see, won't you?'

Lexi shook her head. 'You're a tough one, Oliver Whimsy.'

He gave a slight shrug. 'So I've been told. Now, seeing as I'm not going to tell you anything more about the book, why don't you tell me a bit the photos your father gave to you.'

Lexi stopped walking. It took Oliver several steps before he realised that she wasn't beside him. 'What's the matter?' he asked, before retracing his steps and standing in front of her. 'Did I say something wrong?'

Lexi shook her head thoughtfully.

'Then why are you looking so pensive?'

'It's just occurred to me that I think my father might be giving me some sort of message by handing over the box of photographs.'

Oliver frowned. 'Like what?'

She couldn't be certain, but although her father was non-confrontational, and obviously more desperate to please Gloria than Lexi had ever imagined him to be, by passing on the photos he'd been holding since her gran had died ten years before, he was telling Lexi he wanted her to remember happy times. There had been so many. Her eyes filled with tears.

Oliver's eyes widened. 'Oh, hell. I'm sorry. Please don't get upset.'

Lexi sniffed. A snowflake landed on her nose.

He raised his hand. 'Look Lexi, it's begun snowing. Come along. Take my hand and let's get a move on up this hill. We can warm up in your living room and you can show me your family photos if you want.'

Lexi wasn't sure what to do. She didn't want to let him see how emotional she was or do anything to ruin the friendliness that had built up between them during their walk.

'Lexi?'

Oliver's deep voice snapped her out of her thoughts. She noticed he was holding his hand out for her to take. Without thinking, she grasped his gloved hand in hers and let him almost pull her up the steep hill towards the cottages.

Once inside, they took off their coats, hats, scarves and gloves and she indicated for Oliver to take a seat near the wood burner. She went to the kitchen area and put the kettle on.

'May I look at these?' he asked, giving a nod towards the photos.

'Yes, go ahead.'

She made them both a coffee, glancing over at him every so often. As she carried their drinks to the table, she placed each mug on a coaster and realised he was staring intently at a photo in his hand. He looked like he'd seen a ghost.

'Are you alright?' Lexi asked, wondering what had caused such a reaction.

He took a moment to reply. Then seemed to consider his next move, before turning the photograph to face her. It was one she hadn't noticed before. In the photo a young woman, no more than nineteen was sitting on the lawn in front of the middle cottage. Next to her was a handsome, dark-haired man, who looked to be in his mid to late twenties. The girl had her eyes closed and a beatific smile on her pretty face, her head resting on his shoulder.

'They look very much in love,' Lexi said gazing at the sweet couple. She supposed her grandmother must have taken the photo, or her mother. 'They look like honeymooners,' she added, when Oliver didn't speak. 'Did you know that Jersey was known as the Honeymoon Isle in the fifties and sixties?'

She reached out and took his wrist lightly in hers, pulling it closer to study the photo better. 'Although, by the look of his high-waisted jeans and her dress, this seems to have probably been taken in the eighties rather than the fifties or sixties.'

'They were,' Oliver said eventually.

'Sorry? Were, what?'

'Very much in love.'

Lexi was taken aback. She hadn't expected him to react so dreamily. If it had been Bella, or even Sacha, then she could have understood it – both were great romantics – but Oliver Whimsy hadn't given her the impression he was like that. She wasn't sure what to say next.

Eventually, he looked across the table at her. Then he stared at the photo a moment longer, before sitting upright and gazing at her.

'These are my parents,' he said, in a matter of fact tone.

Stunned, Lexi's mouth fell open. She was delighted for him, especially after all that he had told her earlier.

'I'm so happy you've found a photo of them.'

'So am I,' he said, staring at it wistfully. 'My mother worked here in eighty-nine.' He gave the photo some thought. 'I remember her mentioning a Thea.' He smiled across at Lexi. 'Was that your grandmother's name? She used to change the beds, clean, that sort of thing.'

'Yes, that was Gran.' Lexi realised what a treat it was for Oliver to find this picture, especially on Christmas day. The perfect gift, in fact. She peered at the photo in his hand. 'She was very pretty.'

'She still is. Although a lot more glamorous looking now.'

'And your father?'

'He was the laird's son from the ancestral hall in the highlands,' he said, his voice quiet as he thought back. 'He'd been invited to attend a twenty-fifth birthday party on a yacht, by a friend he had met years before when they both attended the same boarding school. He met my mother on his last day here, when he came down to the boardwalk to swim.'

'So, he was a posh chap then.' Rather like Oliver, she thought. 'They met on the last day of his holiday?' she repeated, studying the photo once more. 'It must have been love at first sight.'

Oliver laughed. It was a gentle, far away laugh that seemed filled with love and sadness for some reason. 'This wasn't taken that day,' he explained. 'Dad came back to the island several weeks later, much to his father's irritation. He refused to return home at the end of that visit until he had persuaded my mother to marry him. Then he went back to his family with his new wife, which,' he looked at Lexi, amusement in his eyes, 'did not go down well at all with my grandfather. He was used to people doing his bidding. My mother told me he never completely forgave my father for not marrying one of the upper crust daughters of one of his cronies.'

Lexi thought it was a perfectly romantic story and told him so. 'And, were they happy?' she asked, willing Oliver to confirm that theirs was a wonderful marriage.

He nodded. Yes. They were, well, still are very happy.'

She noted his quick correction and was unsure why he would make it. 'There's more, isn't there?' She could tell that he was holding something back, but ever inquisitive, was desperate to know that things worked out for them.

Oliver sighed. Staring at the photo, he said, 'They are still together and still very much in love. Like I said, my father has vascular dementia and it's breaking my mother's heart to slowly lose him.'

Lexi's heart ached for Oliver and his family. It saddened her to hear that two people so in love would have to face something so devastating. She didn't speak, waiting for Oliver to continue.

'When I told my mother about staying here, she confided that it had always been a dream of hers to return some day with my father. However, they're very private people. Not wanting them to have to share, I decided to buy all three cottages. They can stay in one when they're over, and my sister and I could stay in the others. Or, when my father becomes more unwell, then I thought one of the properties could be adapted for him. I imagined that doors could be fitted into the connecting walls so that my mother could stay on one end of the properties, my father in the middle and a nurse at the other end.

'They're definitely coming to stay then?'

'Yes, but I'm not sure exactly when.'

They spent the next hour looking through more of her photos. Lexi spotted one of her parents together, her father tickling her mother while she lay on the lawn, laughing. A warm feeling crept through her, like an internal hug. It was just what she needed to see to remind her how happy her parents had once been. And would still be, she thought sadly, if her mother hadn't died so young.

'Look, here's another photo of my parents. And another.' Oliver held them up for Lexi to see. During the course of the evening they found another five photographs of his mother.

'You must keep them,' Lexi said, happy to be able to give him valuable memories of his parents.

'Are you sure?' he asked, beaming at her.

Lexi nodded. 'Of course I am. They're such lovely pictures of a happy time. Your mother was so pretty and clearly adored your father, and he adored her too by the look of things.'

'Thank you, that's the best Christmas present you could have given me.'

He smiled and gazed down at the photos in his hands. It was a smile filled with love for the people he adored, and it occurred to Lexi that any woman on the receiving end of such a heart-gripping smile would be very lucky indeed.

After a few seconds Oliver's smile vanished. He looked at her thoughtfully.

'What?' Lexi asked, intrigued.

'I know your dad has hurt you but if he did give you this box of memories to make up for it then he's not such a bad guy.'

'I had never thought he was before the sale,' she admitted. 'Why?'

'Look,' Oliver said. 'Tell me if I'm stepping out of line here, but maybe he's been coerced into the sale somehow.'

'Yes, he has. I'm sure of it. I know he would never have done such a thing without Gloria's encouragement.' She still wasn't certain what Oliver might be getting at. 'Why?'

He glanced down at the photos in his hands and then back at Lexi. 'I think you should do some digging into this woman's past.'

Lexi couldn't hide her surprise. 'You do?'

'Yes. I'd like to help you. It's the least I can do after my involvement in all this.' He stared at her, the intensity of his gaze making her want to agree. 'You don't have to, of course. It's only a suggestion.'

It was a good one, Lexi decided. She had never known her father to be influenced by anyone before Gloria's arrival. Maybe Gloria was not to blame for his decision, but if she was then Lexi wanted to know why this woman was so determined to do all she could to hurt her and cause her and her father to fall out.

'Alright then, let's do it.'

Lexi was grateful to Oliver for his unexpected suggestion and for his help. She stared at him not surprised to discover that he was a man of many sides. Now she really was intrigued by him. She suspected this was only the start of the surprises she was going to receive from Mr Oliver Whimsy.

CHAPTER EIGHT

Boxing Day

Oliver's Christmas Day revelations had intrigued Lexi. She couldn't stop thinking about his parents and their love story for the rest of the day. Nor could she help wondering what, if anything, they would manage to find out about Gloria.

The following morning, Lexi decided to check up on him. He had seemed perfectly fine when he left her just before midnight, after sharing the food she had bought for herself, along with some he'd brought over from his cottage, together with a delicious bottle of red wine.

'It's a Chateau Mouton Rothschild,' she recalled him saying. 'A delicious Cabinet Sauvignon.'

Lexi had no idea, but presumed by his tone that it was a special bottle of wine. What she did discover, as she concentrated on taking small sips, was that it was the most delicious wine she had ever tasted.

She didn't have a sore head, and was in a much happier mood than she had been the morning before. The realisation that the box of photographs from her father was probably his gift to her, and that he hadn't forgotten to give her something after all, had helped make her Christmas Day much better than she had anticipated.

Lexi tidied up the photos, putting those of her family neatly into a smaller box. She would buy a proper container with a sealable lid when she was next at the hardware store to ensure they would be properly protected from any damp. As Lexi tidied up the other pile, she spotted another photo of Oliver's mother. She was holding up what appeared to be a glass of orange squash in a toast to whoever was taking the photo and Lexi could not help wondering what she might have been celebrating.

Tired but happier, Lexi showered and dressed, humming to herself and looking forward to surprising Oliver with her find. She knew he would be delighted to receive it. As she pulled on her socks and boots, Lexi thought how unexpected it was that she and Oliver had struck up such a friendship. It was a relief to be getting along so well with him, especially after all that had happened. She still found it difficult to quantify how deeply she felt the loss of the cottages, but being upset over them wasn't going to help her get used to the idea. No, she needed to try and be positive. If they continued being friendly and she kept working for him, then hopefully she would be able to remain in her cottage for at least the next few months.

Lexi thought she heard a car engine outside and went over to her bedroom window. She wasn't expecting anyone, so maybe the car had come for Oliver. She peered out and saw him step out of his front door and onto the front pathway. A woman who, Lexi miserably noted, was the most glamorous person she had ever seen, launched herself at him and into his arms.

'Darling, Olly. Oh, how I've missed you.'

Lexi gasped, quickly stepping back in case either the woman or Oliver spotted her watching them. She sat down heavily on her bed. He had said his life was complicated, but what she had just seen didn't look confusing at all. She looked at the photo on her bedside table that she had been going to deliver to his cottage. Now was obviously not the time.

Lexi picked up the photo and stood up. She would just have to hand it to him the next time they spoke. She had been looking forward to popping over to see him and hopefully spend another relaxing day chatting, or maybe going out for a long stroll together. Lexi sighed, surprised at how disappointed she felt not to be able to spend the day ahead with him.

'Who am I kidding,' she said, catching the reflection of her miserable face in the mirror. 'I like him rather more than I had expected to and it's my own fault for being such a stupid romantic.' Right. Enough wallowing. She was going to go down to Sacha's café and see if it was open. Maybe a few of her friends were down there already enjoying their breakfast.

Lexi went downstairs and placed the photo on her kitchen table. She grabbed her purse, put on her coat and hat and went outside. The shock of the cold air took her breath away for a few seconds as she locked the front door. She pushed her hands into her pockets and, head down, walked as quickly as she could past Oliver's cottage to the road. Unable to help herself she glanced through the window and saw them laughing. She felt her mood drop even further. What was wrong with her? How could she even entertain, if only for a minute, that someone like Oliver Whimsy would look at an ordinary women like her, when he had women as beautiful as the one she had seen kissing him earlier, vying for his attention.

'Serves me right,' she mumbled to herself, walking quickly down the hill. She reached the boardwalk and turned right to the café. 'Why would I ever think he wants anything more than to help me sort out my issue with Gloria? Rather I know now though, than fall for that man.'

'Talking to yourself again?' Jack asked.

Startled to find she wasn't alone, Lexi jumped.

'I didn't see you there.'

'Obviously.' He laughed and went to put his arm around her shoulder.

Lexi leapt back. 'Er, no you don't. You're all wet. Surfing again?'

'Yup. I don't feel relaxed until I've been surfing each day.'

Lexi looked at Jack's shiny wetsuit and couldn't understand how he wasn't freezing. 'Why are you going in the direction of the café and not to Bella's to change?'

'Because I wanted to say hi to you first.' He turned to leave her. 'Tell Sacha I'll be there in a jiffy, will you?'

'No problem.' Lexi laughed. Sacha's nutty brother always amused her. When he'd got together with Bella a couple of months earlier, it had seemed to the rest of their friends that they were a perfect match. Bella, a hand model and antique dealer, who coped with her free-spirited mother and ran her small business from her cottage, and Jack, surfer and all-round great guy, loved by everyone. Lexi smiled to herself as she watched him run, barefoot, in the opposite direction, along the freezing boardwalk.

She picked up her pace to reach the café. At least Jack had assumed that Sacha would be there. Then again, she did live in the flat upstairs, but if Jack had asked Lexi to let his sister know he would be there soon, they both knew he would be looking forward to one of her full English breakfasts. Come to think of it, Lexi thought, that's exactly what she could do with too.

She pushed the café door open, and before she had a chance to contemplate taking off her coat, Sacha stepped out from the kitchen, ran towards her and wrapped her in a bear hug. 'Lexi, it's so good to see you. How are you? How was your Christmas? I hope your dad and that ghastly Gloria behaved themselves.'

Lexi hated lying to her friend, so waited for Sacha to let go of her and unbuttoned her coat. 'Christmas was fine actually,' she said, hanging her coat and hat on the stand near to the door. 'But I didn't spend them with Dad and Gloria.'

'Don't you dare tell me you were by yourself all day.' Sacha glared at her not bothering to hide her fury.

'No, I wasn't.'

Sacha frowned. 'Then who did you spend it with?'

Lexi wished she didn't have to tell her friends, but knew they would find out somehow – everyone always did in such a close community. Nothing much stayed a secret for long on the boardwalk. 'I was with Oliver.'

Sacha's mouth fell open and she stared in silence for a couple of seconds. 'Sorry. Oliver Whimsy?'

'Do you know of any other Olivers?'

'Sit your bum down on that chair and I'll

make us both a cup of tea, or would you rather hot chocolate?'

'Hot chocolate for me, please.'

'I'll make them, and then I'll sit with you and you're going to tell me everything.'

Lexi recalled what Jack had said to her. 'Oh, and Jack's on his way here. I think he'll be about five minutes, knowing him.'

Sacha rushed to her usual place behind the counter and grabbed two mugs. 'Then you'd better hurry up and tell me. I'd forgotten he was coming, although I don't know why he asked you to let me know. It's not as if he doesn't end up here most mornings for his breakfast.' She stared at the glass café door for a few seconds. 'He'll probably be fetching Betty on his way here. I invited her to come for breakfast this morning.'

Lexi made herself comfortable and watched as Sacha spooned cocoa powder into the mugs. She already felt more cheerful in this bright, happy space filled with tables and chairs, their paintwork distressed to make them look weather beaten, and the beach-style nets, shells and driftwood, hanging from the ceiling and on the walls adding to the ambience.

'Well, go on then.' Sacha waved for Lexi to hurry. 'Tell me before he gets here.'

Lexi sighed. She knew it wasn't worth arguing with Sacha when she was in this mood. 'There's nothing much to tell, really,' she said honestly.

'He came round to my cottage when he saw my lights were on and invited me to join him for a walk.' She then told her friend about the rest of their quiet but enjoyable day together. 'I have to admit I really enjoyed his company.'

Sacha steamed a metal jug of milk before pouring the foamy, creamy liquid into the mugs and stirring. After shaking cocoa powder on the top, she carried the drinks back to Lexi, placing them on the table and then sitting opposite her resting her hands on the table.

'No.' Sacha said, shaking her head and smiling. 'You're not going to get away with telling me something that vague. How long was he there? What did you chat about?' She pursed her lips. 'What is he really like to spend time with?'

Lexi opened her mouth to speak when she heard voices outside on the boardwalk.

'Typical,' Sacha moaned. 'I might have guessed Jack would get here quickly when I didn't want him to.'

The door opened and Bella stepped in, holding the door open for Betty. Jack followed, quickly closing the door behind them.

Sacha stood. 'How did you get here so fast? I hope you didn't walk here on your own, Betty? It's far too slippery out there.'

Betty shook her head. 'No, lovey. Bella came to fetch me while Jack got changed. He ran along to catch up with us. We're all very hungry this morning, so I hope you've got a lot of food in.'

Sacha laughed. 'Don't I always?' she said as she held out her chair indicating for Betty to sit, while Bella sat down next to Lexi.

'Jack,' Sacha said taking charge as usual. 'You can come and help me make breakfast. Full English for everyone?'

'Yes, please,' they chorused.

'Jools not coming today?' Lexi asked noticing her other friend was absent.

Bella shook her head. 'No, she's having a quiet morning with her gran and that pesky Jack Russell of theirs. I think she had a little more to drink than she meant to yesterday. I saw her on my way to collect Betty and she looked rather peaky.'

It was a shame, Lexi thought. She would have liked to catch up with Jools, but it could wait until tomorrow.

'Alessandro is out having breakfast with Finn. I think they're making plans for the gelateria for next summer's tourist season,' Sacha said. 'They wanted me to join them but I told them I had arranged to see you lot.'

'Well, we're glad you did,' Lexi said, honestly.

Lexi watched Sacha and Jack make their way to the kitchen and leant over the table to give Betty a kiss on her soft cheek. 'Did you have a lovely Christmas?'

'Yes, thank you. I spent it in here with everyone. We had a grand time, didn't we Bella? Although I think your mum got a little carried away with that young chap of hers.'

'Don't remind me,' Bella giggled, rolling her eyes heavenward at Lexi. 'Honestly, you'd think she was a teenager the way she acts. I'm glad she's all loved up but wish she would wait until she got home before kissing him.'

Lexi smiled. Bella's mum had barely been around while her daughter was growing up, leaving her in the care of her beloved grandmother, while she travelled the world, having fun, making the most of the freedom she had missed, having had Bella at a young age. Now, since her return, she had been living with Betty, who insisted she loved the liveliness that Claire brought to her small cottage, especially since she had met widowed fisherman, Tony. The two had fallen for each other in a big way and were planning a beach wedding for next spring.

Lexi was just relieved that Betty had company most of the time, especially since she had fallen and hurt herself a few months earlier. At least this way, Betty kept her independence. They were all relieved the older lady wasn't left to fend for herself now she was in her early nineties and becoming slightly frail. Each of them had tried to come up with ways to help Betty, but she insisted on being as independent as possible.

They chatted a little about Bella's mum, and how she'd got carried away after a few drinks and made her fiancé dance around the café, until

Jack came out of the kitchen. He carried the first two plates of laden with what Lexi knew from experience would be a very tasty breakfast. Sacha followed immediately after him carrying three more. Jack returned to fetch a large plate of toast, then pulled another table over, and settled himself down.

'This looks delicious, thank you,' Lexi said, picking up her knife and fork and cutting into her egg and a piece of perfectly grilled bacon.

Before it reached her mouth, Jack said, 'Sacha tells me that you had an unexpected visitor yesterday.'

'Who?' Bella asked, before putting a forkful of food into her mouth. 'After you got home from your Dad's, or before?'

'She didn't go,' Sacha giggled.

Lexi groaned inwardly. She might have guessed that Sacha would tell Jack. She didn't really mind. The four of them rarely kept secrets from each other. 'I only told you that I was spending the day with Dad and Gloria so you wouldn't all worry,' she admitted. 'I was happy to spend the day at home, reading.'

'But that's not what you ended up doing, was it?'

'No. Oliver Whimsy popped around to my cottage.' Lexi decided to make them wait for more news.

Bella gasped. 'No, really? And, did you invite him in?'

Lexi was enjoying teasing them, now. 'Dad had given me a box containing loads of old photographs of Mum and Gran and lots of other people. They were from the sixties and seventies, when Gran first bought the cottages, and also other photos from the eighties of them and various other people.'

'I remember when Thea bought those cottages in the sixties,' Betty said, wistfully. 'She was such a good sort, your gran. When I think back to those times, it was all fun and laughter, with long-haired hippy types coming and going and having parties on the front lawn. Though how she ever made any money, I've no idea. Thea was such a generous person and we all loved going to visit her.'

'I know,' Lexi agreed. 'Mum always said she didn't know how she survived, but I think the visitors who stayed at the cottages enjoyed Gran's eclectic mix of friends, coming and going.'

'Those were good days,' Betty smiled. 'I remember the summer your dad first came to the island. He was hiring out deckchairs. It was the late seventies, I think.'

'It was.' Lexi loved hearing about her parents and wished she could go back in time and see them as youngsters, meeting for the first time.

'Always going on about how he was going to be a successful artist. Which he was, I suppose, of a sort.'

'He's made a living at it most of his life, so

you could say that he's been as successful as he intended.' Lexi pictured her father's landscapes hanging in the cottages, most of which depicted areas surrounding the boardwalk.

'It's strange to think how much has changed since your Gran died. Is it ten years ago now?' Lexi nodded. 'And your lovely mum, two years ago, already.'

Jack waved a piece of toast in the air. 'Betty, please. No sad stuff, not today. And not,' he added, winking at Lexi, 'until this one has told us about her day with Mr Posh himself.'

Lexi continued eating her breakfast. Swallowing a mouthful, she smiled at him determined to make him wait. 'I'll tell you when I've finished eating. This is too good to waste.'

'Yes, eat up everyone. Lexi's going nowhere until we've heard all about her day.'

Finally, after Sacha and Jack cleared everyone's plates and brought teas and coffees, Lexi told them a little about her Christmas.

'He sounds rather nice,' Bella said thoughtfully. 'He's incredibly handsome, isn't he?'

'Hey, enough of that,' Jack said, feigning offence.

'Shut up Jack,' Sacha said. 'You know Bella only has eyes for you, though why, I can't fathom.'

Bella groaned. 'Will you two be quiet and let Lexi answer my question please?'

'What, the one about him being nice, or

whether I think he's handsome?' Lexi giggled, and knew she had to put her friends out of their misery. They were always trying to pair her up with someone, especially since Sacha had teamed up with Alessandro, and Bella and Jack had finally got together. 'Anyway, before you all get carried away with the imagined excitement of my day, I can assure you nothing remotely romantic happened.'

'What, nothing at all?' Sacha asked, frowning.

'No. And this morning, his girlfriend arrived on his doorstep.'

'Girlfriend?' Bella scowled. 'Are you certain that's what she was? Couldn't she be a sister, or something?'

'No, his sister is in Scotland apparently. This lady grabbed hold of him kissed him and called him darling. I think we can safely say she's a girlfriend. Although, thinking about it, he did seem a little taken aback to see her, but he invited her inside and, well, that was that.'

Yes, she thought miserably, that really was that.

CHAPTER NINE

Late December

Lexi typed up the final paragraph of Oliver's dictation and sat back in her chair, listening to the rain pounding against the living room window. It hadn't stopped since Boxing Day. She had made the most of her time at home by catching up with her work, and a little reading.

She re-read Jools' note, which she'd found lying on the hall floor, supposing her friend must have dropped it off in a rush at some point the evening before.

Sacha asked me to invite you to her party at the café. She said that you were allowed Christmas Day off, but she's not allowing you to wallow alone on New Year's Eve. Invite Oliver Whimsy and his girlfriend if you think he should be included in the fun. Finn and Charlie will also be there. See you there at 8.30pm, latest.

Lexi hoped the weather would clear up before New Year's Eve. She hated spending time getting ready for a party only to turn up looking like someone who had fallen, fully clothed, into the sea. It was cold outside, and would be warm in the café, and she couldn't decide what to wear for the party.

She hadn't heard from Oliver, nor had she expected to. As far as she was aware, his house guest was still staying with him. He had been so lovely on Christmas Day but she wanted to show him that he needn't worry about her being alone. If, in fact, he did. She was more than happy to be a singleton and was pretty used to it by now. Yes, she decided, she was going to show him just how self-contained she really was. She didn't need a man for anything, not even her father, and she certainly didn't want Oliver to think for a second that she did.

In fact, she would put on her coat now, run along to his cottage, and invite him and his friend straightaway, before she could think of a reason to put it off any longer.

Lexi picked up the invitation and put on her parka, pulling up the hood so it covered her hair, before running to Oliver's front door. She banged lightly a couple of times and waited. Within no time at all, her jeans were soaked and clinging to her legs.

'Eugh.' A gust of wind almost blew her hood from her head, so she reached up to pull it back and hold it in place. When there wasn't an answer, she gave the door one more heavy knock and turned to go back to her cottage.

'Lexi? Oh hell, you're soaking. Quickly come in,' Oliver said. He'd opened the door suddenly and, without giving her a chance to speak, took hold of her hand and pulled her into the cottage. 'How long have you been out there?'

She stood dripping in his hallway and opened her mouth to answer, when the beautiful woman she had seen arriving a few days before appeared at the living room doorway. She stood open-mouthed her perfectly manicured hand resting on her chest.

'Olly, what are you doing, leaving the poor girl standing there? Take her coat and bring her in where it's warm.'

All thoughts of disliking the woman vanished as Lexi watched her turn and walk towards the kitchen area, saying, 'I'll pop the kettle on while you sort yourself out.'

Lexi looked up at Oliver, unsure what to do next. She supposed she should unzip her parka and do as his guest had instructed. As she pulled the zip down, it occurred to her how in charge of Oliver the woman had seemed. They obviously knew each other very well. She sounded more like a wife than a friend.

Lexi shrugged her heavy, wet coat from her shoulders and Oliver caught it as it fell.

'Let me hang this up for you. Right, now let's

do as Portia says and get you into the warmth.' As he waited for her to go ahead of him, Lexi wished she'd stayed at home. Then again, perhaps while she was here, she could find out more about Portia and what she was doing on the island.

'We've only got coffee, I'm afraid,' Portia said, indicating a smart coffee machine Lexi hadn't noticed before. 'When the rain calms down a little I'm sending Olly out with a decent shopping list. I'm dying for a cup of Earl Grey.'

'That's fine, thank you. Milk, no sugar for me, please,' Lexi said, irritated when her teeth began to chatter, making her sound a little odd.

'Sit in my chair,' Oliver said, motioning for Lexi to take the seat closest to the log burner.

She did as he asked and shortly after, Portia brought over a steaming mug of rich looking coffee for her. 'I've been looking forward to meeting you, ever since Olly told me about you,' she said, sitting next to Oliver on the sofa and crossing the longest legs Lexi had ever seen. They put her much shorter ones to shame and she had to concentrate on not staring. Beautiful, glamourous and nice; no wonder Oliver seemed to like her.

'Is everything alright?' he asked, frowning. Before Lexi could answer, he added, 'I meant to come over and thank you for a lovely time the other day, but—'

'I arrived,' Portia interrupted, grinning mischievously. 'And ruined everything.' She looked at each of them. 'Sorry, but it couldn't be helped.'

'Couldn't it?' Lexi asked, horrified when they both looked at her and she realised she had spoken the words out loud. 'That is, I mean. Sorry, I don't know what I mean. I think the cold and rain has confused me.'

Portia laughed. It was a tinkling laugh, as if someone had tapped the side of a crystal glass. So delicate. How were there such perfect women? Lexi wondered, aware that she had no chance at all of competing with someone like Portia for Oliver Whimsy's affections. Why had she even imagined for a second that he might like her? She felt a giggle rising in her throat and coughed to cover it up.

She realised Portia was speaking to her. '...so poor Olly had no choice. I arrived and he, being the perfect gentleman that he is, invited me to stay with him for the holidays.'

Oliver turned his head to look at her and raised his eyebrows. 'I invited you? As I recall it, you invited yourself.'

Portia playfully pushed his shoulder and grinned at Lexi. 'He pretends he's cross, but he's not really. Are you, Olly?'

He sighed. 'No, I suppose not, but I had been intending to work while the phones were quieter and everyone was busy getting on with family parties.' He smiled at her and then turned his attention back to Lexi. His cool blue eyes gazed at her and her stomach did a traitorous flip. You can stop that right now, she thought to herself. 'So, Lexi, what brings you out in this horrendous weather?'

She had been so busy scrutinising Portia that she had forgotten her reason for coming. 'Oh, yes. Well, Sacha,' she looked at Portia. 'She's my friend and runs the café down on the boardwalk,' she explained. 'Sacha's having a New Year's Eve party and asked me to invite you both. If you want to come, that is. I know it's Hogmanay in Scotland, so you might have other plans, Oliver.'

His lips slowly drew back in a lazy smile. 'I have no plans at all and I, for one, would love to come to Sacha's party. How about you, Portia? Want to come?'

Rather than looking horrified at the thought of spending New Year's Eve in a beach café, Portia surprised Lexi by beaming at her. 'I'd simply love to,' she said. 'Thank you. Do you mind me asking about the dress code?'

'It'll be come as you like,' Lexi assured her. 'Although, I was wondering what I should wear. I suppose as it's horribly cold out there I'll probably wear trousers and a top of some sort, but it's up to you to wear whatever you like. I'll call for you just before seven-thirty, if you like?'

'Marvellous, I'm looking forward to it already.' She pointed to the mug in front of Lexi. 'Now, you'd better drink some of that coffee. Are you warming up at all yet?'

Lexi nodded. Her jeans still stuck uncomfortably to her legs, but at least the material was warm now instead of cold.

Portia leaned forward and rested her elbows on her knees. 'Olly tells me you live in the cottage at the end and have been working for him since he arrived.'

Lexi took a sip of the hot drink and swallowed. 'That's right.' She wondered whether he had told Portia that she used to own the cottages, but doubted it.

'Typing up his exciting notes about his business knowledge,' Portia laughed. 'I haven't been allowed to read any of it, so I'm going to have to come to you to find out more about the skeletons in his business closet.'

Lexi was mid-sip and, breathing suddenly in horror, spluttered embarrassingly as some of the coffee went down the wrong way.

'How silly of me to tease you when you're drinking,' Portia said with a gasp. 'Although, I will try to find out more. I'm intrigued about it all, you see.' She gave Lexi a wink.

The one thing Lexi knew about working for someone was that she would be loyal to them. If Oliver hadn't already told Portia about the contents of his book, Lexi had no intention of doing so either. 'I'm sorry, I've been sworn to secrecy,' she said, giving Portia her most angelic look. 'If you want to find out anything, I'm afraid you'll have to get your information from Oliver.'

Portia wrinkled her nose in disappointment. 'Oh, that's no fun at all.' She gave Oliver a sideways glance. 'Why are you always so secretive?'

He grinned at Lexi and she knew she had given the right answer to Portia's probing. 'I'll give you a copy of the book when it's eventually published. Anyway, it's not nearly as exciting as you no doubt imagine it to be.'

Portia sighed and smiled at Lexi. 'That's rather dull. Is it dull to type up, Lexi?'

'Oh no, not at all. It's…' She closed her mouth, realising she had nearly given something of the book away. 'That was rather clever, Portia,' she said, aware that her friends were going to enjoy Portia's company when they met her at the party.

'I know,' Portia said, beaming at her and displaying her perfect white teeth. 'But you have to give it a try, don't you?'

Lexi wasn't sure if she was still referring to the book, or Oliver's attentions. Either way, despite only just meeting her, she already knew Portia well enough to believe that she could get anything she set her mind on.

They chatted on a little more, but although Portia and Oliver were perfectly charming and welcoming, Lexi couldn't help sensing that she had interrupted something. She finished her coffee and stood. 'Right, I'd better get back and leave the pair of you to carry on with your day.'

'There's no need to rush off,' Oliver said, standing up.

'No, really there isn't.' Portia uncrossed her legs and stood. She took Lexi's mug from her hand. 'But if you really must dash off, don't be a stranger, will you? I hope you'll pop round again before the party. We can chat a bit more.'

Lexi grinned. 'I'd like that. But don't think I'll be giving away any Whimsy business secrets.'

'Spoilsport.'

Oliver followed Lexi into the hall. 'She won't let you get away with keeping information about the book to yourself, you know.' He lifted her sodden parka from its hook and held it open for her to put on.

Lexi pushed her arms through the sleeves and zipped it up. 'I'd worked that out. I'll do my best not to let her get the better of me.'

He lifted her hood so that it covered her head and part of her face and laughed. 'I'm sure you will.' He hesitated. 'It was good to see you again, Lexi.'

'Thank you,' she said, trying not to gaze into his eyes. 'You, too.'

'I haven't forgotten about helping you look into Gloria's past.'

'Thank you,' Lexi said, relieved. 'But there's no rush.' She didn't want to admit how desperate she was to find out more about the woman who was making her life so difficult.

He opened the door and, without wasting any

time, Lexi ran back to her own cottage and slammed the door behind her. She stood for a second, catching her breath, before taking off her coat, then locked the door, kicked off her boots and raced upstairs into her bathroom. She needed a hot bath, she decided, bending to push in the plug and turn on the taps. Seconds later, her wet clothes discarded, Lexi poured in bubble bath and pushed her hands through the water to make as much of a lather as possible.

Leaving the water running, she carried her wet clothes downstairs and put them in to the washing machine without bothering to put on a dressing gown. No one could see her in her kitchen area unless they came right up to the living room window, or walked around to the back of the cottages to peer into the kitchen, and on a day like today, she doubted anyone would do that. Once the washing machine was on, Lexi hurried back upstairs, turned off the taps and slowly lowered herself into the hot bubbly water and laid back, closing her eyes. She really needed to give herself a talking to where Oliver Whimsy was concerned. To expect him to take time away from Portia to delve into Gloria's life was selfish. To continue liking him, as she now realised she did – especially now she knew there was a significant other in his life – was nothing short of stupidity.

'Ah well,' Lexi said, picking up a handful of bubbles and blowing on them lightly. 'I've got more than enough to be dealing with, without adding man trouble to my list.' As soon as New Year dawned, she was going to start trying to find somewhere else to live. She would also think of a way to find out more about Gloria and her intentions towards her father. Oliver's book wouldn't take too much longer to type up, she was pretty sure of that, and once it was done, she would need to find another way to make a living.

For now, though, she was going to look forward to the party and make sure she enjoyed every second of it.

CHAPTER TEN

New Year's Eve

Lexi was pleased but couldn't help still feeling surprised when Oliver had agreed to go to the party. She had assumed he would want to spend the time working on his manuscript, or simply being with Portia. She hadn't expected him to be interested in mixing with her friends again, not after the drama of the Halloween Party. After a couple of changes of clothes, she was finally ready when Jools rang the doorbell, shouting for her from the door-step.

'Hurry the hell up, it's bloody freezing out here.'

She ran downstairs and opened the front door, waving Jools inside. 'Come in while I grab my coat. You didn't have to come and collect me, I'm perfectly capable of walking down to the boardwalk.'

'I know, but I was ready early so needed to waste a little time.'

'I won't bother with an umbrella,' Lexi said. 'I don't really mind if it's raining on the way home.' Her little toe on her right foot pinched slightly and she wondered if maybe she had time to change into a lower pair of heels.

'Quickly,' Jools instructed, her impatience obvious. 'Finn Gallichan is there, and I want to meet up with him before he gets settled and ends up chatting to everyone else.'

It was the first time Lexi even had a hint that Jools liked Finn. He had come to work for Sacha's boyfriend Alessandro, in his gelateria earlier in the summer, and everyone had taken to him immediately. The fact that her friend was admitting her attraction for him so readily meant she really was in a rush to see him. Well, Lexi thought. That's a surprise I didn't see coming. She smiled to herself. 'Two secs, I'm coming.'

She took her coat from the hook by the door, picked up the bottle of rosé that she had bought to take with her, and stepped outside. 'We have to knock on Oliver's door on the way.'

Jools sighed heavily, but Lexi couldn't miss the interest in her eyes. It seemed that she was as intrigued by Lexi's inclusion of Oliver to the party, as Lexi had been about her friend's interest in Finn.

'Is he bringing his girlfriend?'

'Of course he is. He couldn't exactly leave her

alone at home on New Year's Eve, now could he?' Lexi giggled. 'I have a feeling this is going to be an interesting party,' she added, linking arms with her friend and running with her the short distance to Oliver's cottage. She raised her hand to knock, just as the door opened. 'Blimey, were you spying on us?' she teased, hoping he hadn't heard what she had just said.

'Not at all,' he grinned, wrapping a neat scarf around his neck with a little difficulty, while attempting to hold on to the six-pack of beer as he held the door back. He sighed and leant into the hallway. 'Come along, Portia.'

'Stop nagging, Olly,' Portia moaned from somewhere upstairs.

Jools nudged Lexi in the ribs, looking as if she was already enjoying herself.

'Anyway,' Oliver added. 'You told me what time you'd be here.'

'But she's rarely on time,' Jools grinned, glancing at him and then widening her eyes at Lexi as Portia finally appeared, looking as if an entire glam team had spent hours preparing her for the event. Oliver didn't seem to notice. As soon as she stepped outside, he locked the door.

'Shut up, Jools.' Lexi said, as her friend stared at Portia. She didn't need Oliver to think she was unreliable, especially as he was essentially her boss. 'I'm not always late at all. Not any more,' she added guiltily, before Jools began arguing with her.

Jool's finally caught up with what Lexi was implying. 'Yes, I know,' she smiled. 'I was only messing with you.'

Lexi realised she should be making some introductions. 'Jools, I believe you've met Oliver Whimsy.' Jools nodded at him. 'This is Portia. She's staying on the island at the moment.' She didn't really know what to say about Portia, so thought that the best idea would be to say as little as she could get away with.

'Wonderful to meet you, Jools,' Portia said, beaming at her. 'Do you live on this famous boardwalk too?'

'Yes, that's right,' Jools said. 'I live in the tiny second-hand bookshop with my gran.'

'How delightful.'

'I like it there,' Jools smiled. 'But then I've got nothing to compare it with as I've never lived anywhere else.'

'Right, shall we go?' Oliver asked.

Portia nodded and immediately linked arms with him. 'I've been looking forward to this evening,' she said as they walked to the road and down the hill. 'The weather's been too atrocious to do anything much at all until tonight, so I haven't been anywhere to meet any of Oliver's new friends yet.'

Lexi felt Jools staring silently at her but did her best to ignore her. She didn't fancy Jools whispering at her like she usually did. Her voice was always too loud, and she never seemed to realise that others nearby could hear what she was saying. Lexi presumed it was because she was used to making herself heard to her grandmother, who was slightly deaf.

'It was kind of your friend to include me in her invitations,' Oliver said.

'And me.' Portia tapped Lexi lightly on the shoulder. 'This isn't the New Year's Eve party I was expecting, but I'm more excited about this one than the one I should have been attending at my friend's family estate in Gloucestershire.'

'Really?' Jools pulled a face at Lexi, who hoped that Oliver and Portia hadn't noticed as they followed them. 'I'm pretty sure I would prefer the other party to this one.'

'No, you wouldn't,' Lexi argued. 'You love Sacha's parties. And at least at this one, no one will tell you off for dancing on the tables.' She gave Jools a wink to show she was joking.

Portia gave her tinkling laugh. 'She's right you know, Jools. This will probably be much more fun.'

'I'm surprised you accepted,' Lexi said looking at Oliver, before having time to think how her reply might come across. She was getting to be like Jools with her quips, she thought with concern. 'I had thought after the last party that you might not wish to spend time with them.'

'Ooh, that sounds interesting. Do tell what happened, Olly?'

Oliver cleared his throat. 'That was an unfortunate event and I don't hold any resentment towards any of your friends for their opinion of me. I would have come to the same conclusion about them it if had been the other way around.'

Lexi was relieved to hear him say so. 'Well, we can all start again and they can get to know you properly tonight.'

The party was in full swing by the time they arrived at the Summer Sundaes Café. Sacha's favourite song, Bad Guy by Billie Eilish was playing and Bella and Jack were dancing. He held her left hand above her head as she spun around underneath, almost bumping into Portia as she entered the café after Lexi and Jools. Other friends were singing along to the music as it pounded through the speakers. Lexi could see they had moved the tables and chairs to the outside of the room to make space for the small dancefloor in the middle.

'Hey, sorry about that mate,' Jack shouted, pulling Bella into his arms and welcoming them. 'Find a table and make it your own. Probably the best thing to do is hang your coats and scarves on the back of chairs. Then come and help yourself to some booze.'

'We've all bought bottles,' Jools said, holding up the one in her hand.

Within no time at all everyone found somewhere to leave their coats and got themselves drinks. Sacha had set up plates of canapés on the counter with a large bowl of bean salad and potato.

Sacha waved for Jack to turn down the music, and when he had she stood behind the counter and addressed them all. 'Welcome new friends and old, to the Summer Sundaes Beach Café party. It's great to have you all here, and I'm relieved that the rain held off long enough for you to arrive without getting soaked. Help yourselves to a plate and cutlery,' she said, indicating the neatly arranged crockery and food in front of her. 'There's hot food on that side, including chicken curry and a veggie curry for those who don't eat meat. I'll leave you to help yourselves and then please make the most of the puddings over in the chiller counter. If you can't find something just ask me or Jack. Enjoy.'

Jack immediately turned up the music once more and the party continued.

Lexi thanked her for all her hard work. 'Give me a shout in the morning when you're ready and I'll come down to help you clear up after this lot.'

'Thanks, I might just do that. Now, you help yourself to some food.'

'Hi Lexi,' Alessandro said, coming out of the kitchen and putting his arms around Sacha from behind. 'You are well?'

'Yes, thanks, Alessandro. How's things with you? I thought you might have gone home to Italy to visit your family over the holidays?'

He shook his head. 'Not this year, but maybe

in a couple of months. Maybe they come here to see me and Jersey.'

'That would be nice.'

Alessandro leant slightly forward. 'I have someone who is looking forward to speaking to you,' he said, tapping the side of his nose.

Lexi was intrigued. 'Who?'

There was a gust of cold air and everyone turned to see Charlie, the assistant manager from the nearby Sea Breeze Hotel where Jack's ex-girlfriend Nicky had caused such a scene with Oliver at her Halloween party. He looked very windswept, Lexi thought, not surprised when she noticed his hair was damp.

'I think it's started raining again,' she said, turning back to Sacha and Alessandro, wondering why Alessandro gave her an odd look and then peered over her head to wave at Charlie. Lexi gasped. 'Charlie? Is he the one you were talking about?'

'Is true,' Alessandro smiled. 'Charlie is a good man. He is on his way over now.'

Lexi hadn't ever spoken to Charlie apart from the odd word, but she liked him as did all her friends.

'Hi, mind if I join you?' a deep voice with what Lexi assumed was an Australian accent, asked.

'Good to see you here, Charlie,' Sacha said, giving him a kiss on the cheek. 'Right, you and Lexi can get yourselves something to eat and then find somewhere to sit. I don't want people to wait too long to eat because if they drink too much first then they won't want to bother having any.'

Lexi turned around and saw the man who she had only ever seen on duty at the hotel when he was immaculately turned out, not a hair out of place. 'Hi, nice to see you here Charlie. Shall we join the small queue before everyone does?'

'That's a good idea.' He followed her and when she handed him a plate and cutlery, he took them and smiled. 'It's good to meet you properly, Lexi. I'm looking forward to being able to enjoy a party without supervising everything.'

'I can imagine.' She explained about the food.

Moments later they were sitting at one of the tables with a plate of curry and naan bread and a drink each. Lexi noticed Oliver glance over at her and then narrow his eyes when he spotted Charlie. She wondered if maybe the two of them had exchanged words after the debacle of the Halloween party. She decided not to broach the subject and began eating the delicious vegetarian curry Sacha was so clever at making.

'Is that Oliver, sorry I can't recall his last name.'

'Whimsy,' Lexi said. 'Yes, that's him.'

'He's with a different woman this time, I see.' He took a mouthful of food and watched Oliver surreptitiously. 'What's he doing back on the island, I wonder? I thought he was some big shot in London, or maybe I've got him mixed up with someone else.'

Lexi wasn't sure what to say. She supposed Charlie had every right to be disgruntled about Oliver, but maybe it was time for him to learn that there was a different side to him, the one she knew now to be the real him. Or at least that's what she supposed it to be.

'I think that night was unfortunate for everyone involved, especially him and Nicky.' She knew what she was saying was a bit of an understatement. 'I've got to know him a little better since then and he's actually not nearly as bad as we all presumed.'

Charlie stopped mid-way to lifting a fork of food to his mouth. 'Really? You surprise me.'

Lexi shrugged. 'It's true though. I thought the same way as you at first, but I've spent some time with him over Christmas and he's an OK guy.'

Charlie ate another mouthful. 'I'll have to take your word for it. Although,' he added, lowering his voice. 'He does appear to be interested in what's happening at this table.'

'What do you mean?'

'He keeps looking over this way and I'm not sure if it's because I had a few stern words with him on Halloween, or if it's you he's watching.'

'It won't be me,' Lexi said, feeling certain that with Portia with him for company, Oliver had no reason to be interested in her.

'Enough about him,' Charlie said. 'I want to

know about you. Alessandro tells me you're also in the service industry.'

Lexi shook her head. 'Sort of, but not to the extent that you're used to.'

'I gather you own three holiday lets and have been running them for the past few years. How's that going?'

Oh dear, Lexi thought. Now she was going to ruin her hard work, trying to make Oliver seem more pleasant, by telling Charlie he'd bought her cottages.

'Well, it's like this,' she began and told him a gentle version of the events that had happened just before Christmas.

Charlie frowned. 'I thought you said he was nice.'

Lexi smiled. 'He is. It's not Oliver's fault my father didn't mention he was selling my home and business from under me. And, what's more, he's been very kind by letting me stay at my cottage for now and employing me as a typist. He didn't have to do either of those things, so I can't really think too badly of him.'

Charlie glared in Oliver's direction. 'Well, that's a matter of opinion.'

Lexi didn't want to discuss Oliver anymore. 'Never mind him, tell me something about you. I guess that you're Australian, aren't you?'

'No. I'm from New Zealand.' He grinned at her. 'Though you Brits seem incapable of telling the difference.'

'Well, now I think about it, your accent is slightly different to any Australian I've ever met.'

He laughed. 'That's probably because I'm not one.'

'True.'

Charlie stopped laughing and looked at her for a moment before asking, 'Would you come out for a drink with me one night?' When she didn't answer right away, he added, 'Somewhere we can chat without trying to be heard over loud music and people enjoying themselves.'

Lexi didn't see why not. 'Why, aren't you enjoying yourself here?' she grinned.

He smiled at her. 'I am,' he said. 'In fact, would you like to come with me to the Burns Night party on the twenty-fifth? It's always great fun.'

'Aren't you going to be working though?'

He shook his head. 'Not this year. I intend to enjoy myself.' He tilted his head to one side. 'So? You want to come as my plus one?'

She didn't have to think for long before answering. 'I'd love to. Thank you.'

'Great. We'll go for that drink before though, shall we?'

'Yes, I'd like that.' She realised she was looking forward to seeing him again and getting to know him a bit better. She finished eating the last mouthful of her food and placed her knife and fork together on her plate.

'Let me take these away. Would you like another drink?'

'You're not at work now, you know,' she said with a grin. 'Yes, I'd love another rosé please.'

'Coming right up.'

He got up and took their plates to the kitchen. Lexi watched him go. He looked different when he wasn't wearing a suit, she decided, and he was nice. She glanced over at Oliver. Portia was leaning into him, her mouth millimetres away from his ear as she said something to him that made him laugh loudly seconds later. Yes, Lexi thought, She would enjoy going for a drink with Charlie and getting to know him a little better.

'How's it going?' Bella asked, pulling out the chair next to Lexi and sitting down. 'I really shouldn't dance so much, I'm all hot and sweaty now.'

Lexi laughed. 'You're always so ladylike.'

'Yes, well, it's true. It's Jack's fault, he has far too much energy for one person. He surfs most days and never sits still for longer than a few minutes. Honestly, I could tell you a few things about—'

'Please, no.' Lexi raised her hand. She knew where this was going and had no wish to hear what Jack was like in the bedroom. 'I haven't had a man in my bedroom for so long, I'm sure I've forgotten what I should do if one ever does join me.'

'Do you want me to come back in a bit?' Charlie asked, passing Lexi a glass of wine.

She felt her face heat up. He must have heard at least some of what she had just said to Bella. Lexi realised Bella had doubled over in hysterics. 'It's not funny,' she said through gritted teeth.

'It is, though.'

Lexi noticed Charlie was still standing there, waiting for her to tell him what she wanted him to do. 'Sorry, no, it's fine. Please sit down.'

He put his glass on the table and held his hand out to her. 'Why don't we have a dance instead.' He looked at Bella and smiled. 'If you've finished your conversation.'

She certainly had. Lexi nodded and taking his hand, raised it over Bella's head. Lexi bent down to her giggling friend as she passed. 'You're not supposed to find my humiliation quite so amusing.'

Bella pulled a face. 'But you know that I love you.'

Lexi shook her head and smiled. 'Yes, but sometimes I wonder why.' She pulled Charlie over to the dance area. 'Come along, let's dance then.'

Charlie pulled her to him as the next record's tempo slowed and Lexi wondered if maybe Sacha or Jack had changed the record on purpose. She looked over to see Sacha give her a thumbs up and decided to ignore them. They had obviously made it their mission to set Charlie and her up with each other. Well she could make up her own mind, she thought realising as they danced that he really was rather good. Maybe it was having to attend so many hotel functions? Then again, if he was on duty, surely he wouldn't be taking part in any dancing. She wasn't sure, but either way, she was enjoying herself rather more than she had expected.

The music changed after a few minutes and when someone tapped her lightly on the shoulder, she looked round to see Portia. 'Having fun?' Lexi mouthed.

Portia nodded. 'Yes, thanks.'

A short while later, Lexi spotted Portia looking sad. A moment later they stopped dancing and Oliver put his arm around her shoulder. Then leading her to the table next to the one where Lexi and Charlie had been sitting sat and he bent his head low and seemed to be attempting to pacify her. Lexi hoped they hadn't fallen out, especially on New Year's Eve. The music tempo sped up slightly and Charlie took her hand and spun her around. Lexi laughed and the next thing she knew she was doing some sort of samba; at least that's what she thought it was.

The next thing she knew, Oliver was accompanying Portia towards the café door. It horrified Lexi to see Portia had been crying. She stopped dancing and rested a hand on Charlie's shoulder. 'Sorry, I'm going to have to see if Portia's all right. I think something's the matter and I can't let her go without checking if she's alright. I won't be long.'

He looked disappointed, but Lexi was too concerned about Portia to ask him. She hurried over to the door where Jack was chatting to Oliver and helping Portia on with her coat.

'Portia, what's the matter?' Lexi asked, noticing how Portia's once perfectly made-up face had been ruined by smudged mascara.

'She's fine. Please don't worry,' Oliver said, slipping his arm around Portia's waist. 'We're going now, but Jack, please thank Sacha for a lovely party. The food was delicious.'

Lexi hadn't seen them eat anything but presumed they must have done at some point.

'Do you need me to come back with you?' she asked wanting to help if she possibly could.

Oliver frowned slightly. 'No, you stay and enjoy the party. I know the way back.'

She nodded. The cottage was only up the hill, so it wasn't as if they could get lost getting home. She placed her hand on Portia's arm. 'Are you sure you're all right?'

Portia smiled at her warmly and sniffed. 'I am, thanks. Don't worry about me. I should have known this would happen.'

'Why? What's happened?'

'It's fine,' Oliver said, reaching to open the door. 'Really.' He looked at Jack. 'Please don't forget to thank your sister for us.'

'No problem, mate. The party's not over yet though.' Jack gave him a cheeky smile and slapped him on the back.

Oliver looked confused. 'What do you mean?'

Lexi wished Jack wouldn't tease and knew what was coming.

'It's the New Year's Day swim tomorrow. As you are our newest resident, we'll expect to see you down on the boardwalk in your trunks. No wetsuit mind you. Eight a.m. sharp.'

He glanced at Lexi and seemed unsure whether Jack was joking or not. 'Seriously?'

'Deadly serious. I want to know how tough you Highlanders really are.'

So do I thought Lexi, hoping Oliver would step up to Jack's challenge.

'Fine,' Oliver shrugged. 'I'll see you then.'

Lexi watched him and Portia leave and wondered what had upset her. She seemed to be fine with Oliver, so what else could it have been? She hadn't heard any commotion and hadn't heard them arguing and there didn't seem to be any angry conversations going on anywhere in the café, so she doubted Portia had been caught up in any spats. Maybe it was something else? Lexi wished she knew what was wrong with her new friend.

CHAPTER ELEVEN

New Year's Day

Lexi set her alarm for seven-thirty, giving her enough time to shower and change and get down to the boardwalk for the New Year's Day dip. She knew to wear her costume under her clothes and take a pair of knickers to change into in the café lavatories as soon as they came out of the sea. Every year she dreaded forcing herself into the incredibly cold water, but always felt invigorated straight after. It was the perfect way to start the year, or that was what her mother and gran had always insisted. She wasn't about to change the tradition this year, despite the extra cold weather.

Lexi dressed as warmly as she could. She knew from experience that she would need to warm up as quickly as possible. She pulled on her thick socks and boots, then put on her parka and gloves, grabbed her biggest towel, and shoved a pair of knickers deep into her pocket before leaving the cottage.

She didn't knock for Oliver on her way past, just in case he had a change of heart. For all she knew, he and Portia could have been up all night, chatting, or whatever else that she didn't like to think about.

Lexi ran all the way down the hill to the boardwalk, hoping to warm herself up as much as possible, and got there in plenty of time to join the crowd of locals gathered on the beach. Their family members who had decided not to take part were waiting on the boardwalk, chatting and laughing, no doubt thinking that the rest of them were mad to torture themselves in such a way.

She spotted Jack and waved. Then hurried to the café to change and leave her clothes where it was warm and dry.

'This place is spotless,' she said, recalling guiltily how she had offered the previous night to go and help Sacha tidy up after the party. 'You must have been up at the crack of dawn?'

'Not really. I did it all last night before going to bed.'

'What? Oh Sacha, you shouldn't have done that. Not after all the preparations you did to entertain us all.'

'Nonsense. Alessandro and Jack helped, so it wasn't bad at all. In fact we were all a little tipsy so we had a good laugh as we worked.'

'I'm pleased they helped,' Lexi said, relieved. 'I know I promised to, but I forgot, like a lousy friend.'

'Rubbish.' Sacha frowned. 'You've got a lot on your mind right now and I think the most important thing is for you to focus on that. And don't forget to look after yourself while you're at it'

Lexi laughed. 'Has anyone ever told you how bossy you are?'

'All the time.' She shooed Lexi away. 'Now you'd better get a move on. You do know you're all mad, don't you?' Sacha laughed as Lexi walked from behind the counter towards the café door.

'You don't want to join us?' Lexi asked, wrapping her towel tightly around her.

Sacha shook her head. 'Not me. I have more sense. Anyway, I need to prepare all the hot drinks and pastries for you lot. You'll need them when you come in here sopping wet and full of yourselves for being so brave.'

Lexi giggled. 'We're grateful for being able to come back here afterwards.' She noticed the time on the clock. 'Hell, I've only got a couple of minutes. I don't want to get this far and miss the dip itself. See you later,' she shouted as she ran out of the café and onto the boardwalk.

'Ouch, ouch, ouch,' Lexi grumbled with every step she took. The boardwalk was freezing under her bare feet, as were the granite steps down to the beach and then the cold, damp sand.

'Come along!' Jack bellowed from the water's edge. 'We're waiting for you.'

She ran towards him and the rest of the crowd. 'Sorry, everyone. This is madness,' she winced as her left foot landed on a shell. 'I'm not doing it again next year.'

'You said that last year!' Jools yelled.

Lexi went to give her a mouthful when she saw that her friend was standing next to Finn Gallichan. She wondered if maybe they had got together during the party the previous night and made a mental note to ask her when she was next alone with her friend.

She reached a large rock where everyone had dumped their towels and dropped her bright pink towel nearby. 'Right, here goes nothing,' she mumbled, running the last few metres to the water's edge where the others were waiting.

She rubbed her upper arms and danced from one foot to the other, desperately trying to keep warm. She wished Jack would get on with it so she could run into the sea, paddle for a few seconds and exit as quickly as she could.

'You look about as happy as I am to be here this morning,' said a deep voice next to her.

She turned to see Oliver smiling down at her. She had never seen him anything less than fully clothed before. Seeing him standing next to her in swimming shorts, his muscled arms and torso still slightly tanned from summer, or probably an expensive holiday somewhere, was the perfect distraction from how cold she was feeling at that moment. Lexi had thought Jack was pretty perfect physically, but Oliver looked even better. Maybe, she thought, it's because I fancy him and I just see Jack as, well, Jack.

She remembered he had said something to her and quickly tried to recall what it was. 'I do this every year, but it never gets easier. I think I'm a martyr to Jack's cause.'

Oliver grinned. 'And what cause is that?'

'To persuade us all that swimming in the sea every day is vital for our continued good health.' She waved her hand to encompass the others waiting on the beach with them.

'And do you think he'll manage it?'

'Not a cat's chance in hell,' she giggled. 'Those of us who come down each year, do it because we feel we should for some reason, but most of us only do it this once during the colder months.'

Oliver laughed. 'I don't blame you.'

'But you're a hardy Scot. You should find this easy, surely?'

Jack clapped his hands loudly. 'Right you lot. Here goes. On the count of three I want you all to run as quickly as you can into the water and stay there for at least a few minutes if you can. One... Two... Three.'

Oliver smiled at Lexi and reached out to take her hand. 'Come along, let's do this. Brace yourself.'

Lexi took his hand and shrieked as they began running the short distance into the sea. 'Argh,' she yelled as the cold water hit her feet and quickly moved up her body as she ran deeper into the rough water with Oliver.

He let go of her hand. 'Right, let's swim for as long as we can to satisfy your friend.'

Lexi laughed. She watched Oliver as he set off and started swimming. He was obviously a strong swimmer and extremely comfortable in the water. 'You don't look too bothered about the cold.'

'Years of being made to swim in rivers near my parent's home in the highlands. It toughens you up, whether you like it or not.'

Lexi kicked her legs back and forth as she moved her arms around to keep afloat. 'Maybe I could have done with some of that early training.'

Every second felt like a minute and soon she was too cold to keep going. Oliver Whimsy was certainly attractive to look at but the thought of getting out of the sea and sitting in the warm café was far too tempting to keep her in the sea any longer.

'Right, sod this. I've had enough. I'm off to get dressed.' She turned and began swimming back to the shore.

Within seconds of her reaching the damp sand, Oliver reached her and taking her hand in his led her at a run to the rocks to collect their towels.

'Thank heavens for that,' he smiled as she grabbed her towel and wrapped herself in it quickly. 'I was beginning to think I'd have to give in first.' He reached for his towel and dried his hair and then wrapped it around himself.

She didn't know if he was teasing, but it was so cold that she guessed he might be telling the truth. 'Have you left your clothes at the café like most of us did?'

He nodded. 'Jack suggested I do that, which was thoughtful of him.'

'He's one of the good guys, Jack is,' she said, noticing that someone was taking photos of Jack from the boardwalk with a rather impressive looking camera. 'Right, let's get back to the café before hyperthermia sets in.' She glanced over her shoulder. 'Or at least before the rest of them come out of the sea. There'll be a long queue for the café loos as soon as they decide to dry off.'

They ran up the beach, up the granite stairs and along the boardwalk, reaching the café in a couple of minutes. Oliver opened the door and waited for Lexi to go inside. She smiled her thanks and sighed with relief as the warmth in the brightly lit room wrapped itself around her.

'Thank heavens for that.'

Sacha looked up from behind the counter

where she was putting pastries on a large tray. 'Good, you've done it. Well done, you two. You're the first two back here.'

'That's a relief,' Lexi said, picking up her bag and making her way to the Ladies. 'Oliver, I suggest you get in the Gents right away, they'll all be coming back in here in the next few minutes.'

Five minutes later, they were sitting at a corner table, a cooked breakfast in front of each of them and a hot drink. Lexi could never understand someone choosing coffee over hot chocolate and said so.

'I don't really have a sweet tooth, I guess,' Oliver said, tucking into one of the sausages on his plate. 'This is delicious. I was tempted to have a pastry, but this is much better.'

Lexi began to eat and slowly felt her body warm up. Now that she was no longer hungry or cold, she felt good about having made herself take part in the dip. It always felt satisfying afterwards, she remembered.

After they had finished their food and sat nursing their drinks while the rest of the swimmers returned to change, or from their homes where they'd dried off and dressed, Lexi wondered what had happened to Portia.

'How is Portia this morning?'

'Fine, why?' Oliver stared at her looking confused, as if he hadn't had to escort Portia out the previous evening, mascara smudged under her large pale eyes.

Lexi wasn't sure if she should push the point but was too nosy not to. 'Do tell me to mind my own business if I'm poking my nose into yours.'

'Go on.' He took a drink from his mug.

'Portia seemed terribly upset last night. I wondered what was wrong. Did you have a falling out, or something?'

Oliver stared at her as if he were trying to work out how much to say. She wished he would hurry up and put her out of her misery. There was something odd between him and Portia, but she couldn't quite put her finger on what it was. 'Look, don't feel you have to tell me,' she said eventually. 'I'm just concerned for her. I thought she might have come down with you this morning to see you swim.'

He shook his head. 'No. Portia doesn't do the cold if she can possibly help it. Unless she's skiing, maybe. She's up at the cottage.' He finished his coffee. 'In fact, I wanted to ask you something, which is why I was happy to leave her be and didn't encourage her to accompany me this morning.'

Lexi was intrigued. 'Go on. Ask me.' What on earth could it be? she wondered impatiently.

'Would you mind if Portia moved into the middle cottage? Just for a few weeks, maybe a month.'

Lexi wasn't sure what she had expected him to say, but it hadn't been that. Why would Portia want to come and stay on the island, especially in the middle of winter? She had so many other exciting places she could visit that Lexi assumed would suit her better – like London, where she was sure Portia must have friends.

'Why are you asking me? The cottages belong to you,' she replied, trying not to show how difficult it was for her to recognise the fact. 'I don't have any say in the matter.'

Several other swimmers were carrying food and making their way towards the table next to them. Oliver leaned towards Lexi and lowered his voice. 'They were your home,' he said. 'I don't want to offer Portia the use of a cottage if her staying there will make you uncomfortable.'

Lexi was confused. 'Sorry, I don't understand. Why should I mind?'

He shrugged. 'I was just checking.'

'Whatever you decide is fine with me.' She couldn't understand why he didn't simply invite Portia to stay with him. It didn't make much sense, but it wasn't as if there was anyone booked into the middle cottage, so there was no reason for Portia not to move in.

'I'll freshen it up and make up the bed after I've finished here.'

He shook his head. 'No, that's fine. I'll do it and Portia can help me. She'll be the one using it.'

It didn't seem right to let the person staying in the cottage make it up, and Lexi said so. 'Leave it with me. Give me until lunchtime and then she can take her things round there.'

'No. I'll do it. Anyway, I don't know if she'll be happy to move in there yet, so there's no point in you wasting your time, especially on New Year's Day.'

It all sounded a little confusing, so Lexi shrugged. 'Fine, if you're happy with that.'

He reached out and took her hand in his. 'I am. And thanks for offering, Lexi. I appreciate it.'

Her hand felt hot and tingly in his. She stared at it, and he must have noticed her doing so because the next thing she knew, he had let her hand go and moved away from her. She was dying to ask why he didn't want Portia to stay with him but knew that to do so would be nosy.

'I'll go and pay for this and then we should probably go back. Unless you intend staying here for a bit longer?'

'No, I'm ready to go home,' she said. 'I need a good walk up the hill to help this lot digest properly.'

She stacked their plates and took them with their empty mugs to the kitchen. Sacha had enough to do, feeding the swimmers, to have to clear up after her and Oliver as well. 'I'll pay for mine,' she said when he stepped back to let her in front of him.

'No, it's my treat for you being such a good sport and letting Portia stay on.'

Lexi stopped and turned to him. 'Really, you don't have to. And I don't expect you to ask me about using the cottages for guests either. They're yours. I've accepted that now.' She didn't wait for him to answer but walked on towards the kitchen, stopping as she reached the counter and smiling at him over her shoulder. 'Go on then, I've decided that I will let you buy me breakfast. Just this once.'

He laughed, sounding relieved. 'Good. That makes me feel much better.'

Lexi shivered as they walked up the hill. 'We must have been mad to swim earlier,' she said, a cloud of frosty breath coming out of her mouth as she spoke. 'It's much colder this year than it usually, I'm sure of it.'

'I don't know about that, but it is pretty cold.' He linked arms with her. 'Come along, let's pick up the pace a bit, it'll warm us up.'

'You're not on a mountain trek now, you know,' she joked. 'And you can slow down a bit. My legs are shorter than yours, so this hill is double the work for me.'

'Stop whinging.' he laughed but slowed his pace to meet hers. He grinned at her. 'Can I ask you something?'

'Another request? This is getting a little tedious,' she teased.

'Cheek.' He ruffled the top of her hat, making it lift slightly off her head.

'My ears are cold now.' She removed her arm from his and pulled her woolly hat back down over her ears. Then linking arms with him again, said, 'Right, I'm listening now.'

'I wanted to ask if you'll be my partner at the Burns Night Party. There's one being held at the Sea Breeze Hotel on the twenty-fifth.'

Lexi stopped walking, shocked. 'How can you ask me that?'

'Sorry?' He frowned and looked confused for some reason she was unable to fathom.

Did he really not know how wrong his question was? 'Portia? What about her?'

'She can come with us, if she's still here,' he replied frowning. 'She does tend to change her mind in an instant. She might have returned to London by then.'

So that gave him the right to ask her out instead? 'Sorry. I don't get it.'

'Keep walking,' he said. 'We're nearly there.'

Sacha didn't move. She hated the thought of Portia overhearing their conversation. 'No. I think we need to settle this here before we get too close to the cottages.'

Oliver shook his head. 'Whatever's the matter?'

Had she missed something? 'Won't Portia mind you inviting me?'

'Why should she?'

For pity's sake, Lexi fumed. What was wrong with this man? She hadn't wanted to have to spell it out but was infuriated on Portia's behalf with him for acting so wantonly. 'Because if I was your girlfriend and you asked out another woman, I'd be bloody furious.'

'What?' He took a step back and stared at her. His mouth seemed to be moving but no words came out.

She had shocked him, although had no idea why. 'Oliver?'

Slowly his lips drew back into a smile and his eyes twinkled as he began to laugh. 'You think Portia is my girlfriend?'

'Well, isn't she?'

'No.'

She couldn't have misread the chemistry between them on Boxing Day and the night before, could she? 'But I thought…'

'Go on.'

She didn't dare embarrass herself any more than she already had. 'Why don't you tell me what she is to you then, because you seem to be very close.'

'Please can we keep walking while I explain everything to you?'

She shook her head. She didn't want Portia to discover what she had imagined about the two of them. It would be too mortifying. 'I don't want her overhearing us speaking about her behind her back. Tell me now.'

He folded his arms and stamped from one foot to the other. 'Don't you feel the cold?'

'Not when I'm angry. Now tell me.'

He widened his eyes. 'Fine. Portia was almost my sister-in-law.'

'Why almost?' As soon as the words left her

mouth, Lexi realised that Portia must have been his late brother's fiancée. 'Oh, I'm so sorry. She was your brother's…'

'She was.'

Lexi's heart ached for what Portia must have gone through. 'Did something happen to her over Christmas then?' she asked, feeling desperately sorry for the poor woman who had lost the man she loved so tragically.

'Yes. It was the anniversary of my brother's accident. Portia usually goes up to stay with my parents but didn't like to now my dad's so unwell. That's why she turned up on my doorstep on Boxing Day. She knew I would never turn her away. We spent the time sharing memories of Alistair and comforting each other,' he sighed miserably. 'It helped being with someone who loved him as much as I did.'

'I can imagine,' Lexi said quietly, reaching out to take his hand in hers. 'I'm so sorry, Oliver. I completely misread the situation. I'm glad you had each other to help you through such a difficult time.'

He smiled at her. This time the smile didn't reach his eyes. 'Thank you. It helped.'

He bent down and kissed her lightly. She was so taken aback by the unexpectedness of it that she didn't know how to react and just stood there before kissing him back.

'Now that you know you don't have to worry about Portia's feelings being hurt romantically where I'm concerned, will you consider coming with me to the Burns Night Party?'

'Ahh,' Lexi said, reeling from the sensation of Oliver's lips on hers. She wished she hadn't been so quick to accept Charlie's invitation the night before. 'I'm afraid I can't.'

His broad shoulders drooped slightly. 'Charlie?'

Lexi nodded. 'Yes, Charlie.'

'I can't say I'm not disappointed. I guess I'll just have to see you there then?'

'I suppose so,' she said miserably.

He linked arms with her again and began striding the rest of the way up the hill. 'Come along, before we freeze to death.'

He didn't sound very disappointed to her, Lexi thought as she jogged to keep up with his lengthy strides. Maybe he was putting on a brave face? She hoped so.

CHAPTER TWELVE

Mid-January

Lexi arrived at Oliver's cottage the following morning a little bleary-eyed, but ready to continue typing up the next few pages that he had dictated to her. It had been a very quiet couple of weeks, and the beginning of January was exactly what she had imagined it would be. The weather had been wet and stormy and most people chose to either stay at home during the bad weather, or leave the island to visit family on the mainland or go on holiday somewhere warmer.

She hadn't seen much of Oliver because he had gone to Scotland to spent a couple of weeks with his parents. It had been strange without him around and she even missed Portia who, after only one day without Oliver around, took herself back to London, promising to return before the Burns Night party. She had heard him being dropped off by taxi late the previous evening and presumed he must have caught the last flight back to the island.

It was freezing outside but she didn't bother wearing a coat for the short commute to work. Lexi reached his door and knocked a couple of times.

'Let yourself in,' he bellowed from somewhere inside.

She did as he asked and walked straight through to the living room. 'Good morning,' she said, placing her laptop on the small round kitchen table. 'How are you?' She noticed that his usual jovial manner when he greeted her each morning had gone. His face seemed pale and his expression dour. He looked dreadful. 'Are you all right? Shall I make you a coffee? Or maybe I can fetch you a couple of headache pills?'

Oliver shook his head slowly. 'No, thanks.'

Concerned, Lexi went and sat on the arm of the nearest chair. 'Has something happened?' She didn't want to pry, but he seemed upset and she wanted to help, if she possibly could.

He sighed. He was staring at his phone screen. 'They can't come, Lexi.'

'Your parents? Do you mean?'

He nodded. 'I was hoping to finalise their first trip here while I was staying with them.'

She knew now how important the buying of these cottages had been to him. It was the same importance that had helped her come to terms with them not belonging to her family anymore.

'Oh, Oliver, I'm really sorry. Do you want to tell me what's happened? Or would you rather not speak about it?' she asked, dreading how bad the news might be. She had lost the two closest women to her and knew only too well how it changed a person's life forever, regardless of any attempt to put on a brave face, trying to carry on without them.

Oliver seemed to re-read the message on his phone before placing it face down onto the coffee table in front of him and sitting back in the chair. He closed his eyes.

'My mother did say during one of our chats before Christmas how much my father had deteriorated, but she has a tendency to exaggerate sometimes where he's concerned. I was hoping he wasn't as bad as she made out. When I arrived in Scotland and saw him, I could see for myself that she was right.' He took a deep breath and didn't continue for a moment. 'Apparently, when she told my father's doctor that she was planning to bring him here for a few weeks, hoping that the sight and smells might evoke memories for him so that they could both remember together, his doctor refused to allow him to come.' He gazed miserably at Lexi. 'He's lost too much of his memory now to be allowed on holiday. Their doctor said that rather than help him remember, bringing him somewhere new, somewhere he hasn't visited for over thirty years, would more than likely distress him.'

'That's so sad. Your poor dad.'

'I know,' he said sadly. 'He's really gone down hill since I last saw him, Lexi. He finds it difficult to cope at home where everything is familiar. To bring him here could frighten him and neither of us want that.'

'No, of course you don't.' Her heart ached to see him so sad, and to think of the young, besotted couple in her gran's photos now having to live with only one of them aware of how much they shared. It was heart-breaking.

She saw Oliver quickly brush away something from his cheek and was desperate to hug him but didn't know him well enough to be sure he would welcome such a thing. He seemed such a private man and not one to be open to an unexpected display of affection.

'I'm so sorry, Oliver.'

He opened his eyes and looked at her. 'Thank you. I know you are.' He stared at her thoughtfully for a moment. 'I'm devastated to think that my mother will never realise her dream of returning here with Dad.' He reached out and took Lexi's hand. 'I also feel guilty that my part in trying to do this thing for my parents has meant you've lost something you treasure. If they can't come here then everything I've done and you've gone through seems futile and unnecessary.'

She understood why he thought as he did but he couldn't have known what would happen. 'You didn't know me or my circumstances when you bought these cottages,' she said, wanting to make him feel better. 'You were doing something kind and thoughtful.'

He gave her hand a gentle squeeze and forced a smile. 'Maybe, but in trying to turn my mother's dream into a reality I've forced her to face the terrible realisation that something she has dreamt of doing for thirty years will never actually happen. By trying to make her dream come true all I've done is crush it. And in turn, yours.' He let go of her hand and shook his head. Then standing, he quietly added, 'I'm going for a walk.'

Lexi watched him leave the room and seconds later heard him zip up his jacket and then the clunk of the heavy door closing behind him. She hated that he needed to leave his home for time alone. She wished she had thought to offer to work from her cottage for the morning and give him time to think, but he had already gone, and she didn't want to disturb his solace by chasing after him.

Lexi stared at Oliver's phone wondering exactly what his mother had said this morning but had no intention of breaking his trust by picking it up and reading her message. How heartbroken he must be right now, she mused. His sense of achievement after coming to the island and tracing his parent's footsteps back to where they'd first met and fell in love and, not only locating the cottages, but managing to purchase them and present them as a gift to his mother, must have felt like an enormous achievement. And all for nothing.

Lexi stood up and went to the window. She spotted Oliver's tall figure walking slowly down the hill in the direction of the boardwalk. It looked like he was making for the beach. She would do exactly the same thing if she were him. However difficult life became, the smell and sounds of the beach, and in the warmer months the sensation of the sand under the soles of her feet and the sea lapping over her toes, always helped give her the strength to carry on and face whatever it was that had upset her.

Feeling the need to breathe in the familiar salty air, Lexi went to the hallway and opened the front door. It was freezing, but she didn't care as she took a long, slow deep breath and relished the freshness of the air around her.

Oliver had reached the boardwalk now and Lexi saw Jack walking over to him and stop to chat. She hoped that Jack would persuade him to go with him for a coffee at Summer Sundaes Café but after a couple of minutes Jack patted him on the back and they went their separate ways.

Lexi shivered. It really was freezing, and she remembered, she was being paid to work. She went back inside and closed the door, rubbing her arms as she returned to the warm living room. She made herself a drink, found Oliver's Dictaphone and then sat down at the kitchen table, logged on and began to transcribe his latest thoughts.

About an hour later, Lexi heard the front door and waited for Oliver to remove his coat and join her.

'How are you?' she asked, taking a sip of her stone-cold coffee and grimacing. Her life seemed to consist of countless cups of tea and coffee that she made for herself and then forgot to drink. He looked wretched she decided as she placed the half-filled mug onto the table.

'I'm OK, thanks. Just sad really, I guess.'

She wasn't surprised. 'That's only to be expected. You must be frozen. I need a fresh cup of coffee,' she said, standing and picking up her mug. 'Can I make one for you now?'

He nodded and went to sit down in front of the log burner rubbing his hands together to warm them up. 'That would be nice. Thanks.'

She boiled the kettle and once their drinks had been made took them over to where he was sitting and handed his to him, sitting down in the opposite chair.

'I wish I could think of something helpful to say,' Lexi admitted, hating to see him so downcast.

He placed his cup down onto the coaster. 'You've been more than generous already.'

'I have?'

He stared at her as if he was seeing something new about her. 'You know what Lexi? You have to be the kindest person I know.'

She frowned, unsure how he had come to such a conclusion. 'How do you work that out?'

He shifted on his chair to face her. 'I've taken your most precious possession.'

'Not this again. Look, we both know you didn't do it on purpose,' she said, interrupting his flow before he could say anything further. 'And anyway, you did what you did for the very best of reasons and I understand that.'

'True, but I've still caused you an enormous amount of pain, whether I meant to or not. I could kick myself now I know it was all for nothing.'

He might be right that she had lost the thing she held most dear to her. This had been her grandmother's home, as well as her own, and the one place where she felt truly connected to all her happiest memories, but she couldn't lay blame at his door. 'If my being upset is anyone's fault it's my dad's. Not yours.'

He stared intently at her lost in his thoughts for a while. 'That's another thing. Dealing with this has made me realise you can't waste a second being angry with your family, it just isn't worth it. I want you to try and find a way forward with your father.' She went to speak, but he raised his hand to stop her. 'I know you don't feel like forgiving him just yet and for what it's worth, I understand how you must feel. But what you need to consider before carrying on with this coldness between you is how you both of you would feel should anything happen to the other.'

She hadn't considered anything happening to her father and shivered. 'That's a good point,' she said. 'You're right.' The thought that she could lose him unexpectedly as she had her mother, chilled her to the core.

'I'm lucky that for the most part, I've always had a close relationship with my dad. I think we all made a special effort after Alistair's death to make the most of each other.' He smiled at her. 'I don't want to sound like the voice of doom, but I just want you to think about it. The worst thing to do when you lose someone is to have regrets.'

Lexi wondered if he might be talking from experience. 'Do you have anywhere Alistair is concerned?'

He nodded slowly and looked away from her to the log burner. 'Yes. We fell out the day before he died over something that at the time I thought very important. Looking back though it was nothing more than male pride. I said some horrible things to him, Lexi. And I'll never get the chance to apologise.'

Lexi couldn't stand watching him suffering for a second longer. He looked so downcast and seemed very alone. Standing, she walked the few paces it took to reach him. Then, crouching in front of his chair, Lexi wrapped her arms around him holding him tightly to her.

'I'm so very sorry this happened to you Oliver.'

He didn't react immediately, but she could feel his arms tense slightly. Lexi wasn't sure if she'd done the right thing by being so affectionate towards him. Then, just as she was about to move away, she felt the weight of his arms as they wrapped around her and held her.

'Thank you.' His voice was barely above a whisper and filled with a deep sadness that made her want to cry for his loss.

After a few minutes, she lowered her arms and moved back, sitting on the edge of the sofa. 'I'm sure your brother knew how much you loved him, despite your row,' she said, believing it to be true and wanting to reassure him.

'That's what Portia said, too.' He looked across at her, his eyes filled with loss. 'And even though I know you are both right, it doesn't take away the guilt I feel knowing that my last words to Alistair were ones of anger. I'll never forgive myself for that, which is why, Lexi, I believe you need to find a way to bridge that gap between you and your dad however you can.'

Lexi thought how dreadful she would feel if something happened to her father and they were still distant with each other. It would have broken her mother's heart to know they had fallen out in such a dreadful way. Even though Lexi knew her mother would be furious with her father for what he had done, she also knew she would insist that family was more important than possessions.

'You're right,' she said, determined to find a way to sort things out with her dad. She just wasn't sure how, but she would think of something. Lexi sensed that Gloria would not like them being close again. She had a sneaking suspicion that her father's girlfriend was making the most of their situation. 'I'll find a way.'

Oliver reached out and took Lexi's hand in his. He gave it a gentle squeeze. 'That's good. I know you'll feel much better once everything's been resolved between you both.'

She smiled at him. 'Thank you for caring, especially when you have so much to deal with.'

'I just wouldn't want you to go through what I have with Alistair. Not when you have a chance to do something about your situation.'

She sensed that he was ready to move on from the conversation and withdrawing her hand from his stood up. 'Right, I think I should be getting on with my work. You've been very busy with all this dictation,' she giggled hoping to lighten the mood. 'I was surprised you'd done so much.'

Oliver rose and walked with her to the kitchen table where his laptop was lying closed. He sat down and lifted the lid. 'I had a lot of time to waste on trains and at the airport while I was away. I thought I may as well keep busy to help pass the time. The sooner the book is finished I can move on from it and focus on something else.'

And the sooner I'll be out of a job, Lexi thought miserably.

She caught him looking thoughtfully over his laptop at her. Then his eyes widened. 'Ahh, I didn't mean that to come out quite as it did.'

'It's fine,' she said embarrassed that he had read her thoughts.

'No, it's not. But as soon as I've sorted this book, I want to put things right with my parents,' he announced, the frown disappearing from his face.

'How?' She hoped he wasn't about to do something that would cause him more heartache. 'I mean, if your dad can't travel here and your mum won't come alone, then I can't see what you can do.'

He grinned at her. 'Three things.' He stood up and began pacing, his mouth widening into a smile.

Lexi was intrigued. 'Go on then, what are you going to do?'

'I need you to film me.'

Film him? 'Doing what?' Was he about to let her into some weird secret?

Oliver grinned. 'Don't look at me so suspiciously. I don't know what you think I'm about to say, but it's nothing... odd.'

'That's OK then,' Lexi replied, trying not to laugh.

'I'm going to do two things. First, I want you to record me here at the cottages. Both inside working, maybe eating, my bedroom and how it looks. I'd like to briefly film all three properties, in fact. Then I want you to record me doing things outside.'

'What things?' She still wasn't quite sure what he was planning.

'Everyday things. Me sitting outside reading a book. Mowing the lawn. Days like today, but also when it's sunny. Me walking down the hill to the boardwalk. The view from the hill of the fisherman's cottages, that sort of thing.'

'Ahh, you want to send a recording of the cottages and everything around here to your mum?'

'Exactly. Then she and Dad can sit and watch it together.' He beamed at her and it was such a relief to see him looking happier again. 'They might not be able to come here physically, but they can enjoy revisiting the place where they met and fell in love. What do you think?'

Lexi swallowed the lump forming in her throat so that she was able to speak without crying. 'I think it's a magical idea.'

'Do you think she'll like it?'

'She'll love it.' She stared at him and sighed. 'You really are very lovely, do you know that?'

His face reddened slightly, and Lexi could see

she had embarrassed him. So, this was the real Oliver Whimsy, she thought liking him even more than she had already begun to do. This is the man behind the enigmatic public face that people knew and imagined had a heart of stone.

'That's very kind of you,' he said quietly. 'I'm glad you think so.'

Lexi began to think of all the ways she could record him for his mother's film as she drank her coffee. Then it dawned on her that Oliver had said he was going to do three things.

'You said three things.'

'Pardon?'

'You said you were going to do three things. What were the other two, or aren't you going to tell me yet?'

He finished his coffee and replaced the empty mug on the table. 'The second thing I want to do is look into Gloria's past, like I suggested we do a while back. Are you still wanting to do that?'

'Hell, yes!' Lexi frowned. 'I don't mind her being with my dad if it's for the right reasons, but I don't want him getting hurt by her.'

'Fine, then we'll think how we can find out more about her. Do you know her last name?'

Lexi shook her head. 'No, and I can't really ask Dad without raising his suspicions.'

'I suppose not.' Oliver stared thoughtfully out of the window. 'We are going to need to know more than her first name though.'

He was right. They could hardly start searching for her on the Internet with only a first name to go on. 'Hang on a sec,' she said recalling Jools mentioning that her gran knew Gloria. 'I can ask Jools' gran. I said I'd call in to see her sometime and I can find out what she knows when I do.'

'Perfect. Let me know whatever you discover from her and we can take it from there.'

'Ahh, yes,' she said noticing Oliver's expression had changed slightly. 'The third thing. What is it?'

He started at her thoughtfully. 'I want you to listen to what I have to say before arguing.'

'Sounds ominous,' she said, intrigued. 'Go on.'

'I want to sign the cottages back to you.'

Lexi almost dropped her mug. Hot coffee spilled down her front and she had to pull at the cotton fabric to keep it from burning her chest. 'What? Why?'

'Because they're yours, or at least they should be.' His smile vanished. 'What's the matter? What have I said?'

She stood up, hurt that he could imagine she would accept something this valuable from him. 'No.' She didn't want to offend him, not when he meant it as a friendly gesture, but couldn't help feeling as if she'd been slapped. 'No. I know you mean well, and... and, that's really kind of you, but I can't let you do that.'

'Why ever not?'

'Because you bought them in good faith, so it wouldn't be fair.'

Lexi marched out of the living room, aware that she was still being paid to work for the next few hours. Barely able to contain her tears, she hurried to the front door.

'Hey,' Oliver shouted, hurrying after her. Lexi heard a loud thump followed by an anguished groan seconds before he arrived in the hallway limping. He stood between her and the front door and reached down to rub his shin. 'Bloody coffee table.'

Lexi could almost feel the pain on his pinched face. She pictured him clamouring over the table in his haste to stop her didn't know whether it was her heightened emotions or what, but began to giggle and then laugh hysterically.

'Well I'm glad you think me damaging myself is so amusing,' Oliver said, looking confused and then amused in a matter of seconds. 'I didn't mean to offend you Lexi. I'm sorry if I did.'

She eventually gained control of herself and calmed down, embarrassed to have made such a scene. 'It's fine,' she panted.

'You'll accept the cottages then?' he asked tentatively.

'No.' How could she? she reasoned. 'But thank you. I appreciate the thought.'

'Will you come back inside and finish working,' he teased, grinning at her.

She sighed, exhausted by the range of emotions she had worked through in such a short time. 'I suppose I should, shouldn't I? I am meant to be working after all.'

'Good. At least we can agree on one thing then.'

A while later Lexi finished typing up a chapter and checked her watch. It was getting late. She needed to leave time to get ready for her date with Charlie. She glanced at Oliver with his head down frowning in concentration as he typed.

Lexi was relieved to have finished the day on a friendly footing with him. She logged out of her laptop and closed the lid quietly hoping not to disturb his concentration.

'Doing anything nice tonight?' Oliver asked without looking up from his laptop screen.

Lexi stood and pushed her chair neatly back against the table. 'I'm going out with Charlie for a few drinks,' she said, surprised when Oliver immediately stopped typing and stared at her.

After a couple of seconds, he smiled. 'That's nice.' He turned his attention back to his screen and continued with what he had been doing. 'Have fun. I'll see you tomorrow.'

'Thanks, I'll do my best,' she said leaving him to continue working into the evening.

She showered and changed into a clean top and fresh pair of jeans. They were only going for a drink at the nearby pub, so she didn't feel there was any need to dress up. Thankfully the pub was close enough for them to not have to worry about using any transport, but Lexi had arranged to meet him there and didn't want to be late.

The tide was out and she was relieved to be able to take a shortcut across the beach. It was sunny but cold and even though it was dark now the sun had set, the moon was bright and lit up the rolling waves. The sight of the sea glistening made her wish she was walking with someone she loved. Why did she always seem to experience the most romantic settings when she was by herself?

The moonlight glinted on something in the sand and Lexi bent to pick it up. She brushed the damp sand off the piece of porcelain with a pretty blue and white design that she thought must have originally come from a beautiful plate. She wondered who might have owned the plate and eaten from it as she walked.

She was a little nervous despite telling herself that she was only meeting Charlie for a few drinks. It had been over two years since she had accepted the offer of a date. Not, she thought amused, that she had been asked out that many times. She liked keeping to herself mostly, but already knowing Charlie, albeit only slightly, Lexi believed that now was as good a time as any to step out of her comfort zone and dip her toes into the dating scene once again. She might even like it, she thought, immediately unsure that she actually would.

Lexi dropped the piece of porcelain into her coat pocket as she neared the slipway taking her up to the car park across from the pub. She quickened her step as she neared the small ancient pub, spotting Charlie as soon as she stepped inside. She was relieved to see him waiting for her. Their eyes met in the mirror behind the bar and Charlie immediately turned and waved.

'I've reserved us a place over there,' he said indicating a table next to the roaring fire. 'I thought it was the best place to sit on such a cold evening. Make yourself comfortable and I'll bring you a drink. What would you like?'

'Gin and tonic for me, please,' she answered gratefully, although she would have preferred to cup her hands around a warm mug of tea until they thawed out a bit.

She settled down glad to be in the warmth once again and watched Charlie. He had a relaxed way about him even though he was speaking to people she sensed he didn't know. Lexi supposed it was because of his experience working in the hotel industry that gave him such a confident way about him. She wished she could be a little more like him. More like Sacha too. She was always confident, as was Jools, although Jools, like Lexi, also enjoyed alone time, in her case so she could spend hours painting.

'There you go,' Charlie said placing her drink on the table and sitting opposite. 'How are things with you?'

They chatted for a while and Lexi realised

that as much as she liked Charlie there really wasn't a romantic spark between them. They chatted for a couple of hours about his work and her temporary job and her friends. Eventually he brought up the subject of Burns Night.

'Are you looking forward to the party?'

Lexi nodded. 'Yes. I know it probably sounds odd, but it'll be the first Burns Night event I've ever been to.' She stared at him thoughtfully. 'You know lots of my friends are going so if you would rather take someone else as your plus one, please do.'

He raised his eyebrows, and she could see he was surprised by her comment. 'You don't mince your words, do you?' he laughed. 'I like that in a person. I hate having to second guess what people are thinking.'

Lexi shrugged. 'I don't see the point in pretending especially when something is obvious.'

'You mean that we would make far better friends than . . .' he struggled to find the words. 'Anything else?'

'That's it exactly.' Lexi liked him even more for not trying to play games or pretend he felt any differently to her. 'Do let me know if you'd rather I went with my friends, won't you?'

He shook his head. 'No, it's fine. I enjoy your company. I've asked you to come with me and I'm looking forward to us going to the party together.'

'So am I,' she admitted. 'It's strange but I feel

like I've known you for years for some reason.'

Charlie nodded. 'I was thinking the same thing about you.'

'Is there someone you like?' Lexi asked, wondering who might have caught his attention.

He screwed up his face slightly. 'Yes, sort of.'

'Well, don't you want to ask them to go with you, or are they already in a relationship?'

'I think she's seeing someone. Anyway,' he smiled. 'I don't know if I'd be her type.'

'You won't know if you don't ask though, will you?'

'No, I suppose not.' He kissed her on the cheek. 'But I'm happy to know I'll be spending the evening with you, so let's leave things as they are. Unless, of course, you'd rather not.'

Lexi laughed amused that the two of them were trying so hard to be considerate of each other's feelings. It made her even more relieved that she had been honest about her lack of romantic feelings for him. 'No, it's fine. I'm happy to go with you.'

By the end of the evening he offered to accompany her home. Lexi thanked him but refused and told him she was happy to make her own way. She left the pub and wished him good night and seeing that the tide was still out walked to the slipway and onto the beach.

She wondered who the woman was that Charlie liked. Lexi hoped it wasn't Jools because she knew that her friend was too interested in Finn

Gallichan to pay anyone else any attention. She took a deep, bracing breath and stared up at the moon for a few seconds as she walked. Whoever the mysterious woman was, she would be lucky to have such a gentlemanly boyfriend as Charlie.

If only Oliver Whimsy liked Lexi as much as she was beginning to realise she liked him. Unfortunately, the world was full of 'if-onlys', Lexi thought miserably as she walked across the moonlit beach.

CHAPTER THIRTEEN

Burns Night

Lexi arranged to meet Charlie at the Sea Breeze Hotel but popped into the second-hand book shop to pick up Jools first.

'You're wearing a dress?' Lexi cried, startled to see Jools showing off her legs for the first time in years as she opened the shop door. As soon as the ridiculous question was out of her mouth, she realised that all this effort was for Finn's benefit and wished she could take it back. She didn't want to chance Jools changing her mind. 'What I really mean, is wow, you look amazing.'

Jools glared at her. 'Is that really what you meant, or should I quickly change?'

Lexi looked at her tomboyish friend, who was more at home in worn jeans than anything else and smiled. 'Don't you dare. In fact, I wish you dressed like this more often, you look really beautiful.'

Jools pushed Lexi's shoulder. 'Fine.' Lexi opened her mouth to add something, but Jools wagged her finger in front of her face. 'Shut up. Let's get going before I reconsider.'

Lexi pretended to zip her lips closed and turned to wait for Jools to exit the shop.

'Night, Gran,' she shouted. 'I won't be too late.'

As they walked, recalled her conversation with Oliver. 'You said your gran knew Gloria.'

'That's right. Why?'

'I was wondering if you could ask her for Gloria's last name. Or I could when I come to visit her.'

'Sure. I'll ask her tomorrow if you like?'

'Brilliant. Thank you.'

Lexi could not wait to find out more about her father's unfriendly girlfriend. If she did discover anything new about Gloria then she intended to tell him about the woman he seemed to trust so easily straight away. The sooner she discovered what it was the better.

She stared at the hotel set back from the boardwalk, the orange glow from its bright lights shining appealingly in the frosty air. 'I bet it's warm in there,' she said speeding up.

'Hey, steady on. I'm not wearing trainers now.'

Lexi slowed and looked down at her friend's feet. 'You're not wearing heels either.'

'No,' Jools glowered. 'But these aren't the same as wearing my usual footwear.'

'I suppose they're not.' Lexi had to concentrate on keeping her mouth shut so that she didn't say anything else to irritate her friend.

'So, why are you arriving with me?' Jools asked. 'I thought you were supposed to be on a date with Charlie? Or has something happened to change that?'

Lexi held the collar of her coat tightly, wishing she had thought to wear a scarf, and told Jools about her evening in the pub. 'He's interested in someone. It just isn't me.'

'That's a shame. I thought he was lovely.'

'He is,' Lexi assured her. 'I had a fun time with him. There's nothing between us though and I'm glad we were both honest about it from the beginning. I'd rather he spent time getting to know his mysterious woman.'

'Did he say who she was?'

'No, and before you ask, I did try to get him to tell me.' Lexi grinned at Jools as they reached the hotel. 'We'll just have to keep an eye on him and see if we can work out who she is.'

They quickly took their coats to the cloakroom and went to join the party. As they reached the large double doors, Lexi could hear music and laughter coming from inside. The doors opened and Charlie stood in front of them.

'Good to see you both,' he said leaning forward and kissing each of them on both cheeks. 'I have to say you both look stunning.'

'Thank you.' Lexi grinned at her friend.

'Your other friends are already here and we're all at one big table.' He pointed to the left of the room by the dance floor where a huge buffet table was laden with food. 'Over there.'

Lexi laughed. 'Were you the one who strategically arranged for our table to be in the best place in the room?'

'How did you guess?' He led the way to their friends. 'I have to have some extra perks, being the assistant manager, don't you think?'

Lexi nodded. 'Most definitely.'

They were near the table when she spotted Oliver. Her stomach flipped and her heart seemed to pause for a few seconds when he looked across the room and caught her eye. He was wearing a red and green kilt and she didn't think she had ever seen anything quite as sexy.

'Breathe,' Jools whispered. 'Come along, let's say hello before people begin to wonder what's wrong with you.'

Lexi forced herself to focus on walking. Oliver was standing next to Portia as she chatted to Jack, Sacha, Bella and Alessandro.

'You're finally here,' Sacha greeted them. 'We've been waiting for you both.'

'Oliver was just explaining what happens during Burns Night.'

Oliver smiled. 'Actually, Portia was questioning me about the food, but I was attempting to tell the others what usually happens at these events.'

'Oh good,' Lexi said doing her best to appear bright and involved despite her pulse racing madly as she went to stand next to him. She breathed in his aftershave, sending tingles through her entire body. She told herself to focus, but it was almost impossible standing so close to someone having such a heady effect on her. She gave Portia a welcoming smile. 'What does happen then?'

'You eat haggis,' Portia said grimacing. 'It sounds revolting.'

'It isn't.' Oliver looked unamused at her insult. 'You told me you've never tried it, so you can't know what it tastes like.'

Portia nudged his arm and grinned at the others. 'He's always so protective of anything Scottish.'

'Take no notice,' Lexi said, smiling at Portia before turning her attention back to Oliver. 'I want to hear more,' she added, trying to encourage him to repeat what he had been telling the others.

'There, Portia. Some people are interested,' Oliver said, giving her a wink. 'I've been chatting to Charlie,' he said smiling at Lexi. 'He's asked me to recite the Burns poem, 'Address to a Haggis' and then we'll carve the haggis for those that want to can try it with a wee dram o' whisky.'

'Sounds interesting. Is that it?'

'No, there's a bit more to it than that, but you'll have to wait and see.'

Lexi couldn't wait to find out more. 'I think this is going to be a fun night.'

Oliver stared at her for a few seconds and then said, 'Yes, I hope so.'

She noticed Charlie watching Oliver and then saw him glance at Portia before leaving the room. He was curious to see her reaction to what Oliver had said, Lexi realised, wondering if Portia was the woman that Charles had taken a liking to. She hoped so. As far as she could tell Portia was a sweet woman and after all she had gone through losing her fiancé maybe it was time for her to fall for someone as lovely as Charlie.

Trays, filled with tumblers of whisky, were taken to each table and handed out. Lexi picked up her glass to try some.

'Not yet,' Oliver whispered. 'That's to toast the haggis.'

She wasn't sure exactly what he was going on about but nodded and placed her glass back down in front of her.

Everyone turned towards the doors as the unmistakeable sound of bagpipes could be heard coming along the hotel hallway. The next thing Lexi knew, two waiters pulled open the double doors and four pipers marched into the room in pairs with Charlie between the first and second pair, carrying a silver platter with what she assumed was the haggis displayed on it.

Oliver stood and went over to the stage and when the pipers stopped in front of the audience, he began reciting a poem that Portia told her was 'Address to a Haggis'. As he came to the end, everyone stood and cheered, holding up their glasses to toast the haggis. Lexi had no idea what she was doing but followed everyone's lead and felt strangely emotional. She supposed it was the emotive music, or the tradition of it.

After watching a few of them, including Jools eat haggis, Lexi realised people were getting up to dance. Oliver took her hand. 'Come along.'

'Er, I've no idea what to do,' she said, staring at people as they began to skip and dance in some sort of order on the dance floor.'

'What? You've never danced Stripped the Willow before?'

'The, *what?'* She could see he was teasing her and knew that if she was ever going to be brave enough to at least try to join in then tonight was the night. 'Fine then. I've no idea what to do, so you'll have to teach me.'

'You'll soon pick it up.' He took her hand and led her to the dance floor.

Lexi heard Sacha and Bella giggling in the distance but all she could focus on was the way the bottom of Oliver's kilt swung from side to side as he strode to join the dance.

'Just relax. Forget that people are watching and give yourself up to the music. All you need to concentrate on is enjoying yourself.'

She wished it was that simple, but then he began to dance and took her by the hand leading her with the rest of the dancers. Every time she thought she had the steps worked out, Lexi mis-stepped. After the first few times of getting it wrong, she forgot that there was anyone in the room apart from her, Oliver and the dancers coming in contact with her. Every time Oliver grabbed her hands and swung her around, his eyes connected with hers and she could see that he was loving every moment of the evening. She was thoroughly enjoying witnessing this carefree side to him.

'Having fun?' he shouted over the music as he swung her round yet again.

'Yes, I'm loving it,' she said, trying to catch her breath. How fit were these people? Most of them were much older than her but had twice the amount of energy.

The music ended to cheering and clapping and Lexi looked up to see Oliver smiling at her.

'Come along, I think we need a breather before we dance again.'

He began leading her from the dance floor. She loved the feeling of his hand over hers and wished the night could last forever.

'You two were amazing,' Jools cheered. 'Well, Oliver was.' She held her glass up to Lexi. 'You weren't bad at all though. I was secretly impressed if I'm honest.'

'Lexi was very good,' he said, pouring her another drink. 'I think the rest of you need to take part in at least one dance before the night is over.'

'Yes,' Lexi laughed. 'If I can do it without tripping up, the rest of you can.' As she joked with them, she noticed Charlie and Portia deep in conversation near the bar and smiled. Good, she thought, they've finally found each other. She could see by the way Portia was flicking her hair and brushing imaginary fluff from Charlie's shoulder that she was as into him as he was to her.

Jools took her phone from her bag and checked it, no doubt Lexi thought to make sure her grandmother hadn't tried to contact her. 'Bloody hell!'

Lexi's heart pounded in fright. 'What's the matter?'

Bella, Sacha, Jack and Alessandro moved a step closer to see what was wrong.

Jools held up her screen. 'Jack's gone viral.'

'What?' Jack immediately looked at Bella and shook his head. 'I haven't done anything. Why would I go viral?'

'Read it to us.' Lexi hoped the impatience in her voice would make her friend do it quickly.

Jools looked back at her screen and mumbled to herself as she read. 'It's one of the online newspapers. That picture the photographer took of you coming out of the sea on New Year's Day, Jack it's one of those. They're calling you the latest hot new thing.'

'What? Let me have a look at that.'

Jools handed him her phone and he read silently, his face flushed with confusion.

'Scroll down, there are loads of comments calling for you to be in the magazines.'

His attention was taken by the sound of a phone ringing. They all checked their mobiles. 'It's me,' Jack said, pulling his phone from his pocket. Lexi watched him excitedly, wondering who could be calling him. 'Hi Dad,' he said, indicating the door and walking towards it to take his call in private.

'I thought it was a magazine editor calling him,' Alessandro said, looking disappointed.

'So did I,' Bella admitted. 'Then I remembered it's late and they're hardly likely to call him at this time, are they?'

Lexi laughed. She had been thinking the same thing but hadn't considered the lateness of the hour and therefore how unlikely it would be for any editors to be calling Jack.

*

By the end of the evening, Lexi had exhausted herself taking part in a few Dashing White Sergeants and couple of Eightsome Reels and watched an impressive display of the men dancing the Gay Gordons. She wasn't sure how she was supposed to walk up the hill to the cottages. Her feet ached terribly, but she couldn't recall ever having so much fun in one evening.

Oliver turned to her. 'I've got an early morning conference call so I'm going to find Portia and leave soon. Do you want to walk back with us?'

The idea of having a conversation with the two of them as they made their way up the hill appealed to Lexi. At least then, she wouldn't be focusing too much on her aching feet as she made her way home. 'I'd love that, thank you.'

'Right. Give me a minute and I'll track her down. I haven't seen her around for a while.'

It occurred to Lexi that neither had she. She thought back, trying to picture the last time she had seen Portia and realised it was when she was standing at the bar flirting with Charlie much earlier in the evening. She wondered where they could have got to. She decided to go and ask Jools.

'Nope, I haven't seen her, or him, for ages come to think of it.' Jools leaned in a little closer. 'It's just as well you both decided there was nothing much between you. I'd be on the rampage right now if I didn't know that and suspected him of going off with another woman.'

Lexi motioned for her friend to keep her voice down. 'Yes, but he hasn't, has he? There's no reason to defend my honour, or whatever it was you were thinking of doing.'

Jools laughed. 'I guess not.'

'Anyway,' Lexi said, trying to see where Finn might be. 'What's going on with you and Finn?'

Jools frowned. 'He's going travelling for a couple of months.'

'That's a shame?' She wasn't too surprised. It was the middle of winter after all and Finn wasn't one for staying where it was cold as far as she could tell. 'He'll be back for the season when the gelateria opens again, won't he?'

'Yes, but that's not the point.'

Lexi supposed not. She would be miserable if the man she was attracted to was going away for months. 'I'm sorry Jools. I thought you two were hitting it off really well.'

'We were. He even said that if he hadn't already booked to go, he wouldn't do so now he's got to know me. It can't be helped. I'll just have to shut up and focus on my painting to keep me occupied.'

Why did their lives never seem to run smoothly? Lexi thought feeling sorry for her friend. She glanced at Sacha and Bella both loved up with Alessandro and Jack. Those relationships had only recently become serious and she was thrilled for them. Poor Jools, she would love to see her happy with someone. She wouldn't mind settling down herself. The thought surprised her. Almost thirty and finally wanting to make a home with somebody. It wasn't like her at all.

Jools gave her a hug. 'I'm going to make my way home now. I don't like leaving Gran for too long. I worry in case she needs me for something and can't reach her mobile.'

Lexi knew not to spend any more time chatting. 'Give her my love, won't you? I haven't seen her for a while. Tell her I'll pop in soon.'

'Will do. See you tomorrow sometime?'

Lexi nodded. 'Yes, see you then.'

She watched as Oliver made his way back to her. He stopped when people patted him on the back every few seconds. She thought back to the brilliant way he had recited the poem and his dance moves, and a thrill shot through her. He really was hot. She took a deep breath and waved at him as he neared their table, an angry expression on his handsome face.

Oh, dear, she thought. 'No Portia?'

He stood right close to her, the muscle in his jaw working furiously. 'I found her,' he said, his cool breath by her ear sending tingles down her spine. 'She was with Charlie.'

'And that's such a bad thing because_?'

Oliver glanced over at the people nearest to them, and whispered, 'You know, like actually *with* him.'

Lexi's eyes widened as it dawned on her what he meant. 'Oh, I see. Where were they?'

Oliver sighed. He seemed to be struggling to stay calm. 'Can I ask you something before I tell you?'

Lexi thought it an odd thing to say. 'Yes, of course you can. Look, what's happened? She's alright, isn't she?'

'Portia is fine. It's Charlie I'm more concerned about right now.'

Lexi noticed how Oliver kept clenching his fists down by his side. 'You haven't done something to Charlie, have you?'

'No,' he said sounding as if he would like to.

Lexi wasn't sure what to think. 'Has Charlie done something he shouldn't?'

'I'm not sure yet.'

She was intrigued and slightly anxious for her new friend. 'Go on.'

'He tells me that you and he are just friends.' Oliver frowned. 'I don't want him messing you and Portia around if that's not the case.'

Lexi wasn't used to having a man look out for her in such a chivalrous way. It felt rather nice. She had to concentrate on not smiling. 'Right.'

Oliver stared at her with an intensity in his eyes that she hadn't seen before. Something had happened she realised, but she couldn't imagine what it could be. 'Look I know we've been dancing together a bit tonight,' Oliver said matter-of-factly. 'That's it though. Anyway, I checked with Charlie whether he minded us dancing before I came over to ask you.'

On the one hand Lexi liked to discover that Oliver had been thoughtful enough to check with Charlie that he wasn't going to upset him by dancing with his plus one, but she still couldn't work out what Oliver was so bothered about.

'Will you just tell me what's angered you?'

He stared at her silently for a moment. 'Tonight is your second date with Charlie, isn't that right?'

'Ahh.' So that was the issue. Oliver had caught Portia and Charlie in flagrante and assumed Charlie was being disloyal to her. Her heart did a quick somersault. 'It's fine, really,' she assured him. 'Charlie and I did go for that drink but we realised quite quickly that there was never going to be anything romantic between us.'

'But you came as his plus one tonight?' Oliver asked, looking confused.

'Yes, but only because I had already accepted his invitation and he didn't have anyone else to bring.'

'I asked you though,' Oliver reminded her, looking hurt. 'You could have come with me.'

Lexi realised how it must look to him. 'I know, but then you'd have had to buy tickets for me and Portia.'

His eyes widened. 'You think I'd mind doing that?'

'Not for one second,' she admitted. 'It would have been unnecessary for you to do that though, so what was the point?'

His fists relaxed and he took her hands in his. 'That's so sweet.'

Lexi smiled. 'I haven't been called that for years.'

'I suppose you're right.' Oliver narrowed his

eyes and grinned at her. 'Does that mean you'll consider coming out with me for a meal or whatever you'd rather do?'

Lexi pretended to give his question some thought not wanting to show Oliver quite how delighted she was to be asked out by him. 'That would be lovely.'

Oliver leant forward to kiss her on the cheek. 'Good. We can decide what and when tomorrow when you come to work. It will give you time to consider what you would like to do.' He took her hand properly in his. 'It's getting rather late. Would you like me to escort you home, young lady?' he asked, bowing theatrically.

Lexi laughed. 'Why, yes, kind sir, I'd like that very much.'

He fetched their coats and after saying their goodbyes to the rest of the group they left the hotel and began their short walk home.

Lexi realised she hadn't heard the full story yet about where Oliver had finally found Portia and Charlie, so asked him.

'In the porter's lodge.'

'Really?' Lexi pictured the alcove behind the desk that raised up to let the porter stand behind it. They couldn't surely have been together in there. 'But there's no privacy.'

'There's a small room behind the desk,' Oliver said, shaking his head as if trying to erase an unwanted memory. 'I called a few times and even knocked on the desk. When there was no reply, I heard a strange sound. Thinking the porter might be unwell, I made my way in there. You know the rest.'

'And they didn't hear you coming?' Lexi asked, getting the picture only too clearly.

'No, they didn't.' He closed his eyes and shook his head. 'I wish they had done. Anyway, Portia was horrified, as was Charlie, to be caught with his pants down, and in the place where he worked.'

She could tell Oliver was a little shocked. 'Wow, I don't know if he's brave or was simply too impatient to wait for a more private place before getting together with her. I knew he was a little besotted with someone, I just didn't know who it might be.' She glanced at Oliver, his face set like stone as they walked. 'You don't mind her moving on from your brother, do you? Is that why you're cross?'

His step faltered for a moment before he continued walking. 'No, not at all. I was just taken aback to find them there like that, I suppose.' He thought for a moment. 'I do like Charlie, he seems like a good bloke. I think that's probably why I was so furious when I thought he was messing both of you around. I would like Portia to find someone to make her happy. She deserves to be loved. I know she can come across as a spoiled princess, but she has a heart of gold. The coldness you sometimes see is only her way of protecting herself. She was broken after Alistair died and I worried that she wouldn't ever fully recover.' He walked on for a few steps before adding, 'It was helping her that kept me going if I'm honest.'

Lexi couldn't mistake the misery in his voice. He was still holding her hand and she gave it a gentle squeeze. 'I'm sorry you both had to lose someone so special.'

He stopped walking and took her by the shoulders. 'I'm sorry that you lost two people so close to you, Lexi. You're very brave, especially when I think how I took your last connection to the two of them when I—'

'Oliver, enough. I don't want to dwell on that subject again,' she cut in wishing she had thought to wear a thicker coat on such a freezing evening.

'Sorry. Let's change the subject.'

'OK.'

'You're shivering,' he whispered, pulling her close to him and hugging her tightly. He kissed the top of her head. 'Let's get going before we both catch hypothermia.'

Lexi wrapped her arms tightly around his waist and stood relishing his warm, firm body next to hers for a few seconds before nodding and resuming their walk.

'Let's quicken the pace,' he said, pulling her with him as he walked faster. Lexi had to run to keep up with him, giggling, relieved their mood was lighter than before.

They reached his cottage. 'Coming in for a coffee before your commute home? Or shall I drop you off at your door?'

She liked him offering but they both knew she was more than capable of walking the remaining few steps to her home. She considered his offer. Would it just be coffee? Was she wise to chance it? Was there any chance she was going to miss an opportunity that might end with her kissing those perfect lips? Not one.

'Alright, I'll come to yours, but only for coffee and only for half an hour. I dare not get to bed too late and risk oversleeping. My boss is a right tartar.'

Oliver's eyes twinkled with amusement. He opened his door and held out his arm to welcome her in. Then stepping in behind her he tickled her waist.

Lexi squealed and wriggled out away from him. 'Stop that right now.'

He did as she asked. He smiled at her, gazing at her intently as he lowered his head to meet hers. 'What was that you said about your boss?'

'He's a lovely man,' she giggled.

Oliver stopped laughing. 'Do you really think so?'

Lexi stared into his eyes and realised it mattered what she thought of him. She took a deep breath to steady herself. 'Hmm, I think I do.'

Oliver pulled her into his arms and pressing his firm lips against hers, he kissed her. Her surprise vanished as he kissed her more thoroughly and it was all Lexi could do to keep her knees from giving way as she kissed him back, until she felt something trembling against her stomach. She stepped back, trying to figure out what it could be.

'What's the matter?' Oliver's voice was husky as he tried to pull her back into his arms.

'I think that thing around your waist is vibrating,' she said, pointing to the bag strapped to his front.

'What?' He looked down and smiled, amusement shining in his eyes. 'You mean my sporran.' He unfastened it and removed his phone. He stared at the screen to see who was calling him. 'Sorry about this, I'm going to have to take it.'

Assuming it was probably his mother, Lexi nodded and moved away to give him some privacy.

'What is it Portia?' Lexi could hear the irritation in his voice and made a point of not catching his eye. 'What, now? Well, why didn't you come back with me if you've had enough already?'

Annoyed that Portia was interrupting their evening, Lexi looked over at him. Oliver sighed and shook his head, mouthing an apology at her. 'I'll come right away. But Portia, please be ready. I don't want to have to come looking for you when I get to the hotel.' He ended the call and sighed. 'I'm so sorry, Lexi. I think Portia is a little embarrassed by what happened earlier. She wants to come home but is nervous to walk by herself. Apparently, Charlie has been called to help with some hotel issue, so can't accompany her.'

Lexi found it difficult not to show her disappointment. She wished Portia had waited a few more minutes before calling. She would have loved to have enjoyed another of Oliver's heavenly kisses.

'It's fine,' she said, trying not to mind too much. 'I wouldn't want to walk home alone if I was new here. There aren't any streetlights, which she's probably used to living in London.'

'Thank you.' Oliver picked up his keys and walked Lexi to her front door. Lowering his head, he kissed her lightly on the lips. 'I'll see you in the morning then. Sleep well.'

'Thanks. You, too.' She unlocked her door and went inside feeling very lonely suddenly. How did a simple kiss make her feel that way? She had always been more than happy to spend time alone, yet she was already missing him. It was crazy.

About forty minutes later, as Lexi was removing her makeup in her bathroom, she heard voices; Oliver's deep one and another, higher pitched. It sounded like Portia was in tears and he was trying to comfort her. It wasn't Lexi's business though. She moisturised her face, trying not to think about what could be happening right now between her and Oliver if Portia's night had gone differently.

CHAPTER FOURTEEN

Lexi thought about popping down to the second-hand book shop to see Jools' gran, but not wishing to disturb her decided to spend her lunch break taking a walk in the nearby woods. They were privately owned but the old Major didn't mind people using them as long as they respected his land and kept it litter free and remembered to close any gates that they opened to walk through.

It was several days since she had kissed Oliver and she was finding it almost impossible to stop thinking about him. It was almost impossible when they sat opposite each other at work. She pictured him smiling over his laptop at her a few times and her stomach flipped over. He had been slightly flirtatious at times, but he hadn't kissed her again Lexi knew that if he didn't do so soon then she would have to take matters into her own hands. The only thing stopping her now was the fact that he was her boss. Maybe he had only kissed her on Burns Night because he was more relaxed than usual after a few drinks. He could even be regretting having done so, she thought deciding that to take charge and kissing him might make things awkward between them especially as they still worked with each other each day.

'Hey, Lexi. Wait!' Portia bellowed from Oliver's cottage doorway. 'I'll join you.'

Lexi heard her and stopped walking. She wished Portia hadn't seen her. She would much rather be left alone with her thoughts and try to process her feelings for Oliver. It hadn't helped over the past few days that Portia seemed to spend most of her time sitting in Oliver's living room each day either tapping away on her phone, or adding photos to her Instagram account, saying things like, 'Don't mind me,' and offering to make them coffee or tea.

Lexi knew she meant well and presumed she was just oblivious either to the tension between her and Oliver or that they were trying to work. Finally, Oliver had suggested that Portia find something to entertain herself with, and Lexi presumed that this walk was what she had come up with. She heard the sound of Portia's heeled boots tap-tapping across the road and turned to give her the friendliest smile she could manage.

'I saw you passing the window and would have caught up with you sooner,' Portia said, flicking her long, perfectly curled hair over her shoulder. 'But I couldn't find the jacket I wanted to wear.'

Lexi grinned at her. 'I shouldn't worry. I doubt we'll see anyone else in the woods today, it's too damn cold.'

'Thanks for letting me join you,' Portia said, stumbling over a stone.

Lexi grabbed her arm to stop her from falling. 'It's no problem,' she fibbed, as Portia regained her balance.

'I wanted to speak to you about something. I can't ask Oliver, because it would feel strange especially as I was engaged to his brother.' She blushed slightly. 'And after everything that happened at the party.'

Lexi didn't say anything. From the way Portia referred to the incident, she presumed Porta knew that she had heard about it. 'Go on,' Lexi said as they passed several clumps of snowdrops and daffodils.

'It's about Charlie.'

She wasn't surprised. 'OK. Go on.'

Portia's face reddened even more. 'I really like him, but I don't know what to do about it.'

Lexi knew she had to tread carefully, especially knowing what had happened between Portia and Charlie after the party. 'Do you know how he feels? Has he said anything to you to confirm either way?'

Portia walked a few steps, bending to pick a daffodil before replying. 'He's suggested he moves in with me.'

Lexi immediately stopped walking and gaped at Portia unable to hide her shock. They had only got together for the first time several nights before. 'At the cottage?' She thought Portia was only supposed to be staying there for a few weeks. Not that it was her business, she reminded herself. 'Isn't that a bit quick?'

'I know, right?'

Was that it? 'But what do you think about his suggestion? Would you want to live with someone you only kissed for the first time four nights ago?' Would she want Oliver to move in? she thought, trying not to be a hypocrite. No, it would be far too soon as far as she was concerned. She would need to know someone a little better before allowing them to live in her home so that she had a chance to discover any annoying little ways they might have.

'That's the thing. I loved living alone before I met Alistair. I've got used to him not being around now and have been happy being by myself. There's something about Charlie though. I feel,' she gazed up at the azure blue sky and sighed, 'connected to him. Like it's meant to be.'

'Wow. It sounds as if he feels the same way.'

Portia clasped her hands together. 'He says he feels like he's been hit by a dumbbell, though

I'm not so sure I like that idea. But I see what he means.'

Lexi smiled at her. For such a polished, glamorous women, Portia seemed so innocent and childlike sometimes. 'Have you mentioned any of this to Oliver yet?' she asked, wondering what he thought about it.

Portia gasped. 'Hell, no. He would think I was mad, or worse, betraying his brother's memory.'

'I don't think he would think either of those things.'

'You think I should speak to him about it then?'

Lexi folded her arms and gave Portia's situation some thought. 'You don't really have any choice but to speak to Oliver really. They're his cottages but I know he'll want to do the best by you.'

Portia nodded slowly. 'You're right. I really don't have much choice.' She groaned. 'I hope he doesn't mind.'

Lexi had no idea whether he would or not but hoped Oliver would react with the care she knew he felt towards Portia. 'You'll only know that when you speak to him, but if you want Charlie to move in then there's really no other way.'

Lexi couldn't help thinking that she was too soft for her own good. She recalled the drama with the paparazzi when she had let celebrity Megan Knight stay at the cottage only a few months before. When had life changed from one of families or couples staying at the cottages to people with chaotic lifestyles? She couldn't help feeling a little nostalgic about how life used to be when everything seemed more ordered and the most dramatic thing to happen was the flight bringing the newspapers to the island being delayed.

They came across a small clearing and saw Jools walking towards them with her gran's cheeky Jack Russell on a lead.

'How are you?' Lexi wished she was alone and could catch up with Jools in private. She would have to wait to find out how things had gone between her and Finn. She bent to stroke Teddy. 'And how are you behaving today, little guy?'

Jools pulled the woolly scarf down to reveal her mouth. 'He's being less of a pain than usual because he's on a lead, but he's not too happy about it.' She held out a small bunch of daffodils. 'I picked these for Gran,' she said, looking at the one Portia was holding. 'At least I bothered to pick more than one.'

Lexi was relieved by her friend's attempt to lighten the mood. Typical of Jools to notice how heavy the atmosphere was between her and Portia.

Portia handed her flower to Jools. 'You may as well have this one and add it to the rest.'

Jools took it. 'Thank you. So, did you both enjoy the party? I noticed that you and Charlie were getting on rather well, Portia.'

Portia gave Lexi a pointed glare. Lexi shook her head. 'Don't look at me, I haven't said anything to anyone.'

'He's a lovely chap, don't you think?' Jools added.

Portia relaxed slightly. 'He is. In fact, I'm sort of seeing him now.'

Jools looked surprised. 'You are? That's great.' Then frowning, added. 'But won't that be difficult with you living in London and him being over here? It'll get expensive, travelling back and forth to see each other.'

'Not if I move over here, it won't.' Portia looked slightly smug, Lexi thought.

'Seriously? You would consider relocating from the big city to this village?' Jools looked from one to the other of them. 'Good for you, if that's what you want.'

'What do you mean by that?'

'Right,' Lexi said, wanting to get going again before Jools said anything further to irritate Portia. 'It's too cold out here to be standing around chatting and I, for one, need to get back to Oliver's and carry on working. I'm only taking a breather and I've already been out longer than I had intended.'

'I'll walk with you then,' Jools said. 'Come along, Teddy.'

Lexi listened while Jools bemoaned Finn leaving the island to go travelling. 'At least he should be back in the spring,' she said, trying to reassure her friend. 'The time will go quickly, I'm sure.'

'It would go far quicker in the summer when the tourist season is in full swing,' Jools argued. 'At least then I'm busy keeping up with my paintings for the shop.' She sighed. 'I suppose I could start working on some now, so that I'm ahead of my schedule when the season starts.'

'There you go,' Lexi cheered. 'That's the way to look at things. Keep busy and he'll soon be back.'

'I suppose so.' Jools gasped. 'I nearly forgot. I spoke to Gran this morning and she told me Gloria's last name is Sweeting.'

'Sweeting,' Lexi repeated, aware that she had seen that name before. The contract for the sale of the cottages. Of course. She had known her name all along. How could she have forgotten? 'That's brilliant. Thanks for doing that for me and please thank your Gran.'

'No worries.'

They reached the hill and parted ways, Jools and Teddy crossing the road to the path outside the cottages.

Portia took Lexi's arm and pulled her gently to a stop. 'Do you really think I should ask Oliver now, or wait to see how things progress with Charlie?'

'You're having a change of heart?' Lexi asked hopefully.

'Well, I've been thinking about what Jools said

about London and living here. It's very different, I guess.'

Lexi thought that rather an understatement. 'I know she annoyed you when she made that comment, but Jools is right. In London you have all the buzz of people, theatres, being able to go by train to different areas of the country. Here, especially in winter, the only sounds are waves, crashing against the beach, seagulls, and the occasional car or tractor going up and down the hill. There's not much going on and the island is tiny. I know of friends who've come to live here from the mainland and found it very difficult after a while.'

Portia chewed her lower lip thoughtfully. 'You love it here though, don't you?'

Lexi nodded. 'Yes, but I was born here. I wouldn't last a week living somewhere busy like London. We're vastly different people and are used to opposite ways of life, so you can't really go by what I enjoy.'

'What do you think I should do?' Portia pushed her hands deep into her padded jacket pockets.

Lexi didn't like to put a downer on Portia's plans but doubted Oliver would be too happy about his friend moving on so quickly with Charlie. Lexi really couldn't see her living on the island for very long and remaining content with the quiet way of life.

'If I was you, I'd live here for a little longer before making any long-term decisions. You don't want to rush things with Charlie, have him move in and then realise that it doesn't suit you. It might be better to keep the excitement with a long-distance relationship. I've heard of other people doing that and it seems to keep things fresh and interesting. It's worth considering anyway.'

Portia hugged Lexi. 'Thank you for your wise words. You're a good friend and I appreciate your honesty.'

The rest of her workday passed with Portia hovering around the living room and kitchen area at Oliver's, and from the way he intermittently looked up and glared at her she was obviously irritating him, too.

'For pity's sake, Portia, what is the matter with you today?' he grumbled eventually. 'You look like you need to say something. Do you?'

She frowned and after a moment shook her head. 'No, I'm alright.'

'Then please sit down and find something to read or go and see one of the others. What's Charlie doing right now?'

'Working.'

Portia picked up a magazine she had discarded earlier that day and flicked through it.

Oliver sighed and closed his laptop lid. 'Lexi, you may as well go and catch up with your own bits and pieces. I can't see that we're going to be able to concentrate very much today.' He looked over her shoulder at Portia and pulled a face.

'If you're sure, then thanks.' Not wanting Portia to ask any unnecessary questions, she wrote down Gloria's full name on a piece of paper and pushed it across the table to Oliver.

'What's this?' He glanced up at her frowning.

'Read it.' Lexi smiled at him and then giving a brief wave to Portia, left them to it.

She wondered whether Portia would take her advice about Charlie, or charge straight in and try to persuade Oliver to let him move into the cottage next door with her. Whatever he decided to do, the incident reminded Lexi only too clearly that she was no longer the one in charge or had any say about what happened.

She sorted out her laundry, changed the sheets on her bed and put on a wash. As she watched the water rise through the washing machine window, she heard Portia's shouting outside, followed by the calmer sound of Oliver's voice. She couldn't hear what they were saying but by the tone of their voices he was trying to placate her about something.

Never mind them, Lexi thought, it was time for her to focus on herself. It had been kind of Oliver to give her a job and allow her to stay in the cottage for the time being. She suspected that he might find her more work to do when the book was finished, which she knew wouldn't be too far away. She realised it was his way of making amends to her and as much as she had been relieved to be allowed to stay and be given work, she had no intention of accepting his charity once this project was over. It was time to plan for her future.

She made up her bed with fresh sheets and decided that she should perhaps get an early night. She would be more likely to come up with the next practical step after a decent night's sleep. Lexi showered and made herself a light supper of scrambled eggs on two pieces of toast. Then, after taking the washing from the dryer and folding it, she made herself a milky drink and took it up to her room.

Despite several attempts, sleep eluded her. She stared at the four novels she had bought in the past couple of months and chose one to read. She rarely failed to sleep after an hour or so reading. Plumping her pillows, Lexi made herself comfortable and opened the book.

By one in the morning Lexi couldn't stand how her mind was racing. She had long given up trying to read when she kept going over the same paragraphs as her mind wandered, worrying about where she might find a job, or somewhere to live. She kicked off her covers and got out of bed. Pulling back the curtains, she saw the moon glinting off the sea out in the bay and the light from the red and white painted small lighthouse to the left of the beach at the end of the pier shone brightly on the rolling waves. The tide was out enough for her to walk on the beach and she needed to feel the sand between her toes, however cold it might be.

She hurriedly dressed in her jeans and a sweatshirt and went downstairs to put on her coat, hat and boots. Not wishing to make a sound and alert Portia, or even worse, Oliver, she crept out of her cottage and paced quickly down the hill. When she reached the boardwalk she ran down the steps to the beach and took off her boots and socks.

She leant back against the sea wall and breathed in the cold sea air, feeling a calmness slowly descend. She was relieved to see she had the beach entirely to herself and sighed. It was hardly surprising. Most people had more sense than to get up in the middle of the night and go for a walk. If anyone could see her now they could think her mad to come down here at such a time in the middle of winter, but it had been exactly what she needed. Lexi's feet were cold, so she pushed herself away from the wall and began walking down to the sea. By the time she returned to her bed, she would either be too exhausted to think any more or have come up with a resolution to the next stage of her life.

She reached the water's edge and took a few more deep breaths. She loved it here so much. How could she stand living anywhere else? Then again, she mused, other people did so why not her? She stiffened as she thought she heard footsteps.

'Silly fool,' she whispered, mostly to calm herself for being spooked. Then, hearing a voice that sounded distinctly like Bella's, Lexi turned, expecting to see her friend trying to get her attention from the bedroom window of her cottage. 'What the hell?' she cried, as she saw Bella running towards her along the sand, calling her name in a loud whisper. 'What are you doing down here?' Lexi asked, trying to keep her voice low so as not to disturb any of the locals.

Bella was panting by the time she reached her and bent over, resting her hands on her knees as she regained her breath. Finally, she stood up and stared at Lexi, studying her face intently.

'What?' Lexi asked.

'Why are you down here?' Bella frowned. 'Is everything alright?'

'Yes. Well, no.' Lexi wasn't sure how to answer. Bella knew her well enough to know when she was fobbing her off, so lying wasn't an option.

'Which one is it?'

Lexi shrugged. 'I couldn't sleep and I needed to think.' She began walking.

Bella joined her. 'And you couldn't do that in the comfort of your bedroom?'

'No. Not this time.'

Bella grabbed Lexi's arm and then pointed at her bare feet. 'You're not wearing any shoes. Shit, Lexi, you'll catch your death.'

Lexi doubted it very much. 'I'm fine, stop fretting. Let's keep walking and then I won't.'

'Would you rather come back to my place so we can chat there?'

Lexi shook her head. 'No, thanks.' She smiled at Bella. 'Please don't feel you have to stay here with me. I promise I'm not going to do anything silly. I just really need to think, and this is the place where I do it best.'

Bella pulled her beanie further down over her ears and pushed her hands deeper into her jacket pockets. 'No, let's keep walking. Tell me everything.'

Lexi wasn't sure where to start at first, but then decided that the best place would be how she felt towards her dad after all he had done. 'I suppose I'm just used to it being him and me in our family. We've relied on each other since Mum's death, but now he's got Gloria. Don't get me wrong,' she said, not wishing Bella to misunderstand her. 'I'm very happy for him. It's just that, instead of her coming into our family, he seems to have erased me from it as well as everything Mum loved most.'

'Like the cottages.'

'Yes.' Now she had said it out loud, Lexi didn't think she sounded too unreasonable. Things had changed since Gloria's arrival, and drastically.

'It's only natural that you feel excluded, Lexi,' Bella said, sounding angry. 'There's no need for your dad to not bother with you, but worst of all, he's taken everything from you that gave you security.'

It felt good to hear Bella saying as much. 'I need to stand on my own two feet, Bella,' she said wondering if maybe she should forget her suspicions about Gloria. 'I've got to find somewhere to move on to and a job that will keep me busy and help me pay for all the things I need.'

'You do.' They walked on for a few steps. 'You can always move into my cottage, if you like?'

Lexi smiled at her gratefully, aware that Bella had already invited her to stay. It was typical of Bella to offer space in her tiny home for a friend. 'Thank you, but no. I don't want to impose on your new relationship like that.'

'You wouldn't be. I hadn't told you yet because it wasn't confirmed until late this afternoon, but Jack has been asked away on a few photo shoots and he wants me to go with him whenever I can, so we wouldn't even be there a lot of the time.'

It was good to know that Bella's cottage would be available in an emergency. 'Thank you, I'll bear your offer in mind. But only if I'm desperate.'

'Charming,' Bella laughed. 'No, I'm teasing. Good. You come whenever you want. You know I love having you around.'

Lexi put her arm around her friend's waist. 'You're always generous to everyone and I love you for it.'

'Aww, thanks Lexi.'

'What's this about Jack and some photo shoots?'

Bella laughed. 'Don't look so surprised. I think he's hot.'

'He is good-looking,' Lexi admitted. 'It's just that I can't imagine Jack wanting to take time away from surfing.'

'Neither could he,' Bella said. 'But when he saw how much they were going to pay him he thought he'd be stupid not to accept.'

Lexi stood on a pointed shell and cried out. 'Ouch, that hurt.' She raised her foot and resting one hand on Bella's shoulder for balance, rubbed her damp sandy foot to ease the pain.

'Now will you agree to put something back onto your feet?'

'Yes, alright.'

As they walked back up the beach towards the steps Bella stopped. 'Is that it, or was there something more?'

Lexi wasn't ready to share about her kiss with Oliver, but did confide in Bella about him offering to sign over the cottages to her.

'He did that?' Bella sighed and rested her palm on her chest. 'Why would he, after buying them though?'

Lexi didn't like to tell anyone about Oliver's father's health, so simply said, 'The reason he bought them has gone and he feels badly now he knows how much they meant to me.'

'That's so romantic. I think he's generous to

do that, don't you?'

Lexi was glad it was dark enough that her friend couldn't see her blushing. 'It is rather sweet.'

'Incredibly generous,' Bella said, nudging her. 'Never mind sweet.'

Lexi mumbled her agreement. 'He is much nicer than I ever imagined.'

'Do I sense a touch of affection there?'

Lexi didn't want to admit to her friend that she was developing feelings towards Oliver. 'He's just very kind. He's been very protective with Portia. For a time, I suspected they were a couple, but he simply likes her very much as a friend.' She didn't add that Portia had been his dead brother's fiancée because again, that was for Oliver to share with people if he chose to.

'Did your mum leave a will, Lexi?'

Confused to be asked such a strange question, Lexi shrugged. 'I've no idea, why?'

'Well, I've always believed that your mum wanted you to have her cottages if anything ever happened to her. Isn't that right?'

'Yes.' It was, Lexi thought. 'But when she died, they went to Dad.'

'Are you sure about that? If she didn't have a will then that's probably right, but what if she did and she left them to you? He wouldn't have had the right to sell them.'

Could Bella be right? She had never thought to ask, and it had certainly never occurred to her to question anything he did before Gloria came along.

She was still contemplating Bella's question when her friend said, 'Ooh, I know what you should do.' She glanced at the houses along the boardwalk and lowering her voice. 'I have the answer, Lexi.'

Lexi turned and waited for her friend to share her thoughts. 'Go on.'

'Visit your dad. Speak to him alone. I know him well enough to be certain that now he has had time to think about the repercussions of what he's done, he'll be feeling pretty guilty. And if he doesn't, then ask him about a will.'

'Doesn't that sound a little money-grabbing?'

'Not if he's kept it from you that the cottages were rightfully yours. It's worth a try.'

'I suppose Gloria could have persuaded him that it was the right thing to do.'

'Never mind her,' Bella said dismissively. 'You need to speak to him. Alone. Find a way to see him without her there. Make him listen to you.'

'And?' Lexi wasn't sure what Bella had in mind but needed more than to just go to see him with the intention of having a chat. She needed for them to find a way to clear their differences, which she had to admit would be a relief.

'Ask him to buy the cottages back.'

'What? Lexi stared at her friend.

'He can afford to, can't he?' Bella said. 'After all, Oliver Whimsy paid him for them he'll have the money.' Bella looked so pleased with herself for coming up with the suggestion.

Lexi didn't like to deflate her friend's enthusiasm by suggesting that Gloria had probably persuaded her father to spend the money by now.

'Well? What do you think? Genius isn't it? And so simple.'

'I'll certainly give it a try,' Lexi agreed. There was no harm in asking him, she reasoned and, who knew, maybe he did feel badly enough to want to buy them back. Her father had never been one to covet material things. He hated even having to shop unless it was for art supplies or food. The more she considered Bella's suggestion the more she liked it. Sometimes the simplest solutions were the best. 'You might just have come up with the solution to my problems.'

Bella jumped up and down clapping her hands. 'I knew it. Right, I want you to promise me three things.'

'Go on.' Lexi stifled a laugh. This was the second person to put three things to her.

'First, put your damn boots back on your feet. It's bloody freezing out here tonight and they must be like blocks of ice by now.'

They certainly felt like it, Lexi realised. 'I'm happy to do that,' she said, bending to wipe her feet with her socks and starting to put her boots back on. Her feet immediately felt warmer and more comfortable apart from a few grains of sand that would probably irritate her all the way home. 'And the second thing?'

'Go straight to bed when you get home and try to get some sleep.'

'I think that should be doable,' she laughed.

'The final thing is to promise me that you'll go and speak to your father first thing in the morning, or at least when Gloria's out and you can get him alone.'

'Yes.' Lexi nodded. It wasn't a conversation she would look forward to but as the possible solution to her housing and work problem, she really needed to find out one way or the other if he would agree to do it.

'Good girl.'

She followed Bella up the granite steps and hugged her. 'Now, you get back to that model boyfriend of yours and try to get some sleep. Thank you for coming out to check on me and for always being there for me.'

'It's my pleasure, Lexi. Don't forget to let me know what your dad says.'

'I won't.' She could see Bella had no intention of going home until she was sure Lexi was on her way up the hill, so waved at her and began walking quickly along the boardwalk. 'Please let this idea work,' she prayed quietly, hoping desperately that it would, because as far as she was concerned it was the only realistic option she had of getting her life back on track.

CHAPTER FIFTEEN

Lexi woke the following morning with a strange sense that something was different. She lay in her bed, trying to work out what it could be. She thought back to her chat on the beach with Bella, wondering whether that was the reason she felt slightly odd. Then it dawned on her. The silence. There wasn't a sound outside her window. She turned her head to look at the clock, horrified to see it was almost eleven and that she had overslept.

Lexi pushed off her duvet and swinging her legs over the edge of her bed, sat up. It dawned on her that she couldn't hear the usual sound of seagulls. Even the sea was quiet although that probably meant that the tide was out. She got out of bed, trying to think what reason she should give to Oliver about her lateness. She knew he wouldn't be angry but hated to let anyone down.

Lexi pulled open the curtains. Everything was white.

'What the hell?' She couldn't believe what she was seeing. It wasn't just snowing she was watching a full-on blizzard raging outside her cottage. Lexi could recall previous snowstorms, but nothing as dramatic as this. It was hard to believe she had been walking barefoot on the beach only hours before. Mind you, she thought, it had been incredibly cold her feet and her feet had been almost numb by the time she finally put her socks and boots back on to return home.

She didn't have time to think any longer if she was to get to work before noon. She quickly showered and dressed. She was just about to leave her cottage when there was a knock on the door.

'Lexi? Are you alright in there?' Oliver shouted.

She opened the door. Lexi went to speak; her words vanishing before she managed to voice them. She was too startled by his bright red and white sweater to be able to say anything for a few seconds. Gathering herself, she realised his sweater was quickly turning white from the heavy snow and beckoned him inside.

He studied her face. 'Is everything OK?'

'It is, thanks. I'm sorry I'm running late this morning,' she said as he brushed snowflakes from his shoulders and shook his head to remove them from his hair. 'I couldn't sleep until very late and ended up oversleeping. I rarely ever oversleep and feel a bit bemused right now.'

'Did my sweater help wake you?' he laughed.

Lexi hadn't meant to be so obvious with her surprise. 'Sorry about that. It's lovely,' she said truthfully. 'It's just a little brighter than the sort of tops I would imagine you wearing.'

He pulled the hem out slightly and gazed down at the soft woollen top. 'It's one of my mother's specialities. She always used to make us wear brightly coloured tops when we were younger so that we could be seen from a distance if we ever got lost roaming about the Highlands.'

Lexi loved that his mother was protective of her children. 'I suppose it makes good sense.'

'It did, but she's continued to buy us loud clothes for our birthdays.'

Lexi loved that he had chosen to wear it even when the sweater wasn't something he would have chosen for himself, and said as much to him.

'It was more that this was the warmest thing I had with me. I didn't pack for weather this cold.'

Lexi wasn't surprised. 'We don't usually experience this sort of thing. I think the last time it snowed like this was back in the eighties. I don't remember it but my dad mentioned skiing down the hill a few times. I think he'd probably had a few drinks too many and got carried away.'

Oliver looked astonished. 'He's lucky he

didn't end up damaging himself.'

'He never would have admitted it if he had,' Lexi admitted.

Oliver glanced over at her log burner. Lexi followed his gaze.

'It's not very warm in here,' he said. 'Why don't you come to my place and I'll make you breakfast? I would suggest we go to the café but there are snowdrifts everywhere and I think the road is fairly impassable right now.'

'Thank you.' She followed him out of the house, dragging on her coat and hat as she went. After locking the door, Lexi stood and stared where the path should be. The snow was very deep and completely covered it. The only thing showing the way was Oliver's footprints.

'Should we call for Portia on the way?'

Oliver shook his head. 'She's not at home. We had a bit of a quarrel yesterday afternoon and she stormed off to see Charlie. I haven't seen her since. Knowing Portia, she will have stayed with him.' He opened his front door and waited for her to go inside. 'I'm surprised you didn't hear us, to be honest. We were outside and Portia doesn't have volume control when she's angry.'

Lexi didn't like to admit that she had. 'I was doing housework, so your voices could have been drowned out by the washing machine of the dryer. Was she alright?'

'You know Portia by now, she likes to have her own way.'

He gave Lexi a knowing smile and she nodded. 'Yes, she does.'

Once inside his cottage, Oliver took her coat and hat and hung them in the hallway before following her into the living room.

Lexi walked over to the log fire and rubbed her hands together. 'It's lovely and cosy in here.'

'You sit there while I rustle you up some breakfast.' He switched on the kettle and took a tea bag out of a box in the cupboard. 'Portia made sure I stocked up on some of the tea bags you both prefer.'

'Good for her.' Lexi leant back in the comfortable armchair and watched him as he began his preparations. 'I'm happy with a couple of pieces of toast, thanks. I don't usually have more than that in the mornings.'

Oliver frowned at her. 'Well, seeing as this is more brunch than breakfast and knowing how bitter the weather is outside, I think you should at least have a couple of eggs to go on that toast. Poached, scrambled or fried?'

Lexi could see he wasn't giving her any choice. Now she thought of it, eggs on toast did sound rather nice. 'Scrambled, please.'

She enjoyed watching him work. He seemed happy cooking and she couldn't help thinking that he looked rather sexy making her breakfast. She could get used to this.

Lexi thought back to Bella's suggestion that she ask her father if he consider buying back the properties from Oliver. She had a perfect opportunity to broach the subject with him now that there was little chance of Portia interrupting them. She decided to wait until they were eating.

Shortly after, he buttered four pieces of toast, popped them on two plates and served the scrambled eggs. Then carrying the plate and a cup of tea, placed them onto the coffee table in front of her.

'If you'd rather move over to the kitchen table, feel free,' he said. 'Unless you're happy where you are, which you seem to be. It is the warmest place in the room.'

'I'm perfectly happy thank you.' She picked up her cutlery and her stomach grumbled noisily. 'This looks and smells delicious, thank you.'

'My pleasure. It's nice having someone to share breakfast with occasionally.' He went to fetch his food and then returned to sat opposite her in the armchair, looking slightly embarrassed. 'I didn't actually mean that to come out quite like it did.'

Lexi giggled. 'Don't worry. I'm just glad it was you who said it and not me. I'm usually the one who says the wrong thing.'

They ate in companionable silence passing the odd comment. Lexi relished every mouthful of her food. 'I don't know what you've done to these eggs that's different, but they taste a whole lot better than when I make them.'

Oliver smiled his thanks. 'Scrambled eggs and kippers are the only two things my father has ever cooked,' he said, sounding wistful. 'He used to make them occasionally on a Sunday for Alistair, my sister Eleanor and me when we were growing up. We all looked forward to him doing it. It was always chaotic but great fun.'

'I can imagine.' She thought back to her father's cooking when she was young. 'It's funny what we remember most as children,' she said, suddenly feeling sadder than she had about her distance from her father. 'Dad used to go fishing for mackerel very early sometimes. He would come home and prepare the fish and then drive Mum, Gran and me down to one of the beaches and make a small bonfire to cook them on. I don't think you could do that now, though I'm not certain. I look back at those days now and realise how magical they were and how lucky I was to have experienced such a perfect childhood.'

'So do I.' He ate the last mouthful of his food, placed his cutlery on the plate and put it on the coffee table. 'I look at kid's now, with all the technology they have to hand, and although I'm sure they love every moment of it, I can't help feeling sorry that most of them don't spend as much time outdoors as we used to do. I was forever exploring and coming home cut, bruised and very muddy.'

Lexi laughed. 'So was I. Gosh, listen to us. We

sound like my mum used to do when she'd reminisce about the good old days.'

'We do, don't we?' He studied at her for a while. 'I'm glad I met you, Lexi. You're a breath of fresh air, do you know that?'

She had been called a few things in her time but never that. 'Thank you. It's kind of you to say so.' She didn't want to ruin the mood but felt she shouldn't miss the chance to speak to him while they were alone. 'I wanted to ask you something, if you don't mind.'

He drank some of his coffee. 'This sounds a little ominous but go on.'

'It's nothing bad.' She reassured him. 'It's about the cottages.'

'Right.'

'If you're still happy for me to have them back...'

He smiled and leant forward in his chair. 'You've changed your mind?'

She shook her head. 'No. But I think I might have come up with a solution.'

'Which is?'

'I'd like to speak to my dad and ask him to use the money you paid him for the cottages, to buy them back. If you'd be happy for him to do that?'

Oliver sat back in his chair and pondered her idea. 'I wouldn't have any problem with it.'

She was hugely relieved. She finished the last of her breakfast and smiled at him. 'Thank you. I was going to see him today, but I can't see me being able to get up the hill in this weather. I don't want to phone him in case his girlfriend is there overhears my suggestion. I'm sure she'll persuade him not to do it. I'll have to wait now until I can see him in person.' She smiled gratefully at Oliver. 'But thank you for not minding the suggestion.'

He reached forward and took her hand in his. 'Lexi, I have no problem with whatever you decide to do. You know I would happily sign them over to you. I still would if your father refuses to let you have the money.'

'Thank you,' she said amazed at his continued generosity. 'As much as I'm touched by your kind offer, I couldn't possibly accept such a gift. It would be far too much.'

'If you insist.' He gave her hand a gentle squeeze and then let it go. 'I know how important these properties are to you. Have you thought about what you'll do if your father refuses?'

'Not yet,' she said honestly. The thought of her father rebuffing her suggestion worried her and she suspected Gloria might already have made plans for the money. She seemed to have a huge influence on her father which was why she needed to speak to him as soon as possible and try to persuade him that the cottages should be kept in the family. She wasn't quite ready to give up yet.

Oliver opened his mouth to speak just as the

phone rang. She was so relaxed in his company that the interruption made her jump. He answered the call, and she could tell by his expression that something was wrong.

'No problem,' he said to whoever was on the other end of the call. 'Happy to. Please, don't worry for a second. I'll be there as soon as I can get to you.' He ended the call and stood. 'I'm sorry Lexi but I have to go.'

'Portia?'

'It was her on the phone but she's fine. Apparently, one of the chefs at the hotel has had a suspected heart attack. He needs to get to the hospital straight away but because of the storm there's no way of to get him there by road.'

Lexi wasn't sure how Oliver could help. 'I'm coming with you.' She followed him to the hall and began putting on her coat and hat.

He rested a hand on her shoulder. 'Why don't you stay here where it's warm? It doesn't make sense for both of us to go out in the cold.'

She still didn't really know what they were doing but shook her head. 'I'm not staying here while I could be doing something to help.'

As soon as they were ready, they left the cottage and made their way as quickly as they could down towards the boardwalk. Lexi was struggling to keep up with Oliver's long strides. 'What can you do to help though? Have you got medical experience, or something?'

He stopped walking and turned to look back

at her. 'Sorry, I hadn't realised you were struggling. Here,' he said, reaching out to her. 'Take my hand, it'll be easier.'

She did as he asked. 'It's not easy when you're just a touch over five feet tall.' They walked on for a few strides before she added, 'Why did Portia call you?'

'Someone suggested that as the roads are impassable, the chef is taken to hospital by sea.'

Lexi thought it an excellent solution. 'But don't we have rescue crafts for that sort of emergency?' She was out of breath with the effort of wading through the thick snow.

'Apparently, but they're all out. Or the chaps who make up crews are struggling to get to the boats. Anyway, I'm happy to help.'

'Yes,' she panted. 'But in what capacity?'

He put his arm around her waist and almost carried her the rest of the way. 'They have a boat, but the captain is recovering from a back operation. I gather he isn't allowed to take it out. Portia knows I have a lot of boating experience, so suggested I step in.'

'Really?' Was there anything he couldn't do? Lexi wondered as they reached the front steps of the hotel. 'Can I come with you?'

He pulled the door open and gently pushed Lexi inside. 'Unless you know your way around a boat, an emergency probably isn't the ideal time to start learning.'

'I suppose so.'

They barely had time to stamp the snow off their boots when Portia ran through to the hallway looking uncharacteristically dishevelled.

'Thank heavens you're here, Olly. Are you happy to go straight out again?'

'Yes, sure.'

'Right, come this way.' Without waiting for them to say anything further, Portia began running down the hotel hallway. Lexi followed her and Oliver past reception and through a door to the back of the hotel where Charlie was waiting with Jack, Alessandro, Finn and several others. A very sick looking man was sitting, eyes closed in a wheelchair. He was wrapped up in several blankets.

'Good of you to come,' Charlie said. 'Jack's sorted out a boat and Tony, he's a fisherman from the boardwalk, is waiting on it for us to get to him. The quickest way is out the back.'

'Good luck!' Lexi shouted as they left through the back door. She felt a hand resting on her shoulder and turned her head to find Portia looking very pale. 'Why don't we find somewhere to sit where we can wait for news. In fact, why don't we go to Sacha's café and see if we can wait there. At least we'll be able to watch the boat leave and return if we sit by the window.'

'I love that idea,' Portia said.

A few minutes' later they were knocking on the café door. Sacha spotted them from where she was standing behind the counter and ran to unlock it. 'I'm glad to see you both,' she said waving them inside. 'Come and join me. Bella's here already. We're so worried about the guys having to go off in this weather. They love a drama,

'They do,' Lexi agreed taking off her coat and hat. 'I wish the sea wasn't so rough though,'s she added looking out of the window at the crashing waves.'

'I'm sure they know what they're doing,' Portia said, taking a seat at the window table where Bella was already sitting, staring out of the sea-spray covered window. 'Oliver's great with boats. They're in the best hands.'

'That's good to know,' Bella said, looking relieved. 'I couldn't face anything happening to Jack, or any of the others.' She looked across the table at Portia. 'You saw the poor chef. Do you think he'll be alright?'

'I've no idea. I hope so.'

Sacha made them all mugs of hot chocolate. They sat quietly chatting and comforting each other before she added, 'I've got pastries, too.' She motioned towards a plate in the glass fronted cabinet with a display of croissants, pain au chocolat and pain au raisins covered with a glass dome. 'They're yesterday's, though, so not as fresh as they could be. They'll still be very tasty though.'

None of them were hungry, so declined her offer. Lexi knew she couldn't eat another thing after the delicious breakfast she had consumed only a short while ago before Portia had phoned, calling for Oliver's help.

'How long do you think it will take them to get to St Helier Harbour?' Lexi asked, doubting any of them would know.

'No idea,' Bella said. 'I suspect we won't see them for at least a couple of hours. Maybe we should think about doing something rather than just sitting here? We need to keep ourselves busy while we wait for them to get back.'

'What should we do though?' Portia looked intrigued. 'Play a board game?'

Bella frowned. 'I was thinking more that we could go and check up on the older residents, like Betty.'

'Couldn't you just phone her?' Sacha asked. 'I thought your mum was still living with her. Won't she be looking after her?'

'Yes, but you know how unreliable my mother is.' Bella looked at Portia, whose eyes had widened. Lexi presumed she was surprised to hear Bella speaking about her mother in such an uncharitable way. 'It's true,' Bella added glancing at Portia. 'I love her but she's hopeless unless she's thinking about herself.'

Lexi had recovered enough from her trek down the hill to consider going out again. 'The snow can't be as bad along the boardwalk as it was coming down the hill,' she said, realising it had been much easier walking from the hotel to the café. 'In fact, it's not too bad at all nearer the sea. I'm happy to go and check on Betty and anyone else for that matter. I think it's a great idea.'

Sacha beamed at her. 'I could pack up some of the pastries. What do you think about me making up a flask of hot chocolate and one of tea to take to everyone?'

Lexi loved the idea. 'I think it's a brilliant idea.' She couldn't think of a better way to take her mind off Oliver and what he was dealing with than to visit locals who lived on the boardwalk. 'Let's do it.'

CHAPTER SIXTEEN

Despite being wrapped up warmly, the temperature seemed to have dropped considerably. The sun came out briefly while they were waiting in the café, but now it was snowing again.

'I think we should begin at the other end of the boardwalk, at Betty's home,' Lexi said, holding tightly to the paper napkins she had bought from the shop, her breath coming out in frosty clouds.

Bella, Sacha and Portia nodded their agreement, and each carried something as they set off at as fast a pace as they could manage in the deep snow. Lexi's attention kept being drawn to the rough sea. She willed Oliver to be careful. She thought she knew him well enough to be confident that if he'd offered his services, he must be capable of taking charge of the boat and getting it to St Helier as quickly and safely as possible.

Lexi knew from experience that the main roads would be gritted by now. It was only on the outskirts of the island that they would be impassable like the narrower roads leading to the boardwalk and area around it.

'They won't even have reached the harbour in town yet,' Bella said, quietly falling behind the others to fall in step with Lexi. 'I'm sure Oliver will be fine, and I know Jack is used to being at sea since he's been going out on Tony's fishing boat to help whenever he needed an extra man to help during the summer.' She linked arms with Lexi. 'They'll be back safe, but not for a while yet.'

'You're right, I know you are.' Lexi pulled her scarf up to cover her nose and mouth. 'Hell, it's bitter out here. I thought it was cold last week, but this is another level entirely.'

Bella hugged Lexi's arm. 'And next summer we'll be sweltering in thirty-three-degree heat and dreaming about how lovely and cool it was today, won't we?'

Lexi giggled as she pictured them moaning about the heat next summer. Bella was right. They never seemed to be satisfied with the weather unless it was a particularly balmy spring day or autumn evening. 'One of these days we'll be happy with what we've got.'

'I think we are, for the most part.' They quickened their stride to catch up with the others. 'How are you feeling after last night?'

'Much better.' Lexi smiled at her. 'Thanks again for coming to the beach and chatting to me. You made perfect sense.'

'That's alright. I was happy to. Anyway, you'd do the same for me.' They walked on a few strides. 'Did you manage to get any sleep in the end?'

'Yes, thanks.' Lexi kicked away some of the snow on her boots. 'In fact, I overslept this morning, which was unusual for me.'

'I'm not surprised. You must have got to sleep pretty late in the end. Did Oliver mind when you didn't pitch up on time?'

Lexi shook her head. 'No, he came to my place to check I was alright and invited me to his cottage wanting to make me breakfast.'

'You seem to be getting on pretty well with Mr Whimsy,' Bella said, raising an eyebrow.

Lexi suspected her friends would have been wondering what was going on between her and Oliver, but she was enjoying keeping their growing closeness something special between them. 'There's been nothing for you to pull that face at me for,' she said, frowning. 'Anyway, he's my boss.'

Bella gave her a don't-give-me-that-nonsense look. 'Yes, you keep saying so but I'm beginning to think you might be protesting just a little bit too much.'

'Nonsense. I keep saying it because that's exactly what he is.' Lexi wasn't sure quite why she was bothering to try and deny her feelings for Oliver. Her friend wasn't stupid and could see straight through her.

'Fine,' Bella said, giving her a sideways smile. 'But thinking back to my initial opinion about him from Halloween, I'm beginning to realise I got him very wrong. He seems to be a lot nicer than I gave him credit for.'

'Me, too,' Lexi agreed, thinking how much things can change in a matter of weeks. 'He's always looking out for others, especially those close to him like his parents, obviously, but Portia too. I think it's rather sweet.'

'So do I.'

By the time they reached Betty's front door, flurries of snow were whipping across their faces and it was becoming harder to see far in front of them. Bella's mother, Claire, welcomed them into the tiny living room where Betty sat knitting in front of her fire. She beamed at them and tried to stand.

'No, please don't get up,' Sacha said. 'We're not staying long, we only wanted to check you were alright and to bring you a hot drink and some pastries.'

Betty clasped her hands together as Portia took the lid off the large Tupperware box she was carrying and held them in front of her. 'You are sweet, thoughtful girls. These look delicious.'

'I'll fetch a couple of plates,' Claire said, disappearing into the small kitchen at the back of the cottage.

'Better bring a couple of cups too, Mum,' Bella called. 'We've also brought flasks of tea and hot chocolate to pour you both a cup.'

Lexi loved seeing Betty looking happy and cosy in her cottage, especially after such a worrying year for her. It was difficult to imagine the fragile looking lady as someone who had defied the Nazis during the Occupation of the island. Betty was her hero, as Lexi knew she was for everyone who lived on or near the boardwalk.

'Right,' Bella said, as Portia replaced the lid on the box of pastries and Sacha fastened the cap on the large flask of hot chocolate. 'We'd better get going. But if you need anything at all, either of you,' she looked from Betty to her mother, 'or Tony, then give me or Jack a call and we'll be here in no time.'

Lexi watched as Bella and her mum hugged. What she wouldn't give right now to be able to hug her own mum, she thought, clearing her throat to stop herself from crying. For a moment, she felt very alone. She gave them a quick wave and forced a smile before turning towards the front door to hide her emotion. Bella and her mum might have their issues, but at least they could still spend time together and have fun.

What did Lexi have, now her mum had died, and her dad was no longer as close to her? Get a grip, she thought, taking a deep breath. Now was not the time for maudlin thoughts.

'Hey, you alright?' Portia whispered, joining her by the front door.

Lexi nodded. 'Sorry, yes. I just had a bit of a moment, that's all.'

'I'd suggest we wait outside for them, but it's too damn cold out there.' Portia tucked the large container under her arm. 'I know what you mean though. I think it's this time of year, it always gets me when I least expect it.'

'What does?'

'Grief.'

She was right, Lexi decided. 'Just when you think you're doing well it hits you from left field like a sucker punch to the stomach. Gets me every time.'

'You and me both, sister.'

Lexi looked at the woman, who she probably would never have met, let alone got to know, had it not been for Oliver Whimsy buying the cottages and coming to live there. She liked her straightforward honesty and the way she didn't care what people thought of her.

'I'm glad you came to stay here, Portia.' It was true, she was. They hadn't known each other long but Lexi knew she had found a friend who understood how it felt to lose someone you loved. Like Jools, she had been caught off guard by circumstance and had needed to find ways to cope with the unexpected changes it had brought to her life.

Portia put her free arm around Lexi's shoulders. She was at least ten inches taller than her so had to look down to speak to her. 'And I'm grateful that I was lucky enough to meet you.' She stared at Lexi thoughtfully for a moment. 'I think Oliver is too.'

Lexi presumed Portia meant that he was happy they were friends. 'I can tell he's very fond of you by the way he looks out for you. It's lovely to see.'

Portia frowned. 'He is very protective of me, but that's not what I meant.'

'Oh.' Lexi was confused. 'Sorry, I thought...'

They heard the others saying their goodbyes and coming to join them. Portia bent her head lower and whispered. 'I didn't mean how he is with me, but how he is with you.'

Bella stepped past them and opened the door. 'Right, brace yourselves for the cold, ladies.'

A rush of freezing air gushed into the cottage and the four of them hurried outside and closed the door quickly behind them trying not to let the cold inside.

'Well, that felt good, didn't it?'

Lexi wanted to continue her conversation with Portia, but it would have to wait. 'Yes, I'm glad we came. Betty looked thrilled to see us.'

'Wouldn't you if you were stuck with my

mum all day?' Bella teased. 'No, to be honest, I'm surprised Mum's being so attentive to Betty, especially now that she's in a relationship with Tony. She usually spends all her time giving the man in her life her attention, but she's not doing that so much with him.'

'Maybe she's a little more confident in his feelings for her,' Lexi suggested.

Portia looked confused. 'Who's Tony? I've heard him being mentioned a few times this morning, but I don't think I've met him yet?'

They walked to the next cottage along from Betty's. 'Tony's a lovely guy,' Sacha explained. 'He's a local fisherman who was widowed a couple of years ago. He has two small children. He and Bella's mum have recently discovered each other, which is really sweet.'

'So, why haven't I met him yet? Or maybe I have and I just don't know what he looks like?'

'You haven't.' Bella explained. 'He's spent the last couple of weeks at home recuperating from a back operation. He's fine now but needs to take things easy for a while. Mum, who is the least likely person to act as anyone's nursemaid, has been keeping herself busy looking after things. She's been going back and forth between his house, helping to look after him and cook for his kids, and to Betty's where she's living at the moment.'

Portia looked suitably impressed with Bella's description of Claire's hard work. 'She sounds like a veritable Florence Nightingale to me.'

Bella smiled proudly as she knocked on the next front door. 'She does, doesn't she? I must admit there's no one more surprised than me to see her behaving in such a responsible way.'

They were thanked but not invited inside. After deciding to only visit those where someone lived alone, had small children or were elderly, the women skipped the next two houses. They arrived at the second-hand book shop where Jools lived with her grandmother and rang the bell. Lexi danced from foot to foot, trying to keep her feet warm as they waited for Jools to answer the door.

'I saw you lot wandering around the boardwalk and wondered if you'd pop by to visit us,' she said as she opened the door and motioned for them to step inside.

They walked from the front door directly into a room that Lexi secretly thought looked like a magical library. Built-in shelves on one side faced a varying selection of book on the other side of the room. Each shelving unit groaned under the weight of hundreds of books. At the back of the room was a low counter behind which Jools' grandmother chose to spend her days reading or knitting and passing the time with neighbours in the winter and holidaymakers during the tourist season.

'I can see you've come with supplies,' she added, giving each of them a brief hug as they passed. 'I'm guessing you're on a mercy mission to the villagers.'

'We are,' Sacha, said tapping the large flask she was carrying. 'We have tea here.'

'I've got the hot chocolate,' Bella said giving Jools a wink. 'And Lexi and Portia have pastry treats. We thought you and Mrs Jones might want something to cheer yourselves up if you've got more sense than to venture out in this horrible weather.'

Portia lifted the lid on the container in her arms, and Jools peered inside. 'Ooh, pain au raisin, my favourite. Gran will have one too. Thanks, guys,' she said, taking a napkin from Lexi and wrapping up two of the pastries. 'No need to worry about hot drinks for us, we're pretty organised upstairs.'

Lexi knew from the many times she'd visited the shop that Jools' gran had turned the small front bedroom into a living area with a couple of chairs, a table and her old television so that on days when the shop was closed, she could sit there and take in the view of the small harbour. 'Your gran upstairs today then?'

Jools nodded. 'It's warmer up there and I didn't think anyone would be coming in to buy books today, so I persuaded her to stay in the living room.' She sniffed the pastries in her hand. 'They smell delicious. Thanks for bringing them to us, Gran will be touched by your thoughtfulness.'

'It was our pleasure,' Bella said.

Lexi could tell that Jools was anxious to return to her grandmother, or, she thought, maybe get back to whatever painting she was working on. 'We'll see you soon.'

'Great. You lot take care out there, it'll be slippery on the boardwalk.'

'It is a bit,' Lexi said, going to the door and opening it. 'Bye, Jools.'

As Bella and Sacha walked ahead, Portia slowed down to accompany Lexi. 'Bella doesn't seem to be that keen on her mother, does she?'

Lexi wasn't surprised to hear Portia ask such a question. She knew Bella's history with her mum, and it hadn't been an easy one. 'She has her reasons. They get along well now though, which seems to be the making of them both. It's good to see.' Desperate to ask, she added, 'What did you mean earlier, about Oliver and me?'

'I think my friend Olly has feelings for you.' Portia smiled. 'It's not what I expected at all.'

Lexi was taken aback. It hurt to hear her new friend's shock at the thought that Oliver could possibly have feelings for her. 'Why wouldn't he have feelings for me?' she asked trying to hide how upset Portia's comments had made her. 'Am I that bad?'

Portia took hold of her arm and pulled her back to stop her from walking on. 'I didn't mean it nastily. I just meant that you're not really his type.'

Lexi looked at the tall, elegant woman in front of her. She could still pass as a model from one of the glossiest magazines, despite wearing a strange woolly hat with flaps covering her ears and a thick polo neck pulled up over her mouth. Lexi pictured herself, petite with short, black hair in a pixie haircut. Portia was right, there was nothing glamorous about her. Nothing at all. Lexi could see her point; she couldn't imagine Oliver with someone like her either.

'I see what you mean,' she said miserably.

Portia grimaced. 'I didn't mean it like that either. I just meant that you're not the usual type he goes for.' She groaned. 'That came out wrong too. I meant that I'm not surprised he likes you. Really, Lexi. You're funny, strong, kind and very pretty.'

Portia seemed convincing. 'Er, thanks.' Lexi said, now feeling silly for taking Portia's comments the wrong way.

Lexi was relieved when they finished their deliveries and returned to the warm café. She glanced at the wall clock and then out to the harbour. Surely the men would be back soon, she thought hopefully.

'Stop worrying,' Sacha said, interrupting her thoughts. 'They'll be fine. Come and help me wash these flasks in the kitchen. We need to keep busy.'

Lexi was up to her elbows in soapsuds when she heard Jack's booming voice announcing their arrival, followed by Bella and Portia firing questions at him.

'See, I told you they'd be fine,' Sacha said, sounding as relieved as Lexi felt.

'I'll finish these,' Lexi said, rinsing the first large flask. 'You go and welcome Alessandro back.'

Sacha beamed at her briefly before running out of the kitchen to go and see her boyfriend. Lexi loved to see her good friend so much in love with the new man in her life. They had come a long way in a few months, and it gave her hope that she could do the same with a man. She was so busy thinking about Sacha and Alessandro's initial difficulties that she didn't reach far enough over with the flask and missed the draining board, only realising what she had done as it slipped out of her wet hands.

Lexi grimaced and squeezed her eyes closed bracing herself for the inevitable crash as it hit the tiled floor. When it didn't come, she opened her eyes and saw Oliver standing in front of her, placing the flask onto the worktop. He was dishevelled, his dark hair windswept and his face pinched.

'You look exhausted,' she said quietly her stomach flipping over as she stared at him. 'Did you get the chef to the hospital in time?'

'We did. It was a relief.' He stared at her in silence. 'I heard Sacha mention something about eating lunch here, but I'm shattered. I was wondering whether you were going to stay here like Portia intends to, or if you wanted to come home with me.'

'*With* you?' She wasn't sure if he was inviting her to his home or offering to accompany her back up the hill.

'It's been snowing since we left here earlier today, so the snow will be much thicker going home. The walk is going to be hard going. I'm sure Jack will take you home if you'd rather stay with your friends.'

Did he want her to go back to the cottages with him? She wasn't sure, but now she thought about it, she was ready to go home, either to his or her own. 'I'll come back with you,' she said, happy to see him smile at her reply. 'This morning has been tiring, probably not helped because we were all worried about you guys on the boat in this dreadful weather.' She recalled him catching the flask. 'Oh, and thank you for rescuing Sacha's flask. They're quite expensive and I don't think she would appreciate me dropping one.'

'It was a reflex and I just happened to be near enough,' he said, waiting as she dried her hands.

No one tried to argue with them when Lexi and Oliver told them they were leaving, but she noticed Bella and Portia giving the pair of them a couple of knowing looks. Lexi wasn't sure what they thought they knew, but decided not to bother saying anything and said her good-byes.

She was relieved to see it had stopped snowing, at least for now, as they started the upward trek to the cottages. By the time they reached the pathway to their front doors Lexi was red in the face and panting from the exertion of walking uphill through deep snow.

'You alright?' Oliver asked, looking as if he had merely taken a stroll somewhere pleasant. She nodded. 'Would you like to come to mine? I thought we could plan the recordings for my parents and then I could make you a bit of supper.'

The idea appealed to Lexi but despite the cold, she was sweating under her coat from the exercise she had just taken. All she wanted to do at that moment was soak in a hot bath and try to warm up a bit. 'Can I call by in about an hour?'

'Of course, you can. No rush. Come by whenever you're ready. Don't knock and wait outside either, just let yourself in.'

She thanked him and hurried home.

An hour later, after a long soak in a bubble-filled bath, Lexi arrived at his cottage dressed in her favourite joggers and hoody. It felt a little odd just walking into his home.

'Hi, it's only me,' she called from the hallway before walking into the living area.

He looked up from where he was making

notes as he sat at the end of the sofa, a notepad resting on one of his knees. 'Great. Come here and take a seat by the fire.'

She did as he asked, although the room was warm enough for it not to matter where she sat. 'You're not working again, are you?'

He pointed to the notepad and shook his head. 'No, just making a few notes and trying to think of all the places I want to record for my mother. I don't want to forget anything. You'll know better than me what to include though.'

Lexi supposed he was right. She held her hand out for him to pass her his notes. When he did, she read them. 'You've done really well so far. It's a shame it's been snowing. We could have pretended it was summer outside to remind her of the ones she enjoyed here. Maybe we could show the cottages how they look now, and how they must have looked to her back in the eighties.'

'Good idea.' He took the notepad back from her. 'Has it changed very much around here since then, do you know?'

Lexi thought about the nearby buildings that had been built in the area since she was small. 'A bit, but not nearly as much as you'd probably expect. I mean, the cottages down the hill and around the corner didn't exist back then, even though they look as if they've been there for a couple of hundred years. They replaced a nightclub that I recall Gran telling me used to show cabarets decades ago before it burnt down one night.'

Oliver grimaced. 'I can't imagine a nightclub being allowed in a quiet village like this one.'

Neither could she. 'I suppose they needed to find ways to entertain all the visitors to the island.'

'I'll bet the youngsters enjoyed having a nightclub and a couple of pubs in such a remote area.'

'Remote?' she giggled thinking that on an island only nine miles by five nowhere could truly be classified as remote. 'I'm surprised someone from the Highlands of Scotland could think of anywhere here as such a thing.'

Oliver pulled a face. 'You know what I mean.'

She did but it felt good to tease him a little. 'I remember Mum telling me how she loved the beach barbeque parties her friends held on the beach below the boardwalk.'

'It sounds magical,' Oliver said. 'My mother told me that she and my dad attended a few of those. Also, boat trips around the coast, stopping off in coves, dropping the anchor and going swimming. That sort of thing.'

Lexi sat back in her chair and after slipping off her trainers pulled her legs up underneath her. 'I'd love to go back and experience the eighties, wouldn't you?'

'I suppose so.' He gave it some thought. 'Though I don't see why we can't do all the things they did back then. The two pubs here look as if they've been here for decades and the beach must be pretty much the same. We could have a barbeque when the weather warms up. Invite your friends down there to take photos and do some filming and there's no reason why we can't borrow a boat and visit a few coves, maybe have a picnic.'

'No swimming though,' Lexi groaned. 'That dip on New Year's Day was more than enough for me this winter.'

Oliver laughed. 'And me. It was exhilarating though, don't you think?'

'Maybe.' She pulled a face. 'Then again, maybe not.' She looked around the room. 'You could start off by filming in here. The decoration is a little calmer now that the walls are no longer yellow, and the curtains and bed linen aren't a garish orange flowered pattern, but I think your mother will be able to picture how they were when she stayed here.'

'Good idea. I'm sure she'll love that. '

'You can also intersperse each piece of recording with a couple of photos of your mum, your dad and maybe my gran and mum. I think it'll help give an atmosphere of the past to the recording and be a great way to remind her how it was back then.'

He stared at her, his lips slowly drawing back in a smile.

'What?' Lexi asked, unsure why he was smiling at her.

'You're very creative. I like that idea, very

much. Go on, what else can you think of?'

Happy he appreciated her ideas, Lexi felt encouraged and gave more thought to their project. 'Maybe we can look online and look up the records in the charts when your parents were here together. There's a chance that some of it might help your father remember snippets. It's worth a try.'

Oliver reached out his hand. Lexi gazed at it for a moment unsure what to do, then when he didn't move, she reached out and placed her hand in his. She watched as he closed his fingers over hers, pulled her hand up to his lips and kissed the back of her hand.

'Thank you, Lexi. I know you realise how important this is to me. Your ideas will make this film so much better.' Without taking his eyes from her he kissed her hand again. 'I've enjoyed working with you on this.'

He let go of her hand, but Lexi could still feel the gentle pressure of his lips on her skin. 'It's been fun for me, too.' She wasn't quite sure that fun was the best word to describe what they were doing when the reason was so sad, but she couldn't think of a more appropriate word. 'That is, I mean to say...'

Oliver smiled. 'It's fine. I know exactly what you mean.' He put the notepad on the table in front of him and rested his palms on his knees, leaning forward. 'Shall we start filming then? See how it goes?'

'Sure. It'll be good to start working through that list of yours.'

'Do you mind if I begin by introducing you, and then lead on to your mum and grandmother, Thea, to give some context about who lives in the cottages now?'

Lexi was horrified. She had no intention of being recorded until she was wearing something smarter than her old tracksuit bottoms and woolly jumper. 'Look at what I'm wearing! Can't we wait until I change into something smarter?'

Oliver pointed to his sweater. 'We're filming this for a woman who thought this sweater was perfect for me, and my father is happiest in his father's hand-me-down tweeds. I really don't think they're going to worry about what you're wearing, do you?'

Lexi shrugged. 'I could put on a little lip gloss.'

'Why?'

'Er, to help me look a bit better.'

Oliver took two steps to stand in front of her, took her hands in his and looked into her eyes. His piercing gaze sent thrills through Lexi's stomach. 'Lexi, I don't think you realise quite how pretty you are. If you want to put on lip gloss then I'll happily wait for you to do so, but I don't think you need anything to enhance your looks.'

She wasn't sure if he was being honest or hoping to placate her enough to begin filming.

He laughed. 'I can see you don't believe me.

Well, you'll just have to. I mean, do you even see yourself when you look in the mirror?'

What an odd thing to say, Lexi thought. 'Of course I do.'

'No. I mean really see yourself. See what the rest of us see when we look at you.'

Lexi frowned. Her mum always said how pretty she was, but that was her mum. Mums do that sort of thing. Her dad always told her she had a funny face and Lexi believed him. Either way, she mused, if Oliver thought she was pretty then she was happy to accept he meant it. 'Fine. Shall we begin filming now then?'

An hour and a half later, Oliver was happy with the five-minute clip that they had recorded. This was going to take far longer than Lexi had expected, she realised. Then again, helping Oliver meant spending more time with him and that was something she was more than happy to do.

CHAPTER SEVENTEEN

Lexi finished reading an historical romance that Portia has recommended and wiped away a stray tear. The couple had finally found a way to be together in nineteen-nineteen and she wished that everyone could find their happy ever-after in real life. She placed the book on the coffee table and yawned. She could barely keep her eyes open. Pulling up the chunky knit blanket lying over her legs, she closed her eyes and gave into her tiredness.

She was dreaming about loud banging coming from somewhere. It took a while before she realised that someone was at her front door, calling her name.

'Dad?' She threw back the blanket and got up. Hurrying to the hallway to let him in, she glanced at her watch to see it was twenty past eleven. 'One moment,' she shouted as she unlocked the door, trying desperately not to give in to her panic.

'What on earth's the matter?' she asked, horrified to see his eyes were red. 'Dad? Are you alright?'

He walked past her into the living room and paced back and forth for a few seconds before answering. 'I'm so very sorry, Lexi.' His voice quavered with emotion. 'When I thought about what I've done to you, I had to come here and ask you to forgive me.'

'Dad, it's fine. You need to relax.' His face was white. He looked as if he had been in a state for a while. She gave him a hug, smelling whisky on his breath. It was a relief in a way to know that this was due to him having had too much to drink, but she still couldn't help worrying that if he didn't calm down, his extreme stress might end up causing a heart attack.

'I'm a hopeless father. You've always been a dedicated daughter, and this is how I repay you for your years of love and devotion.'

She took his face in her hands his unshaven cheeks prickling the skin on her palms. 'Dad. I want you to take a deep breath.'

'But I've done a stupid, thoughtless thing and I've upset you.' He cried, hugging her tightly. 'My baby girl.'

'Dad, seriously, take it easy. I'm a grown woman and I really am fine.' She needed to take him home, she decided. He wasn't listening to her and as much as she didn't relish seeing his girlfriend it occurred to her that maybe Gloria might have better luck making him listen. 'Is Gloria at your house?'

He nodded. 'Do you forgive me?'

'I forgive you.' She smiled at him to reassure him. 'Now. I'm taking you home, but I need to know that Gloria will be there to make sure you're alright.'

'She's angry with me for coming here. What am I going to do?'

Lexi had only seen him like this a couple of times before, shortly after her mum had died and when a big sale of one of his paintings fell through and he couldn't cover the mortgage that month.

'You're need to go home and get a good night's sleep. Gloria's probably worried about you. I'm sure she'll forget about being cross with you when she knows you're OK.'

He frowned at her. 'You're sure?'

She wasn't, but he was in no state to hear her say as much. 'Yes. Now, let's get you home.'

A couple of days later, the snow had almost melted apart from lingering grey slush on either side of the road. Lexi had kept busy helping Oliver with more of the filming for his parents but could not find a reason to put off visiting her father any longer. She re-read Bella's text that had appeared on her phone minutes before.

Gloria just took taxi to town. Your father's at home. Now's the time. Bella X

Lexi took a deep breath and lowered the lid of her laptop preparing to leave work and walk up the hill to her father's house.

'Let me come with you,' Oliver said when she told him where she was going. 'I can speak to him. It's the least I can do.'

'No.' She put on her coat and pulled her hat down over her ears. 'This is something I have to do alone. If you're there it'll only make things more complicated. Thanks though, I appreciate you wanting to help.'

'Would you like me to walk with you?'

Lexi smiled. 'I'm fine, thanks. I've been walking up and down that hill for most of my life. I think I could do it with my eyes closed by now.'

Twenty minutes later, she reached the village at the top of the hill. Lexi spotted Betty and Claire coming out of the village shop and gave them a wave, determined not to stop for any reason in case it gave her time to change her mind. She soon arrived at her dad's house. Hoping Bella was right and that Gloria was still out of the house, she knocked on the front door.

'Lexi, what are you doing here?' Her father looked around as if to check they were alone.

'It's alright,' she said, wanting to reassure him. 'Gloria's gone.'

He stood back to let her in. 'You've had someone watching the house?'

Lexi walked through to the kitchen where she always seemed to end up when she visited her dad and leant against the pine dresser. 'No. I'm not a member of MI5 you know.' She hated having to explain herself. Upset to think that their relationship had deteriorated so badly, she added, 'One of my friends knew I was hoping to speak to you alone, she let me know when Gloria left in a taxi.'

Her words seemed to bring him back to earth. 'Sorry, that was silly of me.'

Lexi wanted to reply that he had obviously been spending too much time in Gloria's company. If she hadn't known for certain before that Gloria was filling him with insidious comments about her, she knew now. She had never done anything to offend Gloria, as far as she was aware, and it saddened Lexi to think that Gloria could be so underhand about her.

'It's fine. I know you're worried that she might come back, so I'll get straight to the point.'

He folded his arms across his chest, tapping the toe of his tatty, paint splattered trainer on the floor as he watched her. Lexi was saddened to see him so unsure of her. She needed to get this over with before Gloria sensed something was amiss and returned.

Her pulse raced and she had to take a deep breath so that her voice didn't quiver. She wanted her father to see her strength and determination, not her uncertainty about what she was attempting to do.

'The thing is Dad, I want you to let me have the money Oliver Whimsy paid you for the cottages so that I can buy them back.' There, she had said it. She watched him as he absorbed her words.

He stepped from one foot to the other and then rubbed his pointy chin. 'I can't do that Lexi. I'm sorry.'

She glared at him. They both knew that she would usually give up at this point, but things were different now and she had no intention of him taking advantage of her love for him.

'No, Dad. That's just not good enough.' She didn't want to ask her next question, but it appeared that there was little between them at the moment anyway, so Lexi braced herself. 'Did Mum leave a will?'

'Why do you ask?'

Lexi felt like he had punched her. She knew instinctively that he would have immediately confirmed there hadn't been a will if that was the case. 'So, there was one?'

He turned his back on her nodding slowly.

Lexi's head hurt. It was as if someone had placed a metal ring around her temples and was tightening it slowly.

'Dad, we both knew Mum wanted me to have the cottages, but until now I didn't realize that she had actually left them to me legally.' She could hardly bring herself to ask her next question. 'Did you sell the cottages knowing that you had no right to do it?'

He swung around to face her. 'I needed the money, Lexi.'

'Dad! How could you do that to me? To Mum?'

His face reddened and he looked down at the new tiled floor beneath their feet, which Lexi was noticing for the first time. 'I'm so sorry, love.'

'Why though? You're not a materialistic man.' That was an understatement, Lexi thought, heartbroken to hear her father confirm that he had cheated her.

His shoulders slumped and he turned his back on her again, resting his palms on the pine dresser. 'I can't blame Gloria for what I did, but I did do it for her.'

'Go on.' Lexi took a crumpled hanky from her jeans pocket and blew her nose. She needed to remain composed if she was to get through this. 'What did she need you to do?'

'She persuaded me that it was time I treated myself.' His voice was so quiet that Lexi had to concentrate hard to hear what he was saying. 'We decided to use the money to extend my studio to encompass your bedroom. We've updated this kitchen, as you can probably see.'

Lexi took a moment to look around her. How had she not noticed this new pristine kitchen with the huge cooker that would only be used to cook for the two of them? She struggled to gather her wits. It was devastating to discover how deep Gloria's influence was on her father, especially when she used it in such an underhand, even illegal way. It was so unlike him. Before Gloria came along, he could barely be persuaded to buy anything new to wear despite all his clothes being covered in paint and most of them worn and almost falling apart. Lexi barely recognised who he had become.

'How much money do you have left? Do you even know, or is Gloria already in control of your bank account?' She knew she sounded cold but couldn't help herself. Maybe if her father listened to what he was saying, he might realise how badly Gloria, and he, had behaved?

'I'm not sure.' He turned to face her again, a fearful look in his eyes. 'You're not going to take me to court over this, are you?'

Lexi pushed herself away from the dresser. 'Bloody hell, Dad! What do you take me for? Of course I'm not.' She tried to calm herself and lowered her voice. 'All I want is to find a way to get the cottages back. If Oliver Whimsy is willing to sell them to me for what he paid, and you have the money to enable me to do that, then I'll buy them and we'll say nothing more about this... this nonsense.'

'But I've just told you, I don't have all the money.' He looked close to tears.

'How much do you have?' Lexi asked consciously softening her voice.

He frowned as he thought about her question. 'About two-thirds of it, I suppose.'

Lexi winced. He had managed to spend far more than she had expected. Thank heavens she had forced herself to speak to him now, before he managed to spend it all. She couldn't bear the thought of having nothing left to show for all the years of hard work and saving her gran and mother had put into these properties. She didn't know how she was supposed to make up the shortfall, but at least there was some money left. It was a start.

'Right, I want you to transfer all the money you still have into my bank account. Right now. Do you know how to do that?'

He nodded. 'Gloria's been teaching me.'

Lexi bit back an angry retort. 'Shall we go through to the computer and do it now before she gets back?'

'Yes, we better had.' He walked slowly towards the living room where the battered old computer was set on a table in a corner. 'There's going to be hell to pay,' he mumbled almost to himself. 'I don't know how I'm going to tell her about this.'

Lexi couldn't help feeling a little sorry for him, but he had got himself into this mess by allowing Gloria to take control. 'If she gets too full of herself just remind her that I've agreed not to press charges. She doesn't need to know that I never had any intention of doing so. Hopefully, she'll have enough of a fright to not try something like this again.'

She over her father's shoulder while he sat and logged onto his computer. 'Why didn't Mum's lawyers advise me that I was her main beneficiary?'

'They did send a letter.'

Lexi had a sneaking suspicion what might have happened next. 'You forgot to pass it on to me, didn't you?'

'Yes.' He looked up at her. 'I'm sorry love, I meant to. I put the letter in one of the drawers in the kitchen. I was that upset about losing your mum that I must have forgotten all about it.'

Lexi recalled those dark days only too well. 'Then Gloria found it, I suppose.'

'Yes, she did.'

Lexi didn't need to ask anything more. She could see that the enormity of what he had done was slowly sinking in. She suspected that telling Gloria he had now transferred all the remaining funds back to Lexi would be enough of a nightmare for him to ensure he learned his lesson. She watched as he logged into his bank account. Giving him her bank account details, Lexi waited for him to confirm the transfer and log off.

'Well done, Dad. You've done the right thing. It's what Mum would have wanted.' She gave his shoulder a gentle squeeze. 'Whatever Gloria says, the cottages were never hers nor were they meant to be used to fund her lifestyle.'

'I have to admit I already feel much better.'

Lexi was relieved to hear him admit he felt that way.

'How will you find the rest of the money you need, love?'

'I'm not sure,' she said. 'I'll think of something. I'll have to, won't I?'

She didn't like being at odds with her father. He had done a few silly things over the years. He had driven her mum mad many times when he spent money they had put aside for the mortgage on their bungalow on art supplies, or on an expensive camera that he cast aside within days. She recalled him giving away several valuable paintings instead of selling them, again leaving them short at times, but he had never done anything on this scale. It dawned on Lexi that she wasn't angry with her father for what he had done to her, she was simply disappointed and that, somehow, seemed far worse.

He stood. 'Are we alright now, Lexi?'

'Yes, Dad. We're fine.' They were, she decided, relieved.

She wanted to tell him that it wasn't about the money, but the breaking of her trust that she found so difficult to understand. She couldn't bear to drag things out by trying to explain that what he had done to her made her feel massively let down. Until now, she had always assumed, probably wrongly she now realised, that she came first in his affections. She had never considered that anyone else could ever manage to persuade him to do something that might hurt her. It was shocking to discover how weak he was and how desperate he had been to please Gloria, a woman he hadn't known for very long.

He looked so sorry for himself. 'Is everything else alright, Dad? You know you can confide in me at any time if you want to, don't you?'

'I know that, love. Thanks. I've been a reckless fool and I'll never forgive myself for hurting you.'

Lexi reached out and rested her hand on his arm. 'That's enough now, Dad. What's done is in the past. Oliver Whimsy has agreed to let me buy the cottages and I'll find a way to take him up on his offer. In a few months' time we probably won't even remember this happened.'

It was a fib, but she wanted to make him feel better. Anyway, she thought, glancing at her watch, Gloria might be home at any minute and she didn't fancy getting in the middle of a slanging match with her. She had no need to. This was her father's fight and she was going to let him deal with it in whichever way he chose.

'I'm glad. Hug?' He held out his arms and Lexi stepped into them, wrapping her arms around his bony back. 'That's my girl.'

She kissed his cheek and stepped back. 'Thanks for doing this, Dad. I'd better be going now, but I'll catch up with you soon, alright?'

'Yes, love. Good luck with buying back the cottages.'

She left feeling much better than when she had arrived. At least now she had the remainder of the money in her bank account, safe from Gloria's clutches. She spotted Gloria's taxi turning into the road and quickly crossed over to walk home. It was a relief to have managed to see her father before the return of her nemesis.

As she walked down towards the boardwalk, Lexi looked up at the cloudless, blue sky. It was still very cold, but she loved sunny days like these when the only sounds she could hear were the waves on the cliffs and seagulls. Lexi felt relieved. She might not have found the solution to get her home back but at least she had some of the money. It was a start. She brushed her hand lightly over a dark pink camellia flower on the bank of someone's garden. Just before she turned off to the cottages, Lexi spotted two primroses side by side, a pink and a purple one.

'Spring will be here soon,' she said to herself, feeling much lighter after her difficult meeting. Facing her dad had not been easy but it was the only way she could have made things right.

'How did it go?' Oliver asked as soon as she stepped off the road and onto their path.

Lexi gasped startled to hear his voice. 'Were you waiting for me?'

'I've been outside a few times to look up the hill and see if you were on your way back.'

She liked that he was looking out for her. 'That's kind of you.'

He narrowed his eyes. 'You seem happier. More relaxed somehow,' he said, joining her and walking with her to her front door. 'Can I take it your mission was successful?'

'Partly. He only has two-thirds of the money left, but he did transfer that to my bank account.'

Oliver grinned. 'But that's great. I'll get the papers signed up and we can transfer the properties back to you in the next day or so.'

Lexi raised her hand. 'Not so fast. I'm not taking charity from you. I did tell you that and I meant it.'

'Then I'll have to think of another way to make this right, won't I?'

Lexi unlocked her front door, went inside and turned to face him. 'I suppose you will, although what that might be, I've no idea.'

CHAPTER EIGHTEEN

The next week was spent helping Oliver, intermittently typing up his edits for his manuscript and visiting places on the island that he recalled hearing his mother reminiscing about. They had discovered a photo someone had taken of his parents. They were arm in arm and smiling at each other, standing under the stone arch of the ruins that were once a castle at Grosnez. Lexi explained that it wasn't far and that they could walk to Grosnez from the boardwalk via a small hill to the side of one of the pubs, but in the end they decided to go in her car.

Now here they were, standing in front of the arch of the castle ruins. The shape of the arch reminded Lexi of a heart. It was one of her favourite places to visit, especially in the summer months when the gorse was yellow, and the heather turned purple. On hotter days, if she was lucky, she stood at the edge of the cliffs and was able to watch dolphins playing in the channel below the cliffs.

'I didn't know this place existed,' Oliver said, staring at the archway with the remaining walls on the edge of the cliff face. He pointed through the arch to the islands on the other side of the rough sea. 'Are those other Channel Islands?'

Lexi stared at the view she loved to visit and nodded. 'They are some of the smaller islands. We can visit them one day, if you like. It's best to do it in the summer though as you have to go by boat. You can fly to the bigger islands like Guernsey or Alderney though.'

He stared ahead in silence for a while. 'I never realised there could be so much to see on such a small island. I understand now why my parents fell in love with this place and with each other while they were here. It's an incredibly romantic setting, don't you think?'

'I suppose it is,' Lexi said not having ever thought about it before. She enjoyed hearing him speaking so flatteringly about her home. 'In the fifties and sixties Jersey was a favourite destination for honeymooners,' she explained. 'In fact, they used to call it The Honeymoon Isle.'

'I can see why.'

'So can I now.' She pulled the collar up on her coat. It might be beautiful on the headland, but in early February it was very cold, especially when the wind was howling around them. 'Not the best time to come here probably.'

He put his arm around her. 'It is a bit windy, even for me.' He took his phone from his pocket. 'I'll just film a bit to add to the rest of it and then we'll go.'

Lexi felt guilty to think that her grumbling might have made him rush what was such a special project for him. 'There's no hurry. I'm hardier than I make out. You take your time.'

'If you're sure.' He didn't look convinced as he frowned at her.

'I am. Now, you do what you have to, and I'll take a bit of a walk to keep warm and out of your way.'

She walked a little way along the paths that dogwalkers took, past the gorse that now looked prickly without its bright summer flowers. She stopped to look back watching Oliver filming by the edge of the cliffs and she couldn't help thinking that with his wavy hair he looked how she imagined Heathcliff whenever she read Wuthering Heights. He was filming the sea. Lexi understood why. She was always awed by the turquoise blue of the sea below the cliffs as it crashed against the rocks.

Lexi liked to see him happily going about his day. It was difficult to imagine him as the same man she had thought so abrupt and rude only four months ago. She was glad to have had the opportunity to get to know the real Oliver Whimsy. She loved how he worked hard to ensure his family and friends' lives were as safe and as happy as possible. What a wonderful son he was to his parents and how proud of him his mother must be, Lexi thought, longing to kiss him again.

He seemed to sense her watching and smiled at her. 'Come and join me,' he said waving her over. 'Let's take a selfie.'

Lexi nodded. She certainly wasn't looking her best right now. Her eyes were slightly watery due to the cold wind and her skin was very pale. She hoped he wouldn't share the picture with anyone.

'No excuses,' he shouted as if he could tell she was questioning whether she wanted to have her photo taken with him.

'Fine.' She jogged along the path to reach him, careful as she stepped down the uneven steps into the dip in front of the entrance next to the arch way, and up the few steps on the other side. 'Has anyone ever told you how bossy you are?'

His blue eyes twinkled as he laughed. 'Once or twice, maybe.' He stretched out his arm. 'Come here and let's do this.'

She walked into his arms and he held her close to his side. Lexi put her arm around his back, inside his open coat, enjoying the sensation of the side of her body pressing up against his warm one. Oliver looked down at her and they locked eyes for a moment. Lexi's heart pounded rapidly as he bent his head and kissed her. She barely had time to react before he raised his arm.

'Smile.' He checked the photo.

'Let me see?' She took hold of his wrist and pulled the phone towards her, willing the photo of her to be better than she expected. It was worse. 'You took me off guard.' Not only hadn't she had any time to smile her mouth was open and her eyes wide as if someone had just shocked her. Which Lexi supposed he had. 'That's a horrible photo. Please delete it.'

Oliver studied it. 'I don't think it's that bad.'

'Well I do,' she said, hating to see herself looking so dreadful next to the most photogenic man she had ever met. 'I look like someone's poked me in the bot...' she stopped before she embarrassed herself any further. 'Well, I look shocked, that's all.'

'OK, look, I'm deleting it now. There you go. Satisfied?' His eyes shone in amusement. 'I promise I won't kiss you again before taking this one.'

Lexi looked up at him just as she heard the shutter on his phone click. 'Damn. That'll be another dreadful picture of me.'

'Maybe not,' he said, holding his phone in front of them so they could both look. 'You do look rather. . .' He hesitated and stared at his phone screen more closely. 'I'm not actually sure what that look is you're giving me.'

Lexi studied her image. 'That's how I look when I feel disappointed,' she said honestly. She was quite surprised at being so truthful, but he must see by the way she had been staring at him what had been going through her mind.

'Disappointed? Why?'

Did he not know? Lexi decided to be brave and tell him. She wasn't sure she was about to do the right thing. She preferred keeping her feelings to herself, but this was different. She could imagine her mother saying that if Lexi didn't let Oliver Whimsy know she had feelings for him, then she was being a fool to herself. What did she have to lose anyway?

'That you didn't kiss me for longer,' she said surprised by her own honesty.

It was his turn for his mouth to drop open in shock. She immediately doubted she had done the right thing and watched him as he stared at her for a few seconds. *What now?* Would he laugh off her words to make light of what she had told him, or come up with an excuse to move on from Grosnez to continue with their work?

He put his phone in his pocket and turned her to face him, all the time not taking his eyes off hers. Then, just as she was about to make an excuse for her rash behaviour, he pulled her into his arms and kissed her. Really kissed her. For an exceptionally long time. Lexi had no idea how long their kiss lasted. All she knew was that she had never been kissed quite like that before and did not want it to end.

'Hello there. Excuse me.'

Lexi was vaguely aware that someone was shouting, but too blissfully happy in Oliver's arms to really take note of what the person was saying.

A dog started barking and someone shouted again. 'You two, on the cliff.'

Oliver stopped kissing her and turned. Lexi followed his line of vision.

'Oh hell,' Oliver said. 'I think that chap has had a fall. We need to help him.'

Feeling guilty, Lexi followed Oliver who was pulling off his coat as he ran to help the poor white-haired man.

'Off you get, little guy,' Lexi said, picking up the little dog yapping noisily as he sat on his master's chest. 'You're not helping him by sitting there.' The little dog growled at her as she put him down on the stony ground and held tightly to his lead.

'Stop it, Monty.' The old man looked down at his coat pocket. 'I've got some doggie treats in there if you want to give him a couple to calm him. He's a greedy blighter, so it should work.'

Lexi carefully put her hand in the man's pocket and withdrew three small bone-shaped treats. 'Here you go,' she said, giving them to the dog one at a time.

'Right, let's look at you,' Oliver said, putting his right arm under the man's head. 'Are you hurt anywhere?'

'Just my pride I think.'

'Do you think you can sit up and maybe stand?' The man nodded. 'Good. Take it slowly and if anything hurts tell me straight away. I don't want to cause you any further injury.'

Lexi kept the little dog entertained while watching Oliver taking care of the man. He was gentle and calm, and she realised how special he was. He helped the man sit as Lexi stroked Monty, who thankfully had calmed down. She suspected that the dog's reaction to her before was probably due to panic at his master being on the floor.

Then Lexi noticed Oliver blanche as he spotted blood on his hands.

'You've cut yourself somewhere.' Oliver gave Lexi a meaningful look as he placed his coat around the man's thin shoulders. 'Sorry, I didn't think to ask your name. I'm Oliver Whimsy.'

'Yes, and I'm Lexi Davies,' she said.

The man, Lexi noticed, looked paler than when they had first found him.

'I'm Barry Ross.'

'Can you tell where you might have hurt yourself, Barry?'

He thought for a moment and then reached down to point at his knee. 'Behind there, I think. It's rather sore.'

'That's fine. We'll take care of you, but I think you should go to the hospital,' Oliver said his voice soothing. 'It's too cold to leave you sitting out here and I'm worried to move you in case you've broken something. Can you wriggle your toes?'

Barry stared at his feet and after a moment nodded. 'Yes, I don't think anything's broken.'

'Right, then if you're sure, I think we should take you straight to the hospital.'

Lexi took her keys out of her pocket. 'Let me bring the car as close as I can and put Monty in it. Do you have a car here?'

He shook his head. 'No. I live nearby.'

Lexi wondered if there was someone at his home who could look after his dog and asked him, disappointed when he shook his head. 'Never mind,' she said. 'We can look after Monty for you.'

She ran to her car and drove it as close to the edge of the path as the granite boulders separating the parking area from the rest of the headland would allow.

Oliver put Barry's arm over his shoulder, stooping so that he could half carry him to the car.

Half an hour later they were seated in the surgery's warm waiting room. Oliver went to speak to the receptionist to see how long Barry might expect to be waiting for a doctor to see him.

'How are you feeling?' Lexi asked, hoping that Monty would be fine waiting in the car for them.

'A little shaken, but more because it's occurred to me that I could have been out on the headland overnight if you two hadn't been kissing nearby when it happened.'

Lexi felt her cheeks redden. 'Sorry about that.'

Barry shook his head. 'No. Please don't be. It cheers me up to see two young people in love. It reminds me when I first fell in love with my June. She's been gone these past three years now and although I try to keep myself busy, changing my books in the town library each week and doing regular shops, it's not the same.'

Lexi had to try hard not to give into tears. The thought of this sweet, immaculate man trying hard to keep going without his wife upset her deeply. She was lucky to have support from her friends and other locals on the boardwalk and it was sad to think of Barry feeling lonely. She had an idea. 'Have you ever tried the food at the Summer Sundaes Café?'

He frowned. 'I'm not even sure where that is?'

'Down at the boardwalk. It's not too far from where you live and there's even a footpath from Grosnez if you want to walk.' She didn't want him to take any unnecessary chances. 'I think it probably isn't the best way to get there if you're on your own though. I live up the hill from the café. It overlooks the sea and my friends and I meet there for meals or snacks all the time.'

'It sounds wonderful.'

'Would you like to come and try it sometime

if I picked you up?'

He beamed at her. 'I'd like that very much, my dear. Are you sure you wouldn't mind?'

'Not at all. I'd love to introduce you to everyone. There's a great little community around the boardwalk.'

His smile vanished. 'Truly though, aren't I a little old to mix with your friends?'

Lexi shook her head. 'One of my closest friends is Betty. She's in her nineties and the oldest resident on the boardwalk. I have lots of other friends living there too of all ages, so you're not going to get out of it that easily.'

Barry laughed. It was a joyful sound and Lexi felt much better.

'What are you two up to?' Oliver grinned, sitting down next to Lexi.

'This lovely young lady of yours has invited me to meet her friends in a café on the boardwalk.'

Lexi winced to hear Barry describe her as Oliver's 'young lady'. All they had done was kiss and spend some time together, and that had been mostly spent working. She chose not to correct Barry, not wishing to embarrass him for making assumptions and hoped Oliver wouldn't mind.

'I think you should accept,' he said. 'I've only recently moved to the area and the locals have made me very welcome. The food at the café is delicious, so I'm sure you'll have a wonderful time there.'

'Mr Barry Ross,' a doctor called from the reception area.

'That's me,' Barry said as Oliver helped him stand. 'I'm fine thanks son, I can take it from here.' He looked at Lexi. 'I'd be delighted to accept your kind offer, thank you.'

They watched him go with the doctor to be examined. As soon as the door closed behind him, Oliver asked Lexi for her keys. 'I think I should check up on poor Monty, he's going to be wondering what's going on.'

She took them out of her pocket and dropped them in his hand. 'Hopefully, it won't be too long now until we can give Barry and Monty a lift home.'

The doctor confirmed that Barry was fine to leave. Lexi stopped off briefly at the village shop to buy supplies for him before she and Oliver dropped him and Monty at his house. She made Barry a bowl of soup with two slices of bread and butter, and fed Monty and topped up his water bowl.

'I'll pop up and check you in the morning,' she said. 'Then if you feel up to it, you can come for breakfast at the café with Oliver and me.'

Barry sat in his big armchair in front of his electric fire with his bowl of soup. 'I'll look forward to it.'

As she walked to the car, Oliver took her hand in his. 'You really are the most caring young woman.'

'I am?' Surely, she was only doing what any other person would have done. 'You were the one who practically carried him to the car.'

They got in her old estate and began the short journey home.

'I think it's a lovely thought to bring Barry to the café and introduce him to people. He needs to meet new friends.'

'He does,' she agreed. 'I hate to think of him all alone. There'll always be someone ready to chat to him, or go for a walk with him and Monty on the beach if he gets to know the locals on the boardwalk. I'll check the bus timetable and find out times so he can come and go. He's an independent man and I can't imagine he would want to wait for me to collect him each time.'

'Good plan.' Oliver gave her a sideways smile. 'You know what?'

'Go on.' She wondered what he could be about to tell her.

'I'm glad I met you, Lexi Davies.'

She didn't try to hide how happy his words made her. 'And I'm happy I met you, too.'

'I think I've recorded all I can for my mother now. If you don't mind, I thought I could make us a spot of dinner and, with your creative input, maybe I could finalise it and send it off to her tonight.'

Lexi liked the idea of spending the evening helping him. 'That sounds good to me.'

'Really?' She could hear the smile in his voice as flicked up the indicator and turned the car into her parking space.

'Yes, really.'

CHAPTER NINETEEN

'I think this is the tastiest cooked breakfast I've ever enjoyed,' Barry remarked to Oliver and Lexi, a joyful expression on his face. 'Thank you again for inviting me down here and introducing me to these lovely friends of yours.'

Betty raised her cup of tea to him. 'We're very pleased to meet you, Barry. I hope that now you've spent time with us you'll want to keep coming back.'

Lexi's phone vibrated in her pocket distracting her from hearing his reply. Most of the people who would phone her were currently at the café, so she suspected the caller must be her father. She peeked at the screen. It was. Her mood plummeted. He rarely used a phone, so she knew it must be something important. Taking her mobile out of her pocket, she accepted the call. 'Sorry, I'd better take this,' she said giving her friends an apologetic look before walking over to the doorway to take the call.

'Dad? Is everything alright?'

She could hear Gloria's bossing him around in the background. 'Tell her, go on.'

Lexi's stomach contracted in concern.

Her father mumbled something and then said, 'I'm about to, if you'll give me half a chance.'

A sense of dread crawled up her spine. 'What is it Dad?'

'Gloria and I have got engaged,' he said a forced cheerfulness to his voice. 'Isn't that wonderful news?'

It wasn't and she couldn't bring herself to say otherwise. She glanced towards the table and saw Oliver watching her, a concerned look on his face. *You alright?* he mouthed. Lexi calmed slightly to know he cared enough to ask. She shrugged.

'Lexi.' She heard her father's voice and realised she hadn't answered his question. 'I was hoping for your blessing.'

Why would he want to put that on her? Surely he must have picked up on how much she disliked, or at least distrusted Gloria, and that the very last thing she would want would be to welcome her as a stepmother. Lexi shivered. She dreaded them marrying.

'Lexi.'

She took a deep breath, trying to answer him without being rude, when she heard Gloria's voice again.

'I told you she wouldn't be happy for you, didn't I? Selfish little madam.' Gloria gave a sarcastic laugh.

Lexi closed her eyes to try and calm herself enough to reply. She took a deep breath. 'If that's what you want Dad, then of course I'm happy for you.' It was the best she could do right now.

He was a grown man and what he chose to do was not for her to question. She just hoped he had the sense to know Gloria well enough not to be upset by any future revelations.

'You are? Oh, love, I knew you would be.' She heard a muffled voice and assumed her dad was holding the phone to his chest which he did when he thought he was having a private conversation. 'See, Gloria? I said you were wrong about Lexi.' Then able to hear him breathing again, Lexi heard him add, 'Thanks, Lexi, you've made your old dad very happy.'

'I'm pleased.' She felt a dull ache at the back of the throat and realised she was about to cry. 'I'd better go now, Dad, I'm having breakfast with friends. I love you.'

She ended the call and not wishing anyone to see her upset, quietly stepped outside not caring that she wasn't wearing a coat. Tears ran down her cheeks and she moved to the nearest doorway out of the harsh wind to sob. She pushed her hands deep into her jeans pockets to try and find a tissue.

'Here, take this,' Oliver said quietly, handing a paper napkin to her. She mumbled a thank you but was too upset to be able to speak. The next thing she knew, he was putting a jacket around her shoulders and taking her in his arms. 'I don't know what just happened, but whatever it is, we'll do our best to make it as right as we can.'

His supportive words made her sob even more. Oliver held her tightly, whispering soothing words and kissing the top of her head. 'You'll be alright, Lexi. I promise you.'

Lexi managed to gather herself, wiped her eyes with the napkin and then blew her nose. She was embarrassed to think how dreadful she must look. 'I wish I had sunglasses right now,' she said forcing a smile.

'Why? It's not sunny.'

The confusion on his face made her smile. 'Because my eyes must look all pink and puffy and I want to hide behind them.'

'Your eyes?' he teased, kissing her on the forehead.

'No, the sunglasses.' She stood on tiptoe and kissed him lightly. 'Thank you for coming out here.'

'Do you want to tell me what happened?'

She sighed and explained about her father's phone call. 'I must sound ridiculous. I know Mum's been dead two years now and if I'm honest I would have still been shocked even if it hadn't been Gloria he was engaged to. I just thought he loved Mum so much he wouldn't ever consider marrying someone else. Childish, I know.'

He hugged her again. 'Not at all. We see our parents in a different way to how the rest of the world does or how they see themselves. We might be grown-ups but we're still their children and that sort of thing will always feel strange. Don't beat yourself up about it.'

'I'll try not to.' She realised something was troubling him. 'Something's the matter? What is it?'

He frowned. 'I've heard back from someone who I had asked to look into Gloria's background. I was waiting to tell you after breakfast when we were alone.'

'Can't you tell me quickly now?' she asked impatient to know the worst. 'If there is something Dad should know then now is the time for me to tell him, before he actually marries that woman.'

'I know.' He sighed. 'I may as well just say it, I guess?'

'Yes.'

He frowned. 'She has a history of swindling older, lonely men out of money.'

Lexi gasped. 'I bloody knew it. Go on.'

'That's it really. I know a couple of families have tried to sue her for what she's done, but didn't get very far. She's a very clever woman.'

'She's certainly sly.' She saw Oliver smile. 'What?'

'She must have gone mad to discover that your father had transferred all the money from the sale back to you.'

The thought of Gloria finding out that she now had all the money made Lexi feel much better. 'I'm relieved Bella suggested I do it. Imagine if I hadn't and you hadn't looked into her past life, she might have got away with so much more.'

'But you did see your dad and we have made the discoveries,' he said calmly. 'She hasn't managed to get away with too much this time. And I'm certain that there won't be a next time.'

'Thankfully.' Lexi smiled up at him. 'I'm going to have to tell Dad what we know about her. It's not a conversation I'll look forward to.'

'I can imagine. But you don't have to do it alone, don't forget. I'm happy to accompany you. And I'll have the information my friend emailed across to me to show them as proof of what she's done to other men before your father, should we need it.'

It was a relief to know she wouldn't have to do such a distasteful thing alone. 'Thank you, I appreciate your support.'

'It's my pleasure,' he said. 'Are you ready to go back inside and finish what must now be a very cold breakfast? I also suspect your friends are a little worried about you.' He put his fingers under her chin and lifted it slightly to kiss her again. 'In fact, I almost had to argue with Bella to be allowed to come out here to check on you instead of her.'

Lexi laughed. Typical Bella, that sounded just like her. 'Well, we'd better hurry up and get back inside before she rounds up a search party.'

After breakfast, Lexi and Oliver left Barry and Betty at the old lady's cottage to spend a couple of hours together. 'I'll come and pick you up at one o'clock, so that you'll be home in good time to walk Monty before it gets too dark,' Lexi told Barry. 'And Betty, please let Barry have a shopping list of anything you need. I'll pop to the shops on my way back from dropping him home.'

'Thank you,' Betty said. 'It's probably too icy for me to go to the shops today anyway.'

Relived she thought so, Lexi and Oliver left them to it and returned to their cottages. 'You're more than welcome to come in for coffee,' Lexi said as they got out of her car. 'I lit the log burner early this morning, so the cottage is warm and toasty.'

Oliver nodded. 'I'd like that. I just need to check on something and then I'll come round. See you soon.'

Lexi quickly set up her coffee filter with ground coffee beans for Oliver. She liked her cottage to feel cosy so plumped up her sofa cushions and refolded the blanket she used to cover herself on evenings and cold days, when she would sit in the living room and lose herself in a good book. She thought through Oliver's revelations about Gloria. Although it troubled her to think she had to confront her father with the distasteful information, knowing Oliver would be there with her helped her feel a bit better about it.

Oliver still hadn't arrived half an hour later and she nursed the cup of tea she had made for herself, wondering if he was still coming. Thanks to him, as well as having a good cry, she felt much better and was slowly coming round to the idea that if her father chose to ignore her warnings about his new fiancé then he would carry on with his plans to marry her.

Her thoughts were interrupted by a knock at the door. 'Come in,' she shouted, pouring him a mug of coffee and adding milk.

They took their drinks and sat in the chairs they usually chose. 'Everything alright?' she asked, hoping he hadn't received bad news about his own father since the last time she saw him.

'Sorry I took a while, my mother called.'

'Nothing wrong, I hope?' Lexi asked, concerned.

'No, thankfully.' He seemed happy and she relaxed back into her seat. 'She told me they were delighted with the recording we both did. Apparently, Dad made her watch it four times last night.' Lexi was relieved Oliver's recordings had been received so well. 'She said she loves it.' He gave Lexi a nod. 'She asked me to thank you for all your help and loved your idea of adding the photos you found for her.'

'Why did you say anything about me? It was all your idea and mostly your work.'

Oliver shook his head. 'No, it wasn't. I might have had the original idea, but your creativity made the recording so much more professional and much better. And, what about those amazing photos? No, Lexi, credit where it's due. I couldn't have done it without your input and I'm incredibly grateful for that, as is she.'

Lexi was touched by his kind words. It felt good to be appreciated by someone. 'Thank you then. I'm glad to hear your parents enjoyed the film.'

Oliver laughed. 'She said that she has a feeling my father is going to expect her to play the recording several times every evening from now on. He's already told her it's his favourite thing.'

Lexi felt that familiar ache to the back of her throat. Determined not to cry again, she took a sip of her tea. 'How sweet of him. What a special reminder you've given them. You're very clever to have come up with something so perfect.'

He stared at her. 'I know how much you miss your mother and appreciate how lucky I still am to have mine, even though my father is suffering from this wicked disease. At least right now he can enjoy some memories of their young life together.'

It was true, Lexi thought. Oliver was lucky to have both his parents but they, too, were so lucky to have such a thoughtful caring son as him. She sighed. 'They sound so lovely. I wish they were able to come here as you had hoped. It would have been nice to meet them.'

'I know. I'm sad that it's too late for my father to make the journey, but maybe one day my mother will come back here, and you'll be able to meet her then and show her all the places she remembers. She'd love that.'

Lexi smiled. 'So would I.'

CHAPTER TWENTY

February

Lexi hated February. It was the most miserable time of the year as far as she was concerned, and the weather always seemed to be wet and cold. The only thing in its favour, she decided, was that it was the shortest month and that as soon as it was over spring would be on its way.

She was at Mont Orgueil, having offered to drive Betty and Barry anywhere they wanted for the afternoon.

Oliver had asked to join them. 'I saw this place when I first came to the island,' Oliver said as he and Lexi finished climbing the almost two hundred steps to the top of one of the towers. She took a tentative step towards the edge and peered down at Betty and Barry sitting on one of the benches deep in conversation. 'I paid a taxi driver to give me an island tour and show me all the places a tourist should visit. I saw this enormous castle on top of the hill looming over Grouville bay and am glad that I've actually come here. It's even more impressive close up.'

Lexi had been to the castle a few times over the years, either on school trips, or with her parents or friends as a teenager. 'This view across the bay never fails to amaze me,' she said. 'I sometimes wonder why locals feel the need to travel far away when we have all this on our doorstep. In fact, Bella's mum said that when she went to Santorini and had to work her way to the front of huge crowds to see what everyone insisted was the most beautiful sunset that, as far as she was concerned, nothing could beat the sunset across from St Ouen's bay.'

'Do you agree with her?' Oliver asked.

Lexi shrugged as she peered out over the wide horse-shoe-shaped bay in front of her. 'I've never been to Santorini, so I can't really comment.'

'It says here,' Oliver said, reading from the leaflet he had picked up on their way into the castle, 'that we'll find the medieval wheel of urine if we go to the turrets.' He grimaced, making Lexi giggle. 'I'm not so sure they have anything to compete with that in Santorini.'

'If they do, they probably wouldn't bother advertising it.' She laughed at the notion.

'No, and I wouldn't blame them either.' He studied it again. 'After this, we can go and have our photos taken in the stocks.'

Lexi looked at him thoughtfully.

Oliver laughed. 'What?'

'It's just that you are so different to how I imagined you would be when I first met you. It surprises me sometimes.'

He reached out to her and pulling her to him, kissed her. 'Good. I hope never to stop surprising you.'

She was taken aback by his comment, unsure what he meant. She noticed him staring at her. 'Go on.'

Oliver squinted. 'What?'

'You looked like you wanted to say something to me but didn't know whether to, or not.' She raised an eyebrow. 'I don't miss much. Not often anyway.' She hoped she was right and that he would open up to her.

He rested his palms on the granite wall next to him. 'OK, I've been giving your ownership of the cottages more thought. I think I might have come up with a solution.'

'Ahh.' She wished now that she hadn't been so quick to ask. She didn't see how he could possibly resolve the issue as it currently stood.

A couple came to stand next to them and spent a few seconds looking at the view before the man began fretting about being so high up. Oliver waited for them to walk away before speaking.

'We both agree the cottages should be yours.' Lexi nodded. 'You insist on buying them, but you don't have enough money. I want you to have them back, but you won't let me sign them over to you.'

'That's about the size of it, yes.' She had no idea where his comments were leading.

'How about you take out a loan for the balance, then buy them back from me and we can move on from the whole situation.'

Move on from me? She hoped that wasn't what he truly meant. 'I only have a part-time, temporary job with you and no other income,' she reminded him, wishing she could go with his suggestion. 'Who in their right mind would give me a loan?'

'Me.'

'What?' *Was he mad?* 'No.'

'Not me personally,' he said quickly. 'My company. I could have the contract drawn up legally, if that made you feel better.'

'I understand that you're trying to help, Oliver. I really do and I appreciate it, but borrowing from your company is, to me at least, the same as borrowing from you. Thank you, but the answer is still no.' Lexi smiled at him, but he scowled and turned to stare at the view once more. 'What's the matter?'

She heard him groan before he turned around to face her once more. 'Lexi, we don't come to some sort of arrangement, we're never going to get these cottages back into your name. Do you want them, or don't you?' She opened her mouth to answer, but he raised his hand to stop her. 'I know you do. What you have to decide though, is how much you're willing to compromise to get them back.'

'I don't want to compromise at all,' she snapped more irritated with her principles than with him.

'Then if you insist on paying for them but have no way to obtain the money, how do you imagine you'll ever be able to get them back?'

She didn't know. 'Argh, it's so frustrating.'

'You're not kidding.'

She could see he was exasperated with her. Lexi knew that he was doing his best to help her and couldn't understand why she wouldn't simply give in to one of his suggestions. She was certain that if things were the other way around, he would react in exactly the same way as she was doing now. *Wouldn't he?*

They made their way around the rest of the castle in silence, each lost in their own thoughts.

Lexi heard Betty's laughter and Barry's chatter before she saw them. They were walking back from the eastern side of the castle where they must have been taking in the view of the small bay to the back of the castle. She recalled her father telling years before that in the fifties Rock Hudson had filmed a scene from *Sea Devils* there. As she and Oliver went to meet Betty and Barry, she took his hand in hers.

'I'm sorry for being a stubborn mule,' she said not wishing to ruin their day by quarrelling. 'I know you're trying to help me, and I do appreciate it.'

He lifted her hand and kissed the back of it. 'I know. It's fine. I don't want to force you into anything you're not comfortable with. Let's not worry about it now. We've got the rest of the day to enjoy. Why don't we take Betty and Barry out for a bite to eat then take him home to collect Monty and we can all go for a walk.'

'Good idea,' Lexi said, enjoying having the entire day planned. 'Thank you.'

He smiled down at her. 'What for this time?'

'For being so understanding.'

He put his arm around her and gave her a gentle squeeze. 'I do my best,' he said, giving her a playful wink.

They walked a couple more steps when Oliver held her back and slowed. 'I wanted to ask you another question,' he whispered.

'Go on then.'

'It's Valentine's Day in a couple of days. It's not something I usually bother with, but I was wondering if you wanted to do something with me that night?'

Lexi could think of quite a few things she would secretly like to do with him but took a second to calm herself before replying. 'Yes, sure,' she said as coolly as she could manage. 'That sounds lovely.'

'Great. I'll think of something and we'll make plans.' He smiled at her. 'Or, if there's anything you wish to do let me know. Either way, it's a date.'

A date. A romantic date at that, Lexi mused, feeling much happier than when they had first arrived in the hallway of the castle.

'There you are,' Betty called, waving. 'I hope you two have had as much fun as Barry and me. It's been years since I've visited this place.'

'Me, too,' Barry said, beaming at them.

Lexi's heart almost sang to see the two of them looking happy. 'I'm glad you've both enjoyed yourselves.'

The following morning Lexi walked up to her father's bungalow. She hoped Gloria would be out because she desperately wanted to speak to him alone. After Oliver's kind offer to come with her for moral support, it occurred to her that this was her battle and one she needed to deal with personally.

She stood at the front door saddened to think that until Gloria's arrival she had always felt free to enter her father's home without being invited inside. Now though Lexi felt she needed to knock and wait for her father to invite her in. It was a strange sensation and one she didn't like. She knocked lightly a few times and waited. She was about to knock again when she heard her father's footsteps.

He opened the door and his eyes widened. 'I didn't expect to see you here today. Come in.'

She entered the hallway noticing that it had been freshly painted. Lexi had to admit that it did look much lighter as she followed her father into the kitchen.

'Is everything alright?' he asked. 'You've just missed Gloria, but she shouldn't be too long. She's only popped to the shops for a few bits.'

Desperate to say her piece before Gloria's return, Lexi took a deep breath before speaking. 'Dad, I'm glad I've caught you by yourself, if I'm honest,' she said noticing his initial cheerfulness to see her disappear. 'I'm afraid there's something I need to tell you about Gloria.'

He folded his arms and leant back against the worktop. 'Go on then.'

Lexi wished she didn't feel so guilty about agreeing to let Oliver look into Gloria's past, telling herself that she had done it with the best of intentions. 'I've discovered something about her,' Lexi said quietly. She wished she didn't have to continue but her concern for her father's welfare outweighed her awkwardness at having to speak to him in such a way. 'She has a history of fleecing lonely men.'

'Does she now? And you're telling me this because you think I could be taken in by her charms? Is that right?'

Lexi nodded. 'Yes. I suppose I am.'

'What makes you think I would be fooled by anyone?'

Lexi stared at him, confused. 'Dad, you told me yourself that Gloria was the one to persuade you to sell the cottages to Oliver. Why would she do such a thing when they were nothing to do with her?'

'You tell me.' He glared at her and Lexi had never felt so distanced from her father.

Did he not see Gloria's part in what had happened between them? 'I'm not sure why you're making this so difficult for me? You must know I only have your best interests at heart.'

'Do you though Lexi?'

She gasped, shocked to discover that he distrusted her. 'Yes, Dad. If you're honest with yourself, you would know that. Look. Gloria encouraged you to sell the cottages.'

'You don't know that.'

'I do. I saw her signature on the contract, don't forget. If she had disagreed with what you were doing she wouldn't have witnessed your signature, would she?' He shook his head slowly. 'Then, she persuaded you to knock through to my bedroom to make your studio bigger and by doing so getting rid of my bedroom. She then chose a new kitchen for this house. You told me those things yourself. Surely you can see what's happened here?'

His head lowered and he covered his face

with his hands. 'What you're saying makes perfect sense,' he said miserably. 'I'm not ready to face what's happened though.' He looked at her. 'What are you expecting me to do with this information?'

Lexi shrugged. 'Whatever you think best. It's up to you, Dad. I just thought that you should have all the facts about the woman you've asked to share the rest of your life. Nothing more.'

He stared at her, his hands hanging down by his sides. 'She'll be back soon.'

Lexi understood that he wanted her to leave. 'I'll go now. If you want me for anything, call me. I can be here in minutes. OK?'

'Yes.'

He looked crestfallen and Lexi wished with all her heart that their conversation hadn't been necessary. 'I'll see myself out.'

CHAPTER TWENTY-ONE

Valentine's Day

Oliver arrived at Lexi's an hour earlier than planned on Valentine's Day evening.

'What are you doing here?' she asked, her hair still damp from her shower and no make-up on her face. 'Did I get the time wrong?'

'Can I come in?'

She noticed that it was pouring outside and waved him inside. 'Of course, sorry.'

'Let's go through to the living room,' he suggested.

'Is everything alright?' She hoped he wasn't cancelling on her. She had been looking forward to going out with him, even after seeing the dreadful weather outside.

'I'm afraid I've had a call. There's been a flood at the restaurant. They're having to ring around to all their bookings and cancel. I feel so sorry for them. Of all nights for this to happen.'

Lexi could see he was slightly flustered and as disappointed as her. 'I don't suppose we can get in anywhere else this late?'

He shook his head. 'I'm afraid not. I did phone a few places, but it seems that anywhere decent has a waiting list.'

'Oh, well. It was a nice idea while it lasted.'

'I thought that if you didn't mind, I could order a takeaway and we could eat it either here or at mine. I know it's not the same, but it would be a shame not to do something tonight as planned.'

And it would mean she didn't have to dress up and go out in the pouring rain, Lexi thought, trying to look on the bright side. 'Good idea. I'll light the log burner and we can spend the evening here. I think I have a couple of bottles of wine, but I'm not sure how pleasant they are to drink. I'll have to check.'

'Sounds good to me. Any preference on food?'

Lexi laughed. 'I think we'll have to go with whatever you're can order, don't you?'

'Yes, you're probably right.'

She watched him go and hurriedly lit the fire. Maybe it would be more romantic with the two of them alone together in her living room than among a restaurant full of noisy people. She was getting used to the idea of staying in for the evening.

Her phone rang a while later and Lexi answered. 'That was quick. What are my choices?' she giggled.

'It's Gloria.'

Lexi only just managed not to gasp. She had expected Oliver to be the one on the other end of the call. 'Hello, Gloria.' Her Valentine evening was worsening by the second.

'Your father told me about your visit and your concerns about me.'

'He did?' Lexi said unsure where the conversation was leading.

'He's here with me now.' She heard her father's voice in the background confirming his presence. 'I wanted you to know that I understand why you spoke to him. I have made some silly choices in my past, but that's all over now. I want you to know that I love your father and intend to make him happy.' Lexi wished she could believe the woman. She waited for her to continue. 'That's it really. I just wanted you to know.'

Lexi was at a loss how to reply. She knew she had to say something to acknowledge her understanding. 'I'm glad you've had a chat. All I want is for Dad to be happy and if you are the person to make him happy then that's fine with me.'

'Good. Thank you.' There was a hesitation. 'Your father wants to speak to you.'

'Fine. Bye Gloria.' Lexi waited for her father to speak.

'Hi sweetheart,' he said. 'You heard what Gloria said. We've had a long chat and now you have the money back from the sale of the cottages you know as well as I do that the only money I'll ever possess is for any paintings I sell.'

'True.' She didn't mention anything about his bungalow. Her father was a grown man, and it was up to him how he reacted to Gloria's past.

'We've decided to give our relationship a go, but I want you to know that I'm doing everything from now on with my eyes wide open.'

She was relieved to hear it. 'I'm glad. Thanks for letting me know, Dad and I honestly do hope you'll both be very happy.'

'Thanks love, I appreciate that.'

An hour later, the fire was warming the room nicely and gentle music was playing, almost blocking out the sound of the stormy weather outside. The cottage was warm enough for her to wear one of her favourite dresses and she was beginning to feel much happier about her evening with Oliver.

He arrived looking windswept and carrying two bags. One contained boxes of food and the other two bottles of champagne. 'I hope you like Thai food,' he said. 'I also thought as it was our first proper date that we should celebrate with champagne.'

Lexi lifted the boxes out of the first bag and laid them out on the kitchen table. She decided to wait until another time to tell Oliver about her conversation with Gloria and her father. She intended making the most of their eventing together.

Opening the lids, she breathed in the delicious smells. 'Blimey, you've got all sorts here. And there's so much of it.'

Oliver leant against the work top and shrugged. 'I know, but I wasn't sure what you'd choose, so I picked a few different strengths in heat, some vegetarian, chicken, that sort of thing. I'm hoping you like some of them enough to want to eat them.'

Lexi laughed. 'I certainly will, I'm starving. Let's get some plates and tuck in.'

'The champagne is already chilled because the temperature is so low outside but I'll put the second bottle in the fridge.' He took two glasses from her shelf and opened the first bottle with a subtle pop, pouring them both a glass.

'You look very pretty if you don't mind me saying so,' he said.

'Why would I mind?' She grinned at him, her stomach flipping over as she stared into his eyes.

He handed her a glass of the pale, bubbly liquid, his hand grazing hers lightly. Lexi opened her mouth to thank him as she took the glass, but her stomach rumbled noisily ruining the romantic moment and making her giggle. 'Sorry.

I haven't eaten anything since breakfast. I was saving myself for tonight's meal.'

He pulled out her chair for her. 'Then we'd better get on and eat, hadn't we?'

As they ate their meal and chatted, Lexi kept looking at him, unable to help thinking about how lucky she was to have got to know him. It had been fun spending time with Oliver these past couple of months and even her work for him had been more interesting than she had expected it to be. However, the book was nearly finished and she knew that things couldn't carry on as they were, not for someone like Oliver who, as far as she knew, spent most of the year working on his latest projects and travelling between his different offices.

He finished a mouthful of food. 'You're looking very pensive,' he said, noticing her staring at him a while later.

Lexi didn't want to put a dampener on the mood, but she also couldn't help sensing something was about to change. 'I was thinking that now the book is almost finished maybe you'll be moving on from the island.'

Oliver stilled, his fork of food halfway from his plate to his mouth. He looked at her and slowly lowered his hand. 'And you'd be right.'

She had to concentrate on not showing her disappointment. Suspecting he might be moving on and hearing him confirm that he would be were two completely different things. Lexi felt her heart breaking as she waited to hear more.

'Go on,' she said, hearing the emotion in her voice.

'I'm leaving to visit my parents' tomorrow afternoon. I promised my mother that I'd spend a week with them.'

'That's lovely. I'm sure she must be excited to have you back at home.'

'She's looking forward to it very much.' He picked up his fork and moved his food around on the plate without eating anything more.

Lexi watched him miserably. There was something more, she could tell. 'Is that all?'

He shook his head. 'No. The thing is, I've been away from my office in London for too long. I need to get back and meet with my directors to finalise a few projects for the rest of the year. I've enjoyed working here with you very much, Lexi. I wish it could carry on, but I have obligations that I must keep.' He stared at her. 'I can't put off returning to London any longer.'

'I understand,' she said, wishing he had waited until the following day to tell her.

He reached out and took her hand in his. 'I'm sorry. I know I'm ruining our evening by bringing this up, but I didn't want to drop it on you at the last-minute tomorrow. I will be back in a couple of weeks.'

Lexi took a sip from her third glass of champagne, enjoying the bubbles despite feeling so miserable. She focused on trying to look cheerful. After all, he had gone to a lot of trouble to make the evening special. 'Hey, it's fine. You've got work to do; I get that.'

'Thank you.'

She watched him playing with his food. He looked miserable and wanted to cheer him up. 'I think we've finished eating, don't you?'

'Yes, it looks like it. Why?'

Lexi stood. 'I'm going to change the music and we're going to dance.'

'Dance? Just the two of us?'

'Yes.' She put her hands on her hips. 'You weren't so shy at the Burns Night party, were you?' she teased. 'You were the one insisting I give all those jigs and dances a go. Tonight, it's my turn to tell you what to do. I've only got you for a few hours, so you're mine to do with as I want.'

She knew she sounded a little suggestive but didn't care. Who knew when she would get the chance to have him all alone again? Tonight, she wanted to dance and that's what she was going to do.

His eyes widened and she could see she had surprised him. Oliver stood. 'I'm happy with that.'

'Right, help me move this table and the chairs back to give us a bit more space.'

They cleared the plates and glasses and moved the table back against the wall.

'Ready?' Lexi grinned.

'I am.'

She changed the music to something slow. 'I thought this might be more suited to tonight.'

'Good choice,' he said, moving to stand in front of her. 'Happy Valentine's Day, Lexi.' he whispered taking her in his arms and kissing her lightly.

Lexi gazed up at him for a second. Then, unable to help herself, probably due to the overwhelming emotion of the moment, or the sexy smell of his aftershave, or maybe even the glasses of champagne she'd consumed, she flung her arms around his neck and kissed him right back, losing herself in the feel of his lips on hers.

Eventually, she came up for air and smiled at the stunned, handsome man staring back at her, his dark eyes mirroring her own attraction for him.

'Happy Valentine's Day, Oliver Whimsy.'

CHAPTER TWENTY-TWO

Almost Spring - March

Lexi looked out at the camellia bushes her mum had planted several years before and smiled at the pretty pink flowers, one bush showing off magenta petals, the other lighter pink ones. Spring was almost here, and she looked forward to it. What she wasn't looking forward to was her father's engagement party, but she needed to be there if only to show her support for him. Gloria was his partner of choice, and she had to respect that.

Her phone pinged and she picked it up to see a message from Oliver.

Just landed in Jersey, will be with you soon. O x

Lexi's heart swelled. She wasn't sure where she and Oliver were going with this thing that had been happening between them, but they had certainly moved on from their business relationship. He had been gone for too long and it had surprised her how much she missed him. It was strange to think it had only been a couple of months since he moved into the end cottage above the boardwalk and how she had been determined to dislike him, only for his kindness to turn her feelings around, morphing into something far more special.

She didn't want him to have to pay for a taxi, so decided to text him.

I'll pick you up. See you in seven minutes! L x

Lexi was walking up to Arrivals at Jersey Airport when Oliver spotted her and waved. She looked at the tall, rugged man she had missed so much and hurried towards him.

'How was your trip?'

He put his arm around her shoulder and gave her a quick kiss. 'It was wonderful to see my parents and sister again, but emotional too, as I'm sure you can imagine. Next time I go I'd like you to come with me.'

The toe of Lexi's boot caught on a ridge of tarmac and she tripped, only just righting herself when he grabbed her arm to stop her from falling.

'I didn't expect you to hit the floor in horror,' he teased.

'Very funny. Not.' She pinched him lightly on his waist.

'Ouch. Do I take it that you didn't miss me then?'

Lexi gazed up at him. 'You know I did, I told you on the phone.'

They stopped by her car. Oliver bent down to kiss her again. 'I know and I missed you too, which is why I'd like you to come with me next time I visit my family.'

They got in the car and after queuing to exit the car park, Lexi told him about her dad's engagement party. 'It's only a small gathering in the pub in the village, but obviously I've got to be there to show my support. Will you come with me?'

'Yes, happily.' Oliver smiled at her. 'I'm glad you've forgiven him. This way you can both move on without any animosity. That's how it should be with parents and their children, if at all possible.'

'I agree, although sometimes it feels more difficult than at others.' She was dying to ask him about his trip to his London office. She didn't want him to go, but knew he would have to and couldn't bear the suspense of waiting any longer. 'What happened when you went to London? How did that go?'

For once she didn't mind having to slow down when a tractor pulled out from a field in front of her. She waited patiently for him to reply as the car crawled along behind it.

'I've been waiting to see you to speak to you

about something.'

Lexi's stomach clenched anxiously. 'Go on.'

'I've come up with a plan and if you're happy with it I'll relocate here, at least for the majority of the time.'

She was confused. 'You mean you'll work from here? Stay in your cottage?'

'For now, yes.'

She could feel him looking at her and waiting for her to answer. 'What's the plan then?' she asked, hoping she was going to like it.

He narrowed his eyes briefly. 'Now, I know how determined you are to get your cottages back. And we've discussed how, certainly for the time being, that you aren't able to due to your finances.'

'Yes, go on.' What on earth could he have to suggest? She had refused al his previous offers of help. There couldn't be any other way to resolve the issue, could there?

'How would you feel if I sold you two of them?'

'Sorry, what?' She turned to look at him, confused.

'Lexi, brake!' He pointed ahead of them and Lexi saw that the tractor had stopped to turn left.

She braked so suddenly that both of them shot forward. 'Bloody hell. Sorry about that.'

He took a deep breath and puffed out his cheeks. 'Maybe we should continue this chat in the safety of your home?'

'Funny. No. You've started telling me and I want to hear the rest right now.'

He shook his head. 'We're almost home. I want to tell you when I'm facing you, so I can see for myself exactly how you feel about it.'

Irritated, Lexi wanted to argue but she knew him well enough to know he wouldn't change his mind once it was made up. 'Fine.'

A few minutes later they stood facing each other in his living room.

'Right, I can't cause either of us any injuries now, so tell me this plan of yours.'

He folded his arms across his chest. She could see he was nervous about sharing his thoughts with her. She loved his determination to find a solution and that he kept coming up with ideas despite her continuing to rebuff them.

'I've been trying to figure out a way to resolve this the whole time I've been away. Then yesterday on a train it dawned on me.'

She wished she felt as confident as he sounded. 'Go on.'

'You have two-thirds of the money I paid your father for the cottages.' Lexi nodded, still unable to believe her father had managed to spend so much of the money in such a short time. 'There are three cottages.'

Lexi frowned. 'There are.' Where was he going with this?

He held his hands out, palms upwards. 'It's

simple really. You buy two cottages back from me, yours and the middle one. You'll own both of them outright. Then, in a few years, if you still want to buy the third back, I'm sure you'll find a way to raise the funds to do it.' She watched him studying her face. It was obvious how important it was to him to put things right. 'You don't have to decide straight away,' he added. 'Take your time to consider everything.'

Lexi's mind whirled. She had to admit that his idea was simple, yet so clever. And she had to admit, it was perfect. If he was going to be living on the island, it was understandable that he would want to live in a home of his own. What right did she have to demand all three cottages? After all he had done to help her, surely he deserved to keep one of them? She could still hire out the middle cottage in the summer months if she chose.

'I love it.' She gasped, realising that it really was the perfect solution for them both.

He did a double-take, looking stunned. 'You do? Really?'

'Yes, I do,' she grinned. She took hold of his wrists and pulled his arms apart, stepping in between them. Then, sliding her arms around his neck, she pulled his head down to kiss him. 'You, Oliver Whimsy, are a marvel.'

Her heart swelled at his obvious relief. This brilliant, hugely successful man had been determined to find a way forward for her and she was profoundly grateful to him for trying so hard.

'You're not so bad yourself.' He sighed, his lips drawing back into a wide, perfect smile. 'I must admit I'm massively relieved.'

She kissed him again. 'To tell you the truth, so am I.'

He sat down on the sofa and pulled her on to his lap, kissing her long and hard for several minutes. Eventually they stopped and gazed at each other. 'I was telling my mother all about you.'

'You were? Why?'

He kissed the tip of her nose. 'Because she asked about you, several times. She sensed you were more to me than someone who simply worked for me.'

'She did?' she asked, stroking his neck lightly before kissing it.

'There's something about mothers, isn't there?' he said. 'They seem to know more about you than sometimes you realise yourself.'

Lexi thought back to her wonderful mum and nodded. 'It's true. My mum always seemed to know when I was going to make a big decision and usually before I had decided to make it.'

She rested her head against his shoulder knowing that she would rather be right there than anywhere else.

'Do you know, I'm glad now that I made a fool of myself at the Halloween party.'

'You are? Why?'

'Because if I hadn't needed somewhere to stay, you wouldn't have taken pity on me and let me stay in one of these cottages. I wouldn't have realised this was where my parents had met, and we wouldn't have gone through all we have over the past few months to end up here.'

Lexi grinned up at him. 'Then in that case, I'm glad too.'

He kissed the tip of her nose. 'I love you, Lexi Davies. Do you know that?'

'I do now,' she replied, kissing him. 'And I love you right back, Oliver Whimsy.'

It was his turn to look stunned. 'You do?'

She nodded, not caring that she had just borne her soul to him. 'I do. How could I not after all that's happened?'

The End

A letter to my readers.

Thank you for reading the third instalment in my Boardwalk by the Sea series. I hope you enjoyed Winter Whimsy and getting to know Lexi Davies and Oliver Whimsy.

The fishermen's cottages in this book are based on some in Greve de Lecq, although those are newer, bigger and at the bottom of the hill rather than halfway up where Lexi's are situated in this series. The inspiration for the boardwalk was two places: Greve de Lecq a pretty, small beach with cliffs on one side and a small pier on the other. It's near to my home and where I sometimes walk my three dogs. I also took inspiration from the promenade along the top of the beach at St Brelade's Bay. There you will find the shops, cafes and even a couple of cottages, but not like the ones I've described in this series, they are purely from my imagination.

Next up in the series is the final book, Spring Siren. That book is Jools' story. I'm looking forward to you sharing her world when the book is published in Spring 2021.

For now, though, thank you. If you enjoyed reading about Lexi and Oliver in Winter Whimsy, I'd be very grateful if you would tell your friends and maybe consider popping a short review on Amazon.

Take care and stay safe,

Best wishes,

GEORGINA TROY

Georginax

For more about **Deborah Carr** and her
books written as **Georgina Troy**

Sign up to her newsletter

Coming next from Green Shutter Books...

The Boardwalk by the Sea, book 4
SPRING SIREN

Also in this series:
The Boardwalk by the Sea, Book 1
Summer Sundaes

Book 2, Autumn Antics

Published by **Green Shutter Books**

Also by **Georgina Troy**

The Jersey Scene
(Published in the US/Canada
as The Island Scene)
A Jersey Kiss
A Jersey Affair
A Jersey Bombshell
A Jersey Dreamboat

Published by **Green Shutter Books**

Printed in Great Britain
by Amazon

56932702R00208